STONEWALL INN EDITIONS
KEITH KAHLA, GENERAL EDITOR

Also by Madelyn Arnold:

On Ships at Sea

A Year of Full Moons

Bird-Eyes

Madelyn Arnold

St. Martin's Press ♏ New York

www.stmartins.com

Library of Congress Cataloging-in-Publication Data

Arnold, Madelyn.
    Bird-eyes / by Madelyn Arnold.—1st St. Martin's ed.
        p.   cm.
    ISBN 0-312-26294-9
        1. Lesbian teenagers—Fiction.   2. Psychiatric hospital patients—
Fiction.   3. Female friendship—Fiction.   4. Deaf women—Fiction.
I. Title.
PS3551.R535 B56 2000
813'54—dc21   00-024757

First published in the United States by Seal Press

First St. Martin's Edition: July 2000

10   9   8   7   6   5   4   3   2   1

*To Professor Lois Hudson, who told me not to be too polite,
and to the original Anna & D.A.S.*

1

THEY BROUGHT her into the middle of our ward by the hand, like a child, and left her standing in the hallway, staring around like somebody's little smart dog. That was the first time that I ever saw her: early December, 1964. She was maybe forty and athletic. Her face was wide-awake and kind of nice: bright brown eyes, looking around her constantly. There was this note pinned to her neat round collar: Anna Robeson.

Weird Diane was always the first to meet you on our ward, which sort of set the tone for your arrival. She was coming up behind this New One just about the time that I was noticing her myself, but I didn't say anything. I was thinking about that writing. I hadn't seen them send up any patient wearing a note before, and Weird Diane started yelling, "Hey what's your name" from behind this brand-new patient. Though if she'd been in front of her she wouldn't have known the name, that's what I think. In all nine months I knew her, Weird Diane did not read anything—including

TV ads. She'd point to the screen and yell, *what's that word mean!*

But the New One didn't answer: she was staring. I think maybe at the hemlines which were four inches too long on most of us. And some of us wore socks with our skirts, which nobody did back then except for patients. And then only back ward patients, or old ladies. People that you wouldn't ever notice. She might have been fascinated but that isn't exactly the first word I would think of—she just could not take this in.

"I said your name!" said Weird Diane—and slapped her. The sudden slap nearly knocked her over; she dodged away as graceful as a dancer and flattened quickly up against the wall, with Diane screaming at her, "Whadju say! Whadju say to me!" right in her face. We were kind of enjoying this—you never knew what Weird Diane would do.

"I don't think," said Diane Brown, "she said anything at all. . . ." While Weird Diane was screaming: "Donchu answer a body! Donchu speak no English to a body!"—*very angry*. And someone else said: "She just made this noise, only just made this noise—she didn't even mean to answer you! Well!"

The New One kept her eyes on us—angry, I think, but maybe just afraid.

"Cat gotcher tongue!" said Weird Diane. Loud, in the lady's face.

The New One brought her palms up quick to keep Diane away from her; her fingers spread like eloquent fans—liquid, graceful, bones flowing like tracings in clear water—and she froze again: fingers rigid, fixed and bent like branches of a tree.

She reached down for a pocket but there wasn't one, which must have meant she was used to wearing trousers; she looked again for the pocket that wasn't there, and swallowed hard—looked brave—and opened her mouth to

2

speak. Like an animal with some weird foreign language.

"She's deaf!" I said.

And yes she was. We stared.

And then an attendant—Hart, I think—came up and put a string and pad-and-pencil around her neck. Just like a package.

Some people came in completely crazy of course, like Weird Diane and Vivian-who-never-talks and Spacey Shirley, but most of us came in depressed and not too clear about this place we were committed to; something about benevolent institutions. People coming in from the courts, of course, tended to be suspicious of their families, which makes sense if you think about it. About Anna, though; I never got it exactly straight, but I heard Anna had been depressed about the recent death of her husband (ladies get that way). For several months she had simply avoided people and just worked frantically on the farm, without communicating much with her grown children. Though it's not like she could have called them on the telephone—she would have had to hunt them up, which I guess she wasn't willing to do, so they all went together and took her to this doctor.

He gave her medication, but it backfired; the stuff made her breathing stop. This upset her, and so she would not take it anymore, plus she would not trust him. Nothing upsets a family doctor more than lack of trust. This means you're crazy.

I've always wondered how he tried to communicate with Anna. If this was the guy who delivered all her children. If he knew anything about the place they decided they would send her to; but probably, he didn't. Not his business. So either all of them committed her, or they talked her into signing in herself as suicidal. Imagine this place as heading off a suicide attempt. A contribution to the love of living.

They seemed to think a stay in Eastern Central would erase severe depression, which just shows you. Since she could not read or write too well, I've always wondered what in the world they told her she was signing.

Merry Christmas.

Eastern Central State Hospital Care.

At 5:59 in the morning, all the lights are off except for the little white vents above the floor which line the hallways. In winter, like when Anna came, it's dark except for that glow above the floor. But at six-oh-oh all the lights explode in your face—and the Muzak, loud—you come awake in a sweat with your heart on *drive*. That's the most effective thing in their treatment program.

Anna never did get used to the adrenalin hit that it gives you, when you're shocked awake. But I've always heard that deaf people are kind of jumpy when it comes to lighting. At least she had the blessing that she didn't have to hear that goddamned Muzak.

I hope I meet a Muzak person someday.

All the rest of us did get used to the lights; and some of us, who were really dopey, got to where we could even stay asleep in spite of everything, but Anna was too different from us in this—as in some other things: deaf, you know. What she looked at meant too much to her.

We the rest of us were not very different at all on that ward. Except maybe me, since I was younger. Even our names were not really very different: there were duplicates (or quintlicates, I guess). I don't really know why it's true; maybe the movies were responsible for the naming: but about five years before I was born in '48 everybody named their kids "Diane"; and the girls born in 1938 were all named "Shirley."

So there were five Dianes and at least three Shirleys on

Women's ward D. The Dianes were Tall Diane, Weird Diane, Old Diane, and Diane-with-the-glasses; and it's funny but one of them even got a last name—Diane Brown—but it cost her enough.

(Weird Diane coming up to meet the New One, who is Diane Brown): "Hey what's your name!"

Diane Brown (suspicious of Weird Diane): "Hey yourself."

"I say what's your name? You don't look too crazy to know that!"

(Depressed, fluffing her hair): "I'm Diane Brown."

"We got lots of them," I say, and somebody else says: "How about Dianepink? Look at that hot pink makeup she's got all over."

"Old Diane," says Spacey Shirley, who is old herself. "Tall Diane, Dianewithglasses, Weird Diane."

"Who you calling weird!"

"And a pink one, Dianepink!" says Spacey Shirley, who is black.

"Brown," says Diane Brown. "One of the Brownstown Browns from down around Fayetteville."

"Omy!" Weird Diane says, rolling her eyes around. "One of them Brownstown Browns! One of them how-now-brown-cow-Brownstown-Browns! Miss Diane Brown!"—and suddenly hits her in the teeth. Which was all right with us.

And nobody else was named Latisha, but then I've never been like anybody else.

Well I knew what it was like to wake up with those lights, but not to be deaf in a place like that. You can't know that and you might as well block it out. I do know that the first week is the worst because you are so drugged up that your mind can't move and you can't get used to that; and because you are really looking at where you are, and you can't believe that this could really happen to you. How could this happen. And not only is your body locked up in these solid green walls, but the dope has locked your mind up in this teeny place in your head, and you can't get used to that; and they're going to find your mind in there and stop it cold.

Anna wouldn't take the pills. After what happened to her, she would not trust them, so they gave her shots. And that was bad to watch and so I didn't, except when I couldn't help it. She hated them holding her down, and she hated the shots. She could not only not wake up, she couldn't move. I remembered what that was like when you were locked up in a box inside your head, and couldn't think. Like others here, she began to stand and stare most of the time. If no one moved her, she would stand for hours in one place. But at least she tried to keep from sitting down—you can't get up. She couldn't concentrate on people's faces anymore. She couldn't read the notes they'd write on that little pad she hated, which was stuck on her. I didn't really like that.

If I had only trusted her, I could have helped her out with this: I'd have shown her how you hold the pills in the space beneath your tongue. That's what I did myself, and I saved the pills to trade them off. But I didn't tell her, couldn't have hoped to tell her, which I thought about: I wouldn't have trusted my own face in the mirror.

It was the custom to keep New Ones on the ward for meals during the first week after their arrival. This keeps them from falling in their soup, lets the staff see whether they are going to be a pain or not to manage, and keeps them away from the silverware while they're getting used to us. A good idea. Saves a lot of trouble. So it was the end of the second week before they let her join us down the hall in

6

the cafeteria. The attendants had to hold her up beneath her arms as she was walked.

And she wouldn't eat.

Of course, nobody still sane will touch that stuff the first time they see it. And she tried to hide the fact that she wasn't eating by just messing up her plate and moving silverware— but she really didn't do this very well. Any little kid will do it better. And she started out to act as if not eating was okay; as if they'd let her do just what she wanted to. Well there's nothing they don't interfere with.

The attendants let one meal go by with her messing up her plate. They stuck the next meal forcibly down her throat. I always hate to see it when they do that. So the meal after that she was hiding mashed potatoes in her sweater. It was clear to me that she had to get a whole lot better than that. And so I told her.

Our ward ate at the same time as the guys from the vegetable C ward. Staff schedules this so we ladies are *socializing* with some guys. There were two fat guys between where we were sitting. The man to my right had crosses and nicks of healed cuts on his head from rapid seizures; he was stupid, but he was really useful (if you acted right), though I kept my cup away from him because he'd stick his fingers in my coffee. I leaned way past him, trying to get Anna's attention. I didn't want the attendants or the fat guys to pick up on what I'd tell her.

—*Hey!* (I'm waving).

(Anna is staring, horrified, at the stuff they serve for food: don't look at that *stuff.*)

—*Hey!* I try; I throw a green bean at her.

She looks up.

—*Look!* I point. I scoop up the hard meat parts and most of the beans in my hand. The staff's not looking. I dump it all on the plate of the dumb fat guy, who's to my right. I open my carton of milk and drink a little—til he puts down

7

his orangeade—and then I pour the rest of it in his tall green plastic cup. (Looks awful.)

(Anna stares at me; she's fascinated.)

I mash the rest of my food with a fork, and look up fast to catch her eye.

—*See!* I mouth to her.

I tear the milk container completely open, by its upper seam:—*See!*

(I stare at her):—*Do you catch what I am doing?*

I scoop up the bean mash and the fatmeat mash and the slimy potato gravy into the top of the milk container. (She is studying this.)

—*Understand?* I mouth.

And then the sun's out in her face.

The attendants saying later, "See! Now that wasn't so bad!" And Anna smiling. . . .

It seems like I remember that she wouldn't drink the coffee when she first arrived—her saying that she hated it. I guess the damnfool thought somebody liked it made that way.— *Stupid!* I told her. Whenever I pointed it out, she made an ugh! face. That would make me feel like slapping her. That you don't do what you like in here—but I didn't know how to make her understand me.

That sure it tastes ugly, but you don't worry about taste; what you do is, you put in a spoonful of sugar and three of that white stuff and then at least two of the black coffee powder that looks like powdered coal—or two lumps of it if it's really an old can and has picked up moisture, and only two if the attendants are watching, otherwise as much as you can stand of it, which for me is usually five lumps. Which is why you use the white stuff, straight from artificial cows. It smooths it down so you don't spit all that black stuff out again; so you can swallow it.

8

You try for five and drink it all down fast (it's not for pleasure); if it goes down fast enough it hits at once—and snaps you high, into a sweat on your palms and forehead; your heart rate jumps right up through the top of your head. The caffeine fights the flattening dope they give you here; the flattening stuff will shut your eyes but the coffee props them open. It makes it so every part of you is so heavy you can't move but the caffeine lightens you, it's the only help you'll get. There's surely nothing else that's going to help you on this ward and so you drink it. What the hell it tastes like shit.

—*Stupid!* I told her.

When they bring out the coffee cart at 6:15 in the morning we'd all hit it at once, even the maniacs (I guess they didn't like feeling stupid either), but Anna would just stare at us, like who could drink such garbage? Well I could. I guess she wasn't used to doing things she didn't like. She'd get over it. I would always try to drink at least a couple cups, which I could manage.

That much caffeine really did the trick—except when every now and then some new attendant would see how really fast we'd go through coffee, and then order decaf which is absolutely no damn use at all. You can't drink enough of the stuff to fight that numb-death flatness off your body. Or your brain.

And the first time that happened to me, and I couldn't wake up, I just couldn't make myself adjust right and I really absolutely threw a fit. Screamed and threw the cup against the wall (but the cups are paper) and Hart runs out and tells me what a dirty little whore I am and to wipe it up, wipe it up with my hair I mean, which I refused to do and that gave her an excuse to throw me in the sideroom; which was, I think, the first time I was there. But usually I'm really good at getting over things; you just put them out of your mind and make your body work at something. But then little

9

things will just sort of add up on me; adding up while I'm doing something else. Just a little thing that somebody's maybe done thirteen hundred times will suddenly bother me a lot, and I get this feeling like there's pressure in my head and I get dizzy.

—*Stupid!* I mouthed.

. . . That it did not matter whether she hated the stuff or not, she was going to stay the dead-numb stupid way she was unless she learned to drink a lot of rotten coffee. That tastes don't matter. Or tastes and opinions sure don't matter here. Take it from me, you can put anything in your mouth.

I tried to wide-talk some of this at her, and I tried to write it down on her pad but she couldn't read so well; reading wasn't something she was used to doing and she got mad and started shaking her head real hard: not at me. We were mad at each other but I kept thinking about it: she was miserable. So an idea hit me. I closed my eyes and acted like I was trying to get them open. I acted just like Anna had been looking. Then I acted like my hands were stumbling around looking for the cup, and had found the cup, and that now I was drinking the stuff; and then I had my eyes go pop! open! daylight!—and then I repeated the whole thing over again. She wasn't what you'd call real easily convinced. I repeated it again. Then I pointed toward the really dumb and dopey ones and how they hit the coffee, hard and regularly. And finally with a big-deal sacrifice look she tried the coffee (making the most godawful faces); and of course she did begin to wake up. So she smartened up and had a bunch more and began to look almost human.

Well, you learn.

Except she didn't want to learn.

2

EAST CENTRAL Hospital is built to look like an Iron
Cross. That is, the part that has the patients in it, not the
doctors' lounges and the outbuildings like the laundry shed
and all those little guard houses. Women's D, which had five
rooms with four or six beds, sat on the second floor of the
cross arm to the west, with the little crossbar at the end fash-
ioned from two short hallways. There were shrink offices on
those hallways and a visitors' lounge. Sometime before I came,
D had been an all-male ward. There was a wire porch, like a
dog run, facing west out over the yard, sort of suspended out
from where the little hallways joined to form that crosspart
that makes the floor like a German Cross.

There had been a punching bag out on that porch when
I first came, in September, and I guess everybody must have
known it was out there, but nobody ever used it. So I'd go
out there and pound the living hell out of it. Of course, I
didn't know what I was doing: it took me days to get to
where I could hit it in rhythm, like a fighter—*bammetty-
bammetty-bammetty*—like making screams with the muscles

11

of my arms and back—but then they realized that one of the ladies was using it, which was all wrong, so they took it out. So then I'd go out on the porch and just stare out through the chicken wire walls. And I'd walk around in a sort of X-in-an-O path: catacorner from southeast to northeast and half around the walls; then catacorner from southwest to northeast and half around the walls; then catacorner from southeast and northwest and the other half around; if you did it quick enough, you could get dizzy, which is sometimes therapeutic. But then Anna came, and she wanted to be moving around, too.

I guess I could have just hit her every time she came around; Weird Diane did that (she did that to everybody—that's her interaction, like her socializing). But I knew Anna had to move around, like I do. So instead we'd wad up paper balls and kick them back and forth against the wall, like they were rubber: kickball à la Central—lady-fashion.

But of course not all attendants let us do that, since it isn't very ladylike; you'll notice nobody else would want to do a thing like that. Women don't. You are supposed to wait and life will happen to you. You sit and stare or you play cards, make your face up, or you babble. This shows you that I am just made wrong, and there is absolutely nothing I can do about it. Anna was weird too, but then she couldn't babble and nobody thought that she could play a game with hearing people—where any thinking was involved, like in a card game. And she didn't like disorientation—she hadn't had much booze, like normal people. So medication was harder on her than anybody else. Instead of getting blasted, she was used to working or something; a farmer lady who moved herself around.

When I first came, they gave me these blue pills, several of them, several times a day. It was like having all the strings cut between you and your nerves. They didn't ask me those questions like shrinks ask you in the movies (or maybe when you pay them lots of money) and that was okay because what could I have answered? I wasn't crazy, I was just incorrigible, and besides I was just ripped on medication. I would have flunked those tests where they ask you, hey, what day is this? They gave me those pills, and after three days my heart started pounding real hard; I couldn't sleep or make any sense and my body temperature went down a degree-and-a-half. I shivered constantly: chattering teeth. So then they started giving me brown pills and after a few more days the same thing happened, and this really pissed them off; so they began to give me yellow pills and a little white pill for all the side effects.

By that time I had been there for three weeks and had talked to my shrink, Dr. Kim, and my little social worker, and asked them what the damn pills were for, anyway. And the doctor said a lot of sentences without subjects in them, and without looking at me; and the social worker just said everybody gets pills, take the pills. So I started flushing the damn things down the toilet. I didn't like that dead, drugged-over feeling. I like drugs that make you high, not make you stupid—those things are just no damn good at all. But then I found out that some of the patients like the white pills, they're some kind of amphetamine; so I saved them up and traded them for other things I wanted.

I wish I'd trusted Anna enough to show her about the pills; it might have helped her.

That you swallow hard, to make a dry place under your tongue; this way you don't gag, since they taste terrible (which is probably on purpose). You stick the pills under your tongue and clamp it down, and quickly drink the water in this teeny cup they give you. Then, because they are so clever, they make you talk to show that you aren't holding any pills—which you will prove to them, and everyone is happy. What you do is, you use one of the several answers which do not move your tongue much. Like *I dunno* or *well wadda you think?* You hold your tongue down hard, and swallow over it, continually bailing out your mouth.

Maybe I could have acted all this slyness out for Anna, but it was hard to make long explanations. If I couldn't act things out real clearly, I just gave it up.

At least, though, she was really good at making us understand her. And she could read and write—just not too well. She wrote me out a note: how years have you! (she wrote things out that way) and I wrote back—16; and she was shocked; but everybody always was. After all, I wasn't committed for a suicide attempt or craziness; no one's ever thought that I was crazy—legally crazy. I was stuck on a back ward as incorrigible. I wasn't sent to Juvenile Hall or one of the teenage wards. Incorrigible is catching, like a social disease. I was stuck back there because I was infectious.

One thing. Anna was not supposed to use sign language. Signing was the way that she had talked for all her life; sign was the way she talked to all her family, so they could not often visit. But I think they were not told this was the reason. I think she was not told this reason either. Several times I heard the attendants babbling this over.

It's fortunate that attendants talk continually. This ban on sign was an idea of our doctor's, who had read it in a book some place.

Anna and I had the same doctor; actually a third of us up there had him. There were three docs serving us back wards. Our Dr. Kim was a Korean Mormon whose English was the kind you hear in kamikaze movies. He could read English perfectly well, as well as write it; he spoke it to his satisfaction, but never knew what we were trying to say—which was all right, I guess, since who would want to listen? Fortunately we didn't have to talk to him too much, even when there was something that we needed him for because you only see your shrink for fifteen minutes, twice a month. And with our shrinks, that worked out fine for everyone. When they saw us, they would fill out these little sheets of paper. This way everybody knows that *therapy* had happened. Otherwise, it certainly would be difficult to tell. But anyway.

Kim insisted to Anna that she talk with the mouth like this, not in that animal way (as she had done for maybe forty years). So after a couple attempts to speak (no one could understand her), she stuck her hands in her armpits and just stood around and watched. We weren't to sign to her. So she only watched us.

We weren't too interesting. Not even Weird Diane.

But Weird Diane could blow smoke rings like nobody's business, and so could the attendant, Mrs. Pratt. And after watching some of us for a while, so could Anna. Even though she'd never been a smoker before she came, but everybody smokes in there; you don't have to inhale.

When she'd first come, though, she made her *ugh!* face every time you offered her a cigarette. But there's so much you can do with cigarettes. You can give them to people to help establish friendship (or to ease hostilities); they can give them to you (and that won't mean a Bit Deal—just a kindness). You can collect them or trade them or use them for poker chips. And they give you something to do with your hands and mouth (and make you high) so Anna finally started smoking—just a little bit. It made her look like us, and that was something. About the third week she was there she started to hold the cigarettes while everyone around (but me) was talking. Except the really fargone ones, I mean, who didn't talk.

At least that way you could tell her from the ones like Vivian-who-didn't-talk, who were bananas.

She got so she would sit and hold a cigarette if someone gave her one, watching other ladies in a great big circle sit

15

around and talk. One of the times we were waiting for staff to line us up for dinner, waiting to form that human chain to quick-march down the hall, we were just talking—all of us who ever talked. Except for me. I was just walking around them in a circle, smoking with them. I'd never had any kids, being a kid, and you can bet that teenage kid talk didn't interest them, especially the attendants—who were doing most of the talking, which is what they mostly do.

But Anna is watching how everybody holds her cigarettes. Now imitating, which she is so good at; it's tentatively in her mouth; she's looking at the nib of it; glancing at the others, how they tap away the tip; and now she lights it (everybody giving loud and dumb advice); and then these smoke rings everybody made—she's doing them. Perfectly, chains and figure-8's—she was so good at any gimmick where you moved yourself—great rings, doughnuts curling fat from off her tongue. And she was part of us, for a second she was part of us; friendly with tobacco for a little while.

Smoking was something we were always busy with to some extent or other. It was one way to be busy there. Mostly we sat and blew smoke out our mouths and noses: a greyish haze up the sea green walls. Playing cards, we'd bet with cigarettes. Vivian would eat them sometimes, but that was your own fault if you left them anywhere that she could get her mitts on them. That was just her way of *socializing*.

Anna was to join us and be social. This was supposed to prove she was not depressed. To do this she was supposed to try to talk to us, which she was just as good at as she would have been at opera. No one ever understood her. She knew that and she hated ever trying. But Dr. Kim would tell her that she must not use that old, elaborate way—that ignorant way; Sign was not talking. It was bad, bad, bad, so bad to not communicate; books had told him that this made depression. Books had told him Sign was not a language and to use it was a lunacy. Only apes would use it. We heard him saying this clear out in the hallway.

That day Anna couldn't understand him, or said she couldn't, so he shouted. Dr. Kim was not real fond of shouting; this made his foreign accent sound very much worse. She could not by any guesswork understand what he was saying, and to misunderstand his English just infuriated him. He called in Miss Wykowski from the evening staff to write this down—and to post it in the hallway, like a billboard: *Do not talk with hands.* Anna had talked with hands since maybe twenty years before his birth, but you mind your doctor. At least he hadn't said she couldn't *act.*

An odd thing: signing was the only thing that Dr. Kim was definite about; on this point he was going to be. Involved. In early January he started checking on her progress every morning. When he first came on the ward—and he was promptest of the doctors—he demanded of the ward staff, *was she talking?* Making English orally? Some of the staff would lie, because they hated to be quizzed like that: sure she did—interactive English, orally. Talking a blue streak, only shy around Dr. Kim. Who could know why she was shy? Maybe age. . . . That was fine with Doctor, and he finally let it ride—lots of other issues were taking up his time, and lots of patients. He didn't want to have to deal with this if he could help it. But he didn't want his orders violated. He was the boss. Remember that your doctor is your boss.

He was a busy and fussy gentleman. Also the only doctor who came every working day—even though to a back ward which could not advance him any way. Every morning he would drag his heavy briefcase down the long arm of the hallway, toward the offices' crossbar. His was the office to the left, just around the corner. Every morning, like he was going to face a firing squad. And one morning I looked up,

17

and there were two of him. I almost sucked a cigarette up my nose. Anna was behind him in the hallway—Anna the doctor. She was the funniest mimic I have ever seen. Anna couldn't talk, but communicated.

He hunched his briefcase arm up at the shoulder, from the weight; Anna had her back exactly like him. She was like a blueprint of a fussy little man—a little questioning pull to the side of one eye, the way he squinted around like somebody had just turned on the lights; she had grown down to his five-foot-four and got his jerky penguin walk just perfectly. What can you say to such communication. And maybe that's why. Why should I care.

I had a little cousin I used to see at Christmastime, when I was little. He was deaf. I'd seen him talk a little with his fingers. I had learned a word or two but not too much. It wasn't as if I could really talk to her. Not communication. But of course I like to see her imitate like that, and the ward we both were on was really boring. And maybe it was the challenge that made me want to talk to Anna. Forbid me anything and I'll go right to it.

After her four-week "waiting period," Anna's family was allowed to visit her: this was the usual arrangement for our ward. And it is true that our ward needs adjusting-to. Watching her family visit her was crazy-making for us—we would watch them talk a secret code that none of us had ever quite imagined; it was really very beautiful. Anna had five children who were grown. The youngest was a few months younger than I was. They were hearing, like their dad had been—the one whose death had led to her *depression*—and they seemed to like her well enough. Those people couldn't have known what they were doing when they shut their mother in with us. I still believe they must have loved their mother.

Their talking would marvel us. No one had told them sign

language was ignorant monkeyshines. And how they used it. The expressions.

They sat around in a circle in the northern lounge (just past our doctor's office) and they talked to her: waving of words and strong, emotional faces. You could see that they referred to things and people that you couldn't know, but you'd have sworn you'd have recognized each face. Her kids had Anna faces. Faces like a television screen; laughing and moving and clapping, slapping sounds; now and then a strong emotion breaking in a word or shout. The rest of us, we stared without embarrassment—our private carnival show. A happy family: nothing like our own.

But Doctor Kim would not let the family come too frequently. He only let them visit every now and then because they always signed to her, which he couldn't eavesdrop on. It pained the staff to see her family violate a Treatment Plan, but the family laughed when told they shouldn't Sign to her. After all—that was the way she'd taught them. She was still the mother of them all. They talked to her the way she'd talked to them.

"That's a retarded thing to do," Miss Hart told me. "That's not really talking, it's just like a cat or dog will do. I don't want to see you encourage her to do that kind of talking. Write her, like; she needs the practice."

"Deaf people do it that way," I say.

"No, they can talk, it just takes them more effort. And they get by with gestures, it makes them lazy. They just lazy. Now you got to talk a little slower with them, and you got to repeat yourself, but they got to do their part and pay attention. You got to do real talk to the real world, that's final. Look while I show you. See here? Look at my mouth."

(She mouths something.)

"You said . . . 'how I . . .' something. I didn't get that last."

"No, lookit. See what I do?"

(Flapping lips, facial contortions. Very weird.)

" 'Watch how I . . . how . . .' "

" 'Watch how I talk!' See how easy?"

"Well it isn't all words she does anyway. There's all those imitations, they way she makes her face go—making jokes—"

"You don't do it, that's all! I don't want to catch you talking to her that way when her doctor says not. Is that clear now?"

. . . Oyes. I see.

3

SHE HAD a lot to learn, and it was hard to cue her in about things. Like she had come in at the same time as an old guy who wore green pants, and the first weekend she saw him out in the yard, in the snow. So she wanted to go out in the yard. But that wasn't the way it worked. You had to have these passes to do things. I couldn't tell her that; I couldn't quite explain about the *must* of things, even though the passes part was simple.

When a man came, he either did or didn't get shock treatment: that is where they tie you down and zap you with electricity through your temples. Electro-convulsive therapy, they call it: "ECT," If he didn't get ECT, he got a pass that meant he could walk around outside, inside the gates; that's a pink "grounds" pass. If he did get shocked, then he had to wait till he could get it together to zip his fly again. Then he got it. A man must have a pass so he can function.

Now it's different with a woman. First you had to not leave the ward, and then when they let you, you had to have a blue pass. Some of the really fargone men were supposed to get them, too. The blue pass means you can walk down the hall to eat in the cafeteria. With an attendant. Then you get a yellow one which means you can be alone in the hall. You get a blue one at the end of the first or second week, and the yellow one after a couple weeks more. You have to be good, or you don't get them. Then you can get an orange pass that means you can go to Occupational Therapy or Thursday night dances, or holiday stuff in the gym without being sat with by your attendants. That is good for everybody because who wants to babysit anyway? A woman is supposed to learn the rules.

Anna had to learn that some things are completely illegal, which means it really pisses them off and they really give it to you: sideroom you, clap you in a jacket, shock your head off. If they're really pissed off, they don't completely knock you out when they shock you, and people can hear you screaming all the way out in the yard. These illegal things are: you can't have money on you, you can't go anywhere without a pass, and you can't be queer. It's also true that you shouldn't act too weird—and Anna shouldn't sign. That kind of ban is the personal part of treatment. (She knew about that ban.) And you bat your eyes at the guys, but you can't screw with them. All these bans mean that you violate rules very carefully, when you finally do. It makes things, even sex, more interesting than otherwise. Oh and the pink pass you can get just before they plan to let you out, which they usually don't; and you get a brown one so you can ride the bus in to job interviews in town. But not from our ward. On back wards, you just sit.

I say to her:—*What do you do at home?*
Needle-and-thread.
(You can't do that here, they don't allow it.)—*What do you do at home?*
Sweep with a broom.
(You can't do that—that's what Tall Diane does, it would

22

only make a fight.)—*What do you do at home?*

Sweep-with-broom, wash-with-a-cloth, feed-the-chickens, milk-the-cows, play-tennis, play-with-dogs, run-around-and-around-and-around. . . .

Busy lady.

Anna would take out her family pictures and lay them out on the table. When she thought that we weren't looking, she would stroke and pat the faces, and that always made me feel like stomping on them. But Weird Diane was the one who actually did that. She would always rip up stuff she found. The attendants usually let her—since that kept her out of their hair.

But that one time Anna lost her temper and started to slap her—and I grabbed Anna.—*Stop. Don't.* Anna was stronger than she looked, but you don't beat crazy people up. Crazy people don't know when to quit, and Weird Diane was absolutely crazy. Which I somehow had to explain.

That she was a handful and a headache to the attendants, but she mostly bothered us. So unless there was lots of blood, they'd let her be. If we others had any trouble, they'd eventually punish us; and that was only sensible since we could understand. There was no use punishing Weird Diane—all she'd do was simply knock your head off. Crazy people are pretty good at waiting till you look the other way. But Anna hated her. Anna was absolutely crazy about those pictures. I think she thought that she could have fought off Weird Diane and made her stay away, which wasn't true. Anna had been real active, real athletic. She was used to using her body for her thinking; strong, of course, like any farming wife is going to be. But she wasn't as strong as our other farmer, Vivian-who-didn't-talk: an even bigger lunatic, who followed Weird Diane around the ward.

I did manage to warn Anna off of both of them, which is

harder than it sounds. I knew something about Vivian. Not much. Only that she had begun to see Jesus in the kitchen one morning, and had begun to speak in what she'd said was "tongues." (—*Tongues*, I mouthed to Anna, clasping my tongue:—*Blah-blah-blah*.) Her husband had gone to the stove to get the hotcakes; she was Witnessing, couldn't be bothered; caught sight of him handling the hotcakes and threw hot grease in his face. He was blinded, Miss Hart said. (—*Stick in eyes*, I gestured to Anna, *her man*.) Horrified look from Anna. Didn't fight back after that. Even about the pictures of her family. Which was right. She was too sentimental about them, about her family; about the idea of a husband and a family. But I knew that after a while, she'd forget about them all if she just didn't see them. That after a while, she wouldn't be sure of anything about them, just like the rest of us, although all of us who could be understood lied and said we remembered. That it would come slowly.

First she wouldn't have remembered what their shoes looked like, even shoes she'd picked out, even shoes she'd bought them. Then she wouldn't remember their bedrooms. And then, if there'd been a way to know it, she'd have forgotten how her kitchen was: she couldn't have made a cake, and did she keep the milk in the front or the back of the fridge, on the top or the bottom shelf? She would forget what it felt like outside standing in the yard; how everything looked from a certain place you stand: first you forget the angles and then you forget the things. How it looks from this tree looking in this window, that you could see the canning shelves and dryer. And that it forgets you completely; that once there was a space for you in everything but the space is now filled in and you don't fit there. It's filled in.

In time, none of the streets would look right; away, she wouldn't remember them. All these things of life outside would be less real than a dream and, like a dream, be a little like death, something that pulls you out of the truth of right now and may not give you back, might snap you off like a flower stalk. And then become a far-off pressure like horror, even more horrible than today, because in that dream you are not alive: there is no space for you. Homeless. This may be hell but it is your home. No one will give you another.

4

Anna was smart, though. She watched us smoke, and she learned to smoke, and she watched us play cards. And when one of us looked at her, even out of the corner of an eye, her smile broke out. She had a very deaf smile—with her whole personality in it. I watched her as she watched us. I had time. How she smiled when we were looking at her, and how her face fell blank again, unthinking as a wall, when we looked away. I watched her watch us for several days after her family had first been allowed to visit. Then I taught her to play euchre. To teach her was so much easier than it sounds like it would be. She was so smart.

Taking all the cards, I laid them out. I took out the useless ones, and then I matched up all the others: jack on ten, queen on jack—and then the bowers, the special jacks, on just the aces. I did this only twice and she had got it. Pictures seemed to stick in Anna's head. Which jacks were bowers took the longest, but after she'd got that there was no problem. After the second full hand, she took every trick we played—she had played bridge as she wrote it: *Play bridge school ago many.* And it must have been, since she was pretty old. I wasn't near as good at learning her signs as she was at learning cards. Like:

Three fingers folded down; little finger and thumb out straight like an airplane—back-and-forth. I try to guess this.

You had to move things, you couldn't just place your hands a certain way. I try to guess it:

—*Fiddle?* I mouth. Fiddle around?

(Her bright eyes down to a wolfpoint concentration): *Not! No!* She mouths a word.

—*Fiddle?* I guess again.

Nope. No. She shakes her head. Not what she means. She shakes her head in: I don't know what word you are mouthing.

The question has changed from what *she* means to what word I convey.

—*Fiddle*, I say. I write this down on paper. It is one of the many words she doesn't know.

She looks at my mouth. At the paper.

—*Fiddle*, I say.

And then she is making Jack Benny violin motions. Victory.

And I'm laughing—I meant "fool around," but how do you say it?

She waves the air away from the violin playing. Back to lesson. *Three fingers folded down, back-and-forth, back-and-forth.* Grabs the cards and mouths—"*cards.*" Back-and-forth . . . "*cards*"; back-and-forth . . . "*cards.*"

FIDDLE cards? FOOL AROUND cards? I'm wondering. Yeah, you do fool around when you play cards . . .

"PLAY!" I say.

All that effort to say what we were doing.

Like:

Thumb-and-forefinger: pick, pick.

27

Like this? (*A picking motion, a sort of tweezing action. What does it mean?*)

No. *Up by the mouth, the thumb-and-forefinger: up-by-the-mouth, down-to-the-table, up-by-the-mouth;* so complicated.

(But it's just like a cat or dog will do . . . says Miss Hart.)

—*Little tiny?* I guess.

No.

She writes for me on the notepad: *Ciukin. Brd.*

What?

This all kept us busy, because there was something wrong with both of us (although it was not the same thing) and we weren't like ladies. Well, sometimes you could watch TV, but they screened it first, and I don't like *Love of Life*, which Anna couldn't follow. But that was okay with everybody else. That was okay with all the normal ladies. They were all like my mother, or all like my father's mother.

I always thought they both were nuts.

My mom is this very holy lady who was always so surprised when another one of us showed up. Which we did each year: at least, right up until I left. It seems like I always remember her sitting down. Down to dinner, down for a sermon at the Gospel Evangelical Tabernacle, down in front of the television set. Her belly'd get bigger and bigger in front of the TV screen, and then there'd be this baby. When I was little, I thought there was some connection. Real direct. She sat around, and sat around, and moaned and groaned and bored herself to death.

But then there were the cleanyfreaks like my father's mother, who did the same thing over and over and over like it was the most fascinating thing in the world, like cooking and getting ready to cook and getting over cooking was terrific; but nobody is interested in food unless they're hungry, and men don't give a damn what's clean. And if you don't believe that, go to a bachelor apartment sometime.

I wasn't like either one of them at all, or like my mother's mother, the one who lived with us. I liked them I guess; I mean there were times when I liked them; but I'm not the same kind. I like to keep moving. I really like to keep moving, if I can. If people let me.

Then there was Anna, who couldn't help but move around a lot. She thought by motion.

What they taught the boys at Deaf School in 1936 was how to be printers, how to set up linotyping. And what they taught the girls was how to clean. What else did they need. Who needs any learning. So she was a cleanyfreak like one of my grandmas, but there was nothing to clean on Women's D. Usually. (Well, there was Tall Diane who was sweeping and sweeping the hallway all day long, but she couldn't help it, didn't know what she was doing. Mrs. Pratt told me she thought she ran a boarding house or something.) So neither of us had anything to do, and that *will* make you crazy if you let it.

So we played cards in the afternoons till the evening shift would come around and stare. Especially the head nurse, Miss Wykowski. Wykowski would make it a point to speak to Anna. She used these big expressions and talked so loud, she like to deafened me. "Wellhi!" she'd say. "Wellhowareyou!" she'd say—like Anna was maybe two years old, or really stupid. Wykowski would stare like this Deaf Person was maybe a dog I had trained to look like it was playing euchre. That would make me nervous. I'd go out on the porch. Late afternoons (after Wykowski came on) especially.

If you wore a coat, they'd come and check on you, which is what they were paid to do, so I didn't wear a coat. It was really cold that winter. My fists in my armpits; my sweater wrapped around me almost twice. But I could breathe out there. That porch on the crossbar.

That part of Illinois is flat like a floor and the wind would

29

come straight over the truckstops and businesses and fat white streets from the flat plains grass which is almost prairie, like the schoolbooks say it is. Sometimes on the porch there was an intricate pattern of snow from where the wind had only really gently nudged it through the chicken wire fencing; but mostly the wind slapped sharp snow straight through the cage from the north—gritty crystals of soot and shivered ice, stinging your eyes, making you filthy. Not like the snow you see in pictures in a schoolbook. Like a menace.

Way out in front there was the guardhouse. To one side was the exercise yard where the patients who could walk outside could tramp around in the snow till they got bored. And down below me was the baby ward, an experimental ward, which of course means lots of governmental money. I would lean my head on the grill and watch the little kids below me till my skin stuck to the metal from the cold.

The babies were wrapped in layers and layers of coats. Their attendants brought them out at four o'clock each afternoon, and dropped each one in a clean place in the snow, and it was interesting: red and orange and blue and yellow babies in the snow. There were three attendants, and they brought out thirteen children, one by one. For playing statues, only very convincing. Bringing out these limp kids and laying them down like dolls: one on his belly, face in the snow; one on his side; another, his back; the ones on their butts banged down backwards; and all of them rocking— red and green and yellow and orange, up and down, back and forth, rocking and rocking and never looking up or out or at me or at each other. Just the snow. A very pretty arrangement, very lucky, down below me. Never seeing anything but snow. I watched them for hours. Anna would join me: Anna looking down at them and signing—

(Pats the head of imaginary children): *little kids*. (Making this sign with a wiping motion right under your nose): *snot-nosed-kids*.

Snot-nosed-kids, she points looking questioning at me. *Little-kids (three fingers folded down, back-and-forth), little-kids PLAY? Little-kids (play baseball motion); snot-nosed-kids (shoot marbles motion); snot-nosed-kids (fists in air—), little-kids fistfight?*

But they didn't.

Mrs. Pratt had told me all about them. All you really had to know. That was schizophrenia for kids:

"Them's artistic."

"Say what?"

"Art. Istic. Like little schizies, only they don't give me no trouble."

Right you are.

That's the way to be crazy.

Never seeing anything but snow.

—What was that sign? I look with my face (I hadn't got it . . .).

Pick, pick, Anna answered. Out in the dog run, we could sign in peace. Until they came outside to check on us, I mean.

Pick, pick, she signed.

—No, I don't get it.

There she is pointing—

There, up there—up through diamonds of the screen—

There were *BIRDS* against the big sky;

BIRDS—pick-pick with the thumb-and-forefinger;

—BIRDS, I mouth; and she's flapping her wiry arms: *FLY, BIRDS. FLIGHT—AN EAGLE—SOARING—FREEDOM* . . . My heart pounding—grabbing her by the shoulders, shaking her—*SHUT UP. SHUT UP. SHUT UP!*

5

THEY LET us watch some TV programs after supper: the ones the attendants like, and they had really rotten taste. The TV set was up against the back wall, in the day room, with all the chairs and sofas ringed around it, like the TV is in everybody's home. Usually I sat on the brown sofa between Weird Diane on the one end, and Vivian-who-didn't-talk on the other; the others had their friends they sat with, so I was stuck with the lunatics, in front. I was a kid. Not much in common. Anna sat in the corner and played solitaire for hours and hours and hours, when she wasn't pacing around—but they didn't like us to pace around when we were supposed to be watching TV programs. So we sat. At least, for a while.

After you've watched TV for a while, you sort of know how everything will end—unless you're really drunk or buzzed out, like with reds (and I mean Seconal); so I would stare at the screen until I knew how everybody was going to act, and then I'd go to counting the cement blocks in the green wall behind it. All the walls are green. They had weird blocks. They'll crack along the mortar, but they never crack the same. Each edge is different; you can see a lot of things in them. Like:

There was this house with a little block chimney, only sometimes it was a schoolhouse with these square windows with little bitty panes. If you looked in the cracks of windows you'd see little faces of people trying to see up through these windows—then you stop that.

You could see a bunch of numbers: a one and a three and a backwards four and a couple of eights (and maybe a nine): I could make an X and an A and a capital B out of the broken pieces of bricks; if you do this till you almost think they're there, you have to stop. I always stopped at the B, since it was hardest. You have to stop with the ones you know aren't there.

And then I would let myself start to feel all the parts of my body from the inside, hoping that something was happening to it, something I would have to go take care of. Like that one of my legs was itching, or I was thirsty, or that I had to go to the bathroom or throw up.

You can't let yourself think too much, but I would try to figure out a little bit about the way they had things running there. Sometimes you protect yourself that way; other times, you crazy-make yourself. Every now and again we had these nurse-trainees or interns or someone to talk to, which was fun; and I wasn't the only one who thought that this was interesting; or anyway, less boring. Because when I first came here, there was this girl named Bonny Madden, but then they moved her somewhere else, and when trainees came, she'd make Weird Diane go get them. She'd say like: See those young boys over there? I bet they wanna know your name; I think they *like you* . . . And: See those girls? Well that one thinks you're EVIL. . . . Since we were a back ward, she could make this work out pretty well: most of the trainees only came there once and so they couldn't spot this trick.

What these trainees do is, they come up to you, very solemn and fake, and they talk to you very quiet and very fakey. Tell us about your problems. Scribble, scribble. Or if you have a "brain dysfunction" they read you questions off this little list, like what day is it? Of course, you don't see calendars in here, so this gets tough, even for me. They move across the ward rooms, being solemn; and Weird Diane would watch them, like a rat watches kittens.

And they say—

To Tall Diane, who's sweeping: that's a real nice job you're doing.

Which it isn't.

To Diane Brown: you're really looking nice . . .

She always does.

. . . I guess you must be feeling better?

Better than what?

To Spacey Shirley, who's very old, with grey hair down her back and off in Never-never land—her they loved; they always asked her brain dysfunction questions: What day is it. Did the Yankees win the pennant again this year? Last year? She had been committed in 1954, and had not seen a whole lot of baseball games, which information didn't seem to matter much. Scribble, scribble, scribble.

Tell us about your husband.

What?—she'd say.

Tell us about your husband—have you talked to him today?

Why, what a nice young man! You look like the president!

Where's Henry?

What?

Where's Henry? Have you seen him recently?

Well it's so hot in here—look at all these people!

They love it when you give them textbook answers; everyone would scribble in his notebook and be very satisfied. One time I asked her: Hey, who's Henry? And she says, what? And I go: Henry says hi to you for him, Shirley; and she snorts, oh the blessed hell he does, he's buried fifteen years ago. . . .

You could make up stuff and make their eyes get big. A distraction. For a while I had this trainee Social Worker who looked like Sandy Dennis in *Up the Down Staircase*. She was doing a thesis on incorrigibles, I think. She used to ask me all these *Serious Questions* that she got out of this book called *Casework Problems*, which meant me. Every week for a month we'd talk and she'd laugh and twist her hair around a pencil. I got to the point where I really kind of liked her. And I got so bored that I started to tell her about what really happened, about the things that I was really feeling: that made her sick so she got another job.

I hate to remember telling her any kind of truth.

Most of the patients were either crazy or very crazy, but nobody had ever thought that I was—only legally incorrigible. That's a special thing, because if they'd put me in the Illinois Girls' School I'd have been free at eighteen, and nobody would have let me off that easy. Committed, I had to stay till twenty-one, by which time I'd be like Weird Diane, or maybe even stand and stare like Vivian-who-wouldn't-ever-talk. So they'd all be rid of me. But it takes a lot of things to make you crazy; more than you think, because you fight to save your home and you live in your head.

How to be incorrigible:

You can run away from home and stay away.

You can screw a lot and have a bastard, which the state will take away—or did, in 1964 (and for years before that). Or you could take up petty crime, or dope and drinking, or be listed sociopathic. There are a lot of ways to get that label. Or probably even things I haven't done or heard about.

Piss people off. Make them overvalue you.

Weird Diane hates me:

"You watching me alla time!"

"Not either!"

"Yeah you are, sugarbabe! You keep them voodoo eyes offa me!"

Back off. Carefully.

I'd wait for a commercial and then get up and take a real long shower. They only let me take a few a day, because I really really like it. Being alone, and having all that heat on me.

You really could be alone in the shower except for some of the night attendants, who would come and watch you in the morning—the only men we had worked nights. And Miss Wykowski, from evening shift, but she bothered only me. Miss Wykowski.

I like the smell of green soap: clean and like medicine, like somehow something clean is going to happen.

HOT water.

It's so cold and damp in this building your bones hurt. And the shower has the smell of mineral-water-wearing-stone; a little mildew, a little bleach. You could smell the heat and soap and in the splattering of the water you couldn't hear the Muzak anymore. Cocksucking Muzak.

And I like just rubbing the soap around myself. I rub the jellied stuff around and wherever it slips, it slides across a bone: the bones of hips, and sliding to my ribcage . . . I like my bones; the bonier I was the better. They were my friends and surprised me when I felt them or looked in the mirror, they were amazing to feel under the thin soft skin. Where I ran my fingers, there were bones; wherever I rubbed the soap were pleasing, sharp firm edges, like my friends.

And then (I was never ready) there's Wykowski on the outside of the curtain; (never ready) waiting to say it's time to change the dressings (and I haven't got them wet, now?). Waiting to watch me step out of the shower.

Ever observant. In control.

Everything about Wykowski shines and is very white; shine in her hair like a lady in a movie. Her uniform: white shiny nylon, very white; white hose, very expensive, a little old-fashioned, like white china. Fingernails shine. And she rustles when she walks—a woman sound, two slips together; a little clink of pens and coins (I sometimes picked her pocket); all white light and sound and glowing seamless. The head nurse with the dope keys—all the power you need.

To command we change the bandages, which we do:

(I am sitting on the table in the medications room. She is fiddling.)

"You're behaving yourself now?" (She slaps me on the thigh.)

"Yeah," I smile. Real young and kind of sweet.

"What were you on when you axed yourself?"

"Nothing."

(Slap on the thigh again; she giggles.) "What were you on, now? Don't you give me that stuff."

"Jazz."

The eye that says: o god I love how sexy bad you are; you should be punished.

37

"Heroin!" (She makes a little clicking sound; a lady scandalized. A little pinch, a little too much pulling on the stitches . . .)

"Ow!" (It doesn't hurt this much. I watch her.)

"You cut on yourself. What are you complaining for? This can't hurt."

"Don't—that's pulling—"

(A little pull.)

"Ouch—don't. I was jazzed when I did that. I don't even remember feeling anything."

"Don't pull away like that—lie down. I haven't got four hands and you've got your tape down in these stitches. Heavenly days—here! Lie down or I'll smack you one."

That's what she wants.

And then we would finally be finished, at maybe nine-thirty or ten, and I'd go out in the hall and the feeling from the shower would be gone. What a shame. There'd be Vivian feeling the wall cracks with her fingers; there'd be Tall Diane with her sweeping and sweeping and sweeping, and Weird Diane doing babble-talking and Spacey Shirley standing around, and people who weren't playing cards or something, just sitting. And Anna would be pacing around with her hands, which should be in her pockets, tucked in her armpits. Being silent. Staring at them all, and being silent.

I think she was never sure just what was wrong with everybody; she thought too much, because she couldn't talk. You mustn't think. The trick is to see these things and not get inside them, never to see what Vivian sees, or what you think you might see if you were Vivian; never to imagine what it's not like not to trust where the wall joins the ceiling (little lines like snakes); and never to imagine if they left the ward door open, or a window; or if they left a knife around—because you just can't handle that.

38

That's how the attendants do it. They never see anything, they laugh all the time. The trick is to pretend that nobody is doing anything weird, and that you never could, either, and that what you see is perfectly okay. But it can creep up on you anyway if you get too good at that. You can get so everything's exactly equal: people and walls and Vivian and Diane; the TV and the cement blocks and the way they fold the milk containers; and when everything is equal, what are you? That's when you sit and stare. You have to fight that actively, all that staring; and when you find yourself doing that you have to get up and move. You simply move. Just walk someplace and look back where you were—not far away—and remind yourself that you aren't there anymore. So you are not equal to the way you were; that place is not yourself, and you're still free.

6

OUT ON the street I used to have these great thoughts, like that I was completely free; almost with my head completely weightless. I had never imagined feeling like that before. That usually I went around trying to be happy, I think everybody does, but under the happy part would be the truth. The trapfact of the way things really were. That whatever there was to enjoy, you went back to misery since that was where you actually existed.

I would look up at the buildings which would go straight up around me and think how all the people there were living; rooms I might like, people who might like me, who might even give me money; rooms I didn't know with things inside them I had never seen, even in movies; beautiful things, colorful things; different ways to be; not what I knew. I could look in all directions and not feel that I knew everything already and that it was all on top of me, and like I couldn't breathe.

At my parents' house you could just walk in the door and it would crush you: the too-small rooms with colors that I hated, and everything feeling like my father. He had puffed out and was stuck in everything. First I couldn't sleep in there, and then I couldn't breathe.

But wherever I looked on the street, he wasn't in it. I felt free of him. You can freeze and starve, of course, but you can breathe if you can find someplace where nobody either wants or even knows you. And sometimes on the ward nobody wanted me; and that's a kind of freedom.

Freedom *from*.

One time my father visited—he only saw me twice—and he held his hands out to me through the wire mesh; but then he saw that nobody was looking, so he dropped them.

He had the idea, he told me, that I was getting better. They were going to move me up in front, and he could maybe visit more. Forget it.

I wasn't going up front anywhere. Not for years.

The front wards got the People Going Somewhere—getting better. Better at acting out the things they should be, I imagine. Better at pretending they aren't crazy and they never ever could be. Most of the patients there had been responsible, or it was thought they would be, sometime— skillful people, voters, people with money; workers, fathers of families—Daddy types. Nobody who was deaf, or really nuts, or undesirable, like on our ward. Front wards were like with real citizens who had somehow just screwed up: they were important, and the staff they saw were therefore also important, doing the job of fixing up slightly bent but perfectly workable people. My doctor would have loved me to move to a front ward; he would have come to visit me, he would still have been my doctor—he was stuck with me; and I bet we'd have had a lot more "talks," which God forbid. I saw enough of him. The doctors in front were much more important than our docs; we were not getting better, we therefore weren't important. For this reason what our shrink staff did was also not important. Which makes sense.

41

They were like first grade teachers: embarrassed to say what they did and who they did it to. We just weren't worth the time to fool with us; the very sight of backward types depressed them. Or sure seemed to. Our wards' docs were Dr. Falgus, Dr. Gildenshied and Dr. Kim; the first two were senile, and the third man talked like a man blowing English through a bubblepipe. He heard that way as well, so everything about us either baffled or entirely offended him.

Every morning when he came to work, he'd look at us and sag in every seam. Another day with the living proof his career had wings and was flapping away—real fast—in the wrong direction.

Hard is life.

My father visiting the second time:

(He sits in the visitor's room across from me, behind the chicken wire fencing.)

"Well," (looks hard at me). "I imagine you know how good we was to you, now."

"Yeah," I say. "Where is Mama?"

(Looks around for a staff member but sees none.) "And well, I guess you're pretty well settled in. It looks decent."

"Yeah. When is Mama coming? Or didn't she come?"

"Well," (looks around for staff members and sees one— sudden tears).

"You Ma sure has missed you, sugar." (Attendant listening.)

"I just don't see how you could have done us like you did. You just about broke her trusting heart, but I guess you know that. . . . (Attendant leaves to answer the phone.) Anyway. (Takes out his handkerchief; looks at his watch.)

"Well I want to talk to her then. I mean she is here, isn't she? Is she in the car?"

"What do you want to do that for, ain't things bad enough?"

"I just want to talk to her kind of private. I just want to talk to her a minute."

"Private, hell." (Looks at watch. Holds it to his ear.)

"I don't see why we can't talk a little, private."

"She's talking to that Chinaman of yours, Whatsisname."

"Well that ought to clear up everything for everybody."

"Hunh."

(He looks at me, but I don't meet his eyes. I've never liked to.)

"Still better'n everybody. Still better'n everybody, aren't you?"

I look at the clock.

I think that I can stand him.

For half an hour.

And through a chicken wire fence.

Fortunately I was back ward, and you don't get to have a lot of visitors. I was back ward, I was going to stay as back ward; this has its points. At least the staff isn't *following your progress*—writing down every word or action you might say or do, like Brian says they do sometimes. Brian is a guy I met in there, a man that things have made a professional inmate.

Brian was also back ward, but there are back wards and back wards, like there are public schools and then there are public schools. For example, the women's back wards have fewer raving loonies than the men's back wards do. That's because except for the real crazies, more of the men were worth fixing up. Those guys went up front. And because their back wards had both the real nuts and the guys who just weren't worth it, their attendants saw the difference and treated some of them like men. For instance, Brian.

Brian had a job outside the hospital. He was a dancer in a gay bar. He was twenty-one and had been committed when he was about sixteen, about like me, until he was *cured*, which would be never. He was this light brown *fegeleh* (he liked that better than *faggot*) who had so many things done to cure him that the very sight of him discouraged a lot of the staff. A living failure. They had made their peace with failure by pretending that the things they'd done to him had never happened, which was fine.

There were also other guys on Brian's ward who worked. One had been a carpenter but had had this real bad accident with his head; this had demented him. He could not remember anything of his life before the accident; he was very stupid and now had epilepsy. But if you put the tool in his hand, he could saw like crazy. And he could toe-in these tiny little furniture nails—beautiful work to see when he was finished, you could hardly find the joint. He could only work for an hour or so, and then he'd fall apart; and the people he worked for would stick him in a cab, and he'd come back to us. That was a failure, too.

There also were these real loons on his floor—real dangerous nuts. Like Phillip-the-black-one-with-pens-in-his-pockets. This guy had a collection of nonworkable pens in several folders marked with "STP," and stuck in his work shirt pockets; and one time he stuck somebody's eye out with one of them and they made him stop carrying them for a while, but then they changed staff and he got some more. And one time he was just sitting in the day room, staring out the window, when Brian came in from work and said "hi" to somebody; and Phillip gets up and tries to brain him with a chair. He really nearly got it done. This put Brian in Mercy Hospital with head injuries (and all he could think of was whether he'd have epilepsy when he came out, and whether he'd still have his Irish nose), which was funny because when the staff there found out where he'd come from they didn't want to touch him. They wanted him tied down. Well his doctor wouldn't hear of that, he actually laughed about it; and after that every time they came at Brian to draw

44

blood or change bandages or something, he would draw his head back, real low and hateful, and then snap his head up at them and hiss! like a snake. Which is pretty funny, I think.

But then one time Phillip just came into Brian's room and got in bed with him and he was really good. That's just it: you never really know about the ones who are really lunatics, like Phillip.

There was Ralph, this white man built like a storage tank with whitish hair; Brian said he had once been real pretty with real blond hair; but when I saw him he just had an uneven fringe of it up over the bald, scarred areas like weeds growing over a rutted road. He weighed about 350 and had suspenders. Mostly he sat, and that's what he did; but if you put food in front of him he ate, and that's what he did. For hours, unless you stopped him. He was simple. He had been a construction worker and a falling beam had hit him in the head.

Yes, there are back wards and back wards; you think about that a lot (if you can think). Many of the men on back wards are vegetables, and some are only retarded for some specific reason. Something unpleasant happened to them. Everyone knows that their stay in here is permanent and everyone just forgets them, but the patients go on living here. Just because you're nuts doesn't mean you've left the surface of the earth. You still get holes in your socks; you still get sexy. You watch the Series on television, and that's how you make your way. You just get by. And on the men's wards there are pool tables, bumper pool and exercise equipment; it's okay to move right in and make yourself at home, and just be crazy. Everyone knows that you're not crazy just to get your way, which everybody thinks that ladies sometimes do; everyone knows that a man just couldn't help it. There's a sense of loss when a man freaks out: that a lively, useful thing has suffocated. Not like ladies.

Like I told Brian: mostly we ladies sat. (The idea of boredom seemed to appeal to Brian. He thinks ladylike is easier, which shows you.) But sometimes—only on weekdays—they would schedule things for us ladies to listen to: cheap things for them to offer. Things that we should know, like to put grease in a cup before you measure syrup, or that kind of boring, useful stuff. There wasn't a lot of call to measure syrup on our ward; even they would have admitted this was true. And one time there was this chic young thing from Blaisdell's Ladies Store who showed up to entertain us with two suitcases full of wigs and tubes. A makeup artist. She laid out tubes and bottles and brushes and little bits of lady fuzz and fur, and then started painting up her face and talking to herself in this set of three mirrors with big white bulbs on them, bright lit-up like a theater marquee.

Diane Brown had also been a makeup artist, working for years at Block's department store before she married. After the lady had been jabbering and dabbing away for about fifteen minutes, Diane jumps right in and makes it a dialogue. Giving the lady lots and lots of good advice, one Face to another. This blush, that rouge, some other kind of lipstick; Max Factor, Helene Curtis, names and tubes and plates of little colored stuff you rubbed around to make more bones and take away the lines and little marks. They got very tight about these things, and even talked to me; how I had hollows in my cheeks this stuff would cover. All I did was paint these purple circles under my eyes. And they said: *"Re-e-all-ly, Latisha. Honestly."*

And then Diane Brown started making fun of those thick little-bear eyebrows of Anna's—who'd been standing around the whole time, looking critical. "We ought to paint you up," she said to Anna.

I made *paint-my-face* motions; Diane did the same—as Beautiful Lady. Then Diane made this motion off towards

46

Anna. Nothing doing. Anna made her *tastes-like-horsepiss* face.

And of course we didn't have to knock her down, and we did paint her. But first she stuck her hip out and went *wibble-wibble-wibble* like a hooker.

The little lines around her eyes: erase her age. The darkened places that showed she couldn't sleep. Make those agile eyes so dark she's like a tribal mask; the white erase, the blending of mascara with the fingertips; Anna wouldn't let them clip her eyebrows, though—they were like her punctuation.

And when she looked in the mirror, she made her *tastes-like-SOUR-horsepiss* face; and then she reached to touch the mirror Anna, very carefully, very reflective.

She slid her fingertips across the hair; beneath the chin; briefly on the thigh—watching the mirror. Slyly, slowly, she made sexy-eyes at it. She pulls me out in front of her, to hide behind. Peek-peek, the sexy-eyes in the mirror . . . the Famous Lady. Everyone is standing, clapping loudly. She starts to slink around me in a Famous Lady way (everyone laughs at us—I stand like a post)—eyebrows up; now just one of them, cocked high-living; now she's behind me again, and hidden completely—all you can see in the mirror is me, standing with purple eyes—then arms, an extra pair appear—combing my hair, blubbing my lips, arranging my clothing motions; and then she is unbuttoning me, my new hands in the mirror making me sexy—

"Here!" Miss Hart says. "What do you think you're doing!" I jump away from in front of the mirror and there they are, eyes in a row, all the staff is looking hard at me.

"Playing!" I tell them. "We were only playing!"

I laugh like I think the whole thing's really funny.

Nobody laughing.

Hard to breathe.

The other place you could be by yourself was the sideroom; but even in that teeny grey room you could hear the tinny flat automatic Muzak: *There's a Coconut Grove; My Funny Valentine; Alice Bluegown; Climb Every Mountain; A Day in the Life of a Fool; April Love....* I learned to dissect every single separate sound, to hate them right; to hate the tiny flat minds of inventors. The Muzak played the same tape over and over. And over. And over.

One thing about being sideroomed: it's cold. It's really cold in there without your clothes. It's a six-by-eight-foot room, green of course, that has no windows. For furniture, a bucket and canvas cot without a blanket. There's just the bucket, you don't go to the bathroom—that's a *privilege*.

After a while, you almost think it is. I didn't handle that very well the first time they put me in there. I would try to hold it until there was no one looking in the door; but then I'd look up and there'd be Hart or Wykowski. Or Weird Diane. Or one of the guys—the night attendants.

I felt like I had never known before that I was naked. And I didn't want them to know how well it worked. How cold it was. How helpless. I was afraid that for the first time I would see my fists hit something just like watching someone else. I had to concentrate on not having that happen. One of the things you do is make yourself breathe; breathe in, breath out; counting the bricks (can you make out little cities like the edges of Detroit in little boxes?).

You never bother to look up at the window in the door: *I'm cool; this doesn't bother me.* (You try your best.)

But then I look up and see Wykowski and then I'm banging my head on the floor—bang! slam! it explodes in my head so fine! But then they'd tie me down and I really hate that. You can't have anger; there's no place to put it.

But.

Sometimes your body fights when your mind has given up.

I think that the sideroom usage was not Dr. Kim's idea. He preferred not to see unpleasant things. He considered ugly scenes to be attendants' business; he looked away when people did those things which were undignified, the way most men leave diapering to women. Maybe that was his attitude toward Sign Language—not just misunderstanding: some people think that Sign is not a language, but it is. If someone had just been able to tell him. If he'd listened. He's no listener.

With sign, you can tell *when it happened; how you feel.* You can say the immediate, simple things you use a language for, and you can make it *interesting.* Lots of people can't do that in English.

What I think offended Kim was that he really thought Sign Language looked undignified. Sign is full of facial exclamation points. He kept his face very deadpan, very doctor. He kept his hands to his sides or folded neatly. The attendants drove him crazy with their constant gesturing; and Anna, of course—with her circling words and pictures in the air—he thought was animal-like: something out of caveman-throwback stories. He thought that words were the same thing as ideas, so she could not have a thought or even God. God was the Word and the Word was Love, so she must be an animal; Sign must have made her crazy by itself without the Word. Something crazy, stupid and undignified.

Dr. Kim liked things simple. He liked things very neatly tied together: *You don't talk with hands,* he told her. Nothing she could say. He read this somewhere.

Kim had a very small frame fitted over what he knew about; there were not many things he knew about, and this had made life cleaner. He fitted at the top of the frame, with medicine in general and every other kind of work below him. Work was life.

Mental patients didn't have their own place on the frame, since we weren't working. So we were tiresome, unaccounted for, bizarre. And somehow, unaccountably, Dr. Kim had become a back ward doctor. There didn't seem to be a way to attain his proper place, like in Korea. And this thoroughly discouraged him. I think he was miserable and maybe this made him want to stick to silly rules. At least he was boss. He could feel like things were working. Which they weren't.

Anna made a sign for him: *peer-glasses-squint.*

I thought that was pretty funny. And, of course, the way she walked like him—prince of the penguins. For Anna, talking was creating.

She points to a poster of President Johnson hanging on the wall and signs: *the head-of.*

Of State, I think she means.

A picture hangs in the Nurses's Station of Dr. Gildenshied; she signs: *the-head-of* (he's the chief doc on the back wards); signs: *glasses-squint/the-head-of/you-and-me.*

—"Boss!" I guess.

She pats me loudly.

Yup. That guy's the boss, and we can't sign (much).

I point across the room:—*who/that-person?*

(Twists her mouth up; glares from side to side: *Weird Diane.*

—*Who/that-person?*

(Belly wobble; bloats out cheeks; eyes empty): *Mrs. Pratt.* (Choke on my coffee). . . .

About the ward she signs—a lot: *waste-time, waste-time!* No kidding.

But what were we saving time up for—we're nothing anyway.

Except I guess that wasn't true for Anna. After all, she had had children (once); she had been something (once).

We would practice. She would teach. I wasn't very good at all at sign language. She'd call me: *poker face.* But slowly,

50

stupidly, by January I'd picked up several signs. Not too quickly. I wasn't very good: my fingers stammered. But I kept on trying anyway—*Father, Mother, crazy, alone* and *good-friend*. For *good-friend*, clasp your pointer fingers like little people firmly shaking hands; shake these friends; that's *good-friend*.

If I did it right she was crazy over me—she'd punch my shoulder—head bobbing *yes-yes-yes* like a puppet crazy. *Practice*, she told me: *Lazy! You/need/practice.* And I did practice. At first, I did.

Slyly, I ask:—*Who-me?*

Pick-pick/eyes.

(BIRD eyes? Why BIRD EYES?)—*Why bird-eyes/me?*

Pick-pick/eyes (she acts this out): *you/peek-eyes/same-like/ bird/you/skinny/pick-pick/peek/like/blackbird/eyes.*

Yeah, I do.

7

SHE NEVER looked quite right for a woman her age, not like the mother of a family. Oh, she looked old. I mean she had crows' feet, love lines, places where the sun met a hard wind; but she did not look like a mature woman: fat, baggy, idle.

(My father slapping my mother's fat thigh: *well now that's a real woman.*)

(Not me.)

And you don't play kick-the-paperwad out on the porch when you're a mature lady. Ladies don't. She had those face lines, of course; a little grey in her hair, and a little sagging— mostly where her breasts had used to be. Her bones were right: her shoulders and her hips completely even in a line. It wasn't that she was mannish, just athletic, like a girl can be. Like no grown woman I had ever seen.

But when we dragged her downstairs for Thursday night dances, that's when she looked like a woman—really frumpy. That's when she looked like a patient from a ward. A dumpy, lost old bag of clothing. And that was the staff's fault.

The clothing her daughters had brought her was good enough. In fact, the problem was that it was too good. That was what actually made her look so awful.

Before your clothes came up from Admitting, they got rid of a lot of them. They got rid of belts and ties, not only because you could hang yourself, but because there's no way that any attachment could stay stuck with what it belonged to—not in our ward. You should see what comes back from the laundry, anyway—all that bleach. They threw out all the slacks or jeans, because that's not lady stuff. They certainly don't want to threaten femininity. They check to see which sex you are, before they even consider sending your clothes to you. Then they get rid of the expensive stuff, things somebody might rip off. The only people, of course, who could have got away with that would have to have been on staff, which tells you they are realistic. Then they got rid of half of what was left, because all the room you had anyway was a little space in a closet, and part of a drawer. But then you don't get out much. What do you need clothes for?

And then they put the labels on, so that all over your body you have *Eastern Central Hospital* and your name just like little flags out on a putting course. Well, Anna had had a lot of slacks, and she had had these nice outfits where one part matched the other part. This had made the clothing they allowed her especially bad. When her kids came to visit (and the doctor did not let them come too often; and it was true that she was more upset after they left than if they didn't come at all); when her kids came, they wondered what had happened to her taste. But the Admitting people had only sent up half of the match on all these matching outfits. And besides, some of the outfits had been really nice clothes—too expensive—and so many sets had had slacks; all of which she couldn't have. I wonder if her kids ever asked her why she dressed like that. Probably not, since they were cheerful people. They wouldn't have asked her anything that might have got a bad answer. As it was, what could they make of what she told them about this place? . . . Better to drop it. . . .

What all this meant was that she dressed entirely out of mismatches. It didn't hit you when she was running around, but when she just sat, and that's all she did at dances, then you saw the checks-with-stripes, the flower-patterns-with-the-funny-plaid. She tried at first. But after a couple of months, she didn't care.

Well, the dances were supposed to be a big deal because you got to see patients from the other wards, which translates *opposite sex*. You're supposed to look and giggle but not touch. It's not really all that big a deal, that's what I think. You could see the coherent ones at Snack Bar every weekday afternoon and Snack Bar could be interesting and useful—that's where I met Brian, who helped me so much, later.

The dances are not any kind of big deal, though: almost none of the guys ever has any money. Except Brian. And of course he doesn't count—I mean, with ladies. Though he would be useful. If you pay him later.

At seven o'clock on Thursday nights our ward trooped down to the big locked hall door and they unbarred and unlatched and unlocked it, and then they tied up some of us, and then we all shambled out of our green ward into the brown hall, past the vegetable wards, past the kitchen, past the back hall leading to the attendants' locker room; and then we would turn and there was the stairwell and we'd sort of pour down four flights of brown stairs, straggling out from each other as much as we could; (Weird Diane would manage to pee in one of the corners but sometimes they'd get mad and didn't let her); and then we come to the big firedoor leading to the main floor leading to the basement, and that is also locked, and then we shuffle on into the gym and it is Dance Time. On Thursday they let Women's D, Men's F, and the front wards and two of the wipe-out, vegetable wards get together. Whoopee. The other wards meet other days, like Wednesday and Friday.

As soon as we get there, our staff heads for the other staff and leaves us the hell alone: don't bother me, I don't bother you; get lost and don't do anything I wouldn't do. For that you'd need a big imagination. Sometimes Wykowski hangs around me, though.

On the edge of the big gym floor are the folding chairs, in little wing formations. We got them from a high school fieldhouse and they are red-and-gold, purple-and-gold, green-and-white (with most of the paint scraped off), the colors of somebody's basketball team somewhere.

Our attendants jam together in the good chairs (some even had arm chairs) on the left side of the room; I mean they have their own fish to fry (with male attendants from the men's wards—babyluv). On the right side is the Snack Bar, where the state gives you five dollars a month to buy ice cream and cigarettes and pop without any fizz, and third-day discount doughnuts. They keep your "money" for you in an account book and that way they think they know what your habits are.

They like that. Cigarettes can be traded, sometimes even for money, but the other stuff just tastes like fat people shit. At one end of the room is the stage, with big purple curtains; there's a picture painted on a big screen behind them, but I could never make it out: some kind of scenery. Usually there's this old record player on the stage, which is the Music. The Music is played by this beak-nosed hemiplegic lady who does the Music Therapy, when we have it, which is every other week.

The music is awful but the dance is okay if people will leave you alone, which they sometimes don't. The vegetables mostly sit and rock and rhythmically bang their heads, or lie on the floor and look up at the ceiling, which is peaceful. Some of them are dangerous, and that always pisses me off—

attendants standing around won't ever help you (unless there's really lots of blood). Mostly there'd be waltzes and big band music, and *Barney Google*, and *Alice Bluegown*, and nothing cooler than 1955 when the Music Therapy lady took the stage.

Sometimes the docs come slumming. They'd have staff meetings and drop by the gym to see us Recreate. Doing Socializing. Everybody one big happy family. Especially Dr. Falgus, a little square man with eyes that never focused (at least on me). They all come and stare, and smile and leave. That's therapy. We're seeing movie stars.

Anna would hide in corners and when she could pick up the beat through her feet, she'd keep time. Mostly she hid. That is okay most of the time. And most of the music doesn't have a good enough beat to pick up. And nobody cares.

But sometimes the visitor types will come to give us dance lessons. The Waltz (-2-3 . . .), the Virginia Reel, the Polka . . . the visitors will come up and grab us by the hands and swing these groups of two of us together while they stand and grin like lunatics. Brian has a way that will discourage them. As soon as one of them comes to him and starts this do-good gushing, he starts simpering—index finger on his chin and makes these googoo eyes, bat-bat—real silly, like a woman's supposed to do. He gets so hotshot faggot they will walk all the way around four other people to avoid him. Brian's really good at understanding things.

They have a real knack for fixing you up with somebody you hate. Like one time this string-tied fat man wants me to dance with Bill from F, one of the dangerous vegetables you try to stay away from, and Bill hurt me. He tore off all the buttons on my blouse (he could have just asked); I had to ask for help to get him off me. Everybody all around just laughed. I hate people who won't help you. But Brian kicked him in the balls, which was okay. Brian can be really useful sometimes.

Diane Brown introduced Brian to me in the Snack Bar; I think that was November—before Anna came; I came around and Diane was with the guy from Recreation Therapy and this Brian, whom I'd only seen from clear across the room. She says his name and mine, and I say—"hi," and all he says to me is—

"Hon, how *old* are you!"

The way most people do. And so, I tell him.

"I don't even believe that." (Diane Brown.) "Do *you* believe that?"

> I'm sitting down at the table with them, directly across from Brian. His eyes are very bright but his thin body's real relaxed, so I think: *sopors*.

"I was about your age . . ." he says. And drops it.

"She hustles." (Diane Brown, again.)

> To hell with her.

"Jazz?" he says.

> Oyes.

"Oh *well*," he says. "Some people *do* have all the luck."

> He taps the ashes off with his index finger; skinny fingers like a mesmerist.

"You gay?" I say.

> (Now they're looking smug around the table.)

"Can you keep a *secret?*"

> (They all laugh.)

Recreation Therapy guy: "She can't. None of them can."

"I can!" I say.

"She can't," says Diane Brown.

"Like hell I can't."

"*Can you* keep a secret? Put your *hand* out." Brian is watching me; he smiles a little. He looks from me to Mrs. Pratt (across the room) and back again to me. "Be cool," he says.

> He holds my fingertips just like Prince Charming, in his left hand.

"Be cool . . ." he says.

He taps his cigarette. And almost touches me, the red tip almost brushing.

I'm cool.

I'm cool with the feeling this cannot be happening.

Diane giggles; folds her hands together, like in prayer.

She brings her hands down hard across my wrist. And I can't move. Not without attracting lots of attention.

"Not a sound," he says.

He feints really casually, the tip above my skin, and I can feel it. Not a muscle. They are kidding. I am cool.

The Recreation Therapy guy is looking around like he sees a parade is passing. Turning paler; very blond, very pale.

I'm not moving.

The tip again. The warmth.

But I don't move.

He drops the orange tip against my skin.

I jerk.

(Start counting . . . Breathe in very evenly. . . .)

Diane is holding my wrist. They watch me closely. The electric shock of the pain makes me perspire, the skin pores opening. In the back of my head I think about how my father used to make me play *no flinching* but I don't think that he burned me. Or at least I don't remember that. I try to pull a little; Diane holds me. Pain spreads into bones, and is throbbing as my heart is beating but I stand it. The little hairs on my arms are standing straight . . . on the back of my neck. . . . A sour smell in the air, like burning leather. I think this nausea comes from my not breathing, so I breathe.

They're fascinated.

The burn is almost numb now, pasty white and very deep (and I am shaking but I haven't let them see this.)

Suddenly Brian jerks it up and stares at the lit red end. "Hey," he's saying. "Oh, hey . . ." Shakes his head.

Blinks around him, like he's waking up. "Well yeah," he says. "I guess you can keep a secret. I mean unless you *like* that kind of thing." Puts the cigarette down, smiling at me.

(Sick to my stomach, afraid I might throw up.)

Diane Brown: "I don't think that was really touching her at all."

The wound is a little white crater with grey inside. "I don't think it was really touching skin," she says.

And I reach across and take his cigarette away. I hold it in my numb right fingers against the back of my left hand; it jerks back up. It has a mind of its own; I force it down and hold it there; a burning smell.

The hairs again. Start counting, even breathing.

"Don't"—Rec Therapy says—

It hurts so much it almost makes me vomit.

"Hey . . ." says Brian, elegant; he reaches out and takes the thing away from me. His is an elaborate, graceful motion. Thinking shrewdly; little smile at me. Thinking hard.

(Dizzy feeling taking time to go away again; swallow the nausea.)

"Whatta you—crazy?" Brian says, smiling languidly.

And we all laugh.

What are you, crazy?

But our *observed* socializing was during the dances, which were of course less interesting. And they really were bearable except when we had the Rodeo Club (or whatever it was) that wanted to Help All the Unfortunates and Get Right With God, for two hours a month. Seems that some one of them had had a sister stuck in Eastern Central, but then she went and killed herself, and they wanted to feel better about that. String Tie was the man who yelled out steps for all these dances. String Tie was the guy whose sister croaked herself. He bounced around like a basketball, amazing. And you had to say that *he* was not too horrified to touch us— like you couldn't get him off you.

About February he decided to Help Anna Adjust. That was about the third time he saw her at a dance. I think it was maybe Valentine's Day and there was this big party. She was in the habit of sitting with her fists under her arms, back in a corner out of the way, where none of the goons would see her. She couldn't hear them coming up behind her, naturally. By goons I mean the semi-vegetables who are schizophrenic; sometimes they are very dangerous. They don't let women alone, but at least that's normal. Also they punch a lot so the attendants stay away from them. (*Why fight when you might not win?* they tell us. Then they laugh.) Staff do these mean little pissant things to the ones who never bother them, but the goons they let alone and that can really piss you off. Or does me, anyway. It reminds me of back in high school where the teachers never help you fight off punks (but *you* they'd badger; *you're* much safer). What do you want. If you want protection, get yourself a biker.

Back in a corner, there'd be Anna, hiding. String Tie wants to help her *socialize*; he comes right up and grabs her by the hand (she doesn't know him): *come on honey*! as he hauls her by one hand. But she won't come. Very deaf, smiling very brightly; shakes her head. Very hard she shakes—a great big NO!

Come on! he says; *let's go!* but she shakes NO. Then somebody cues him in that Anna's deaf. Oh.

He thinks a little. Very.

WELL SUGAR, THAT DON'T MATTER—AIN'T NOBODY HERE KEEPS TIME GOOD ANYWAY! YOU JUST COME ON! And then she was caught up in the middle of all these people running and bouncing and yelling. She could get loud music through her feet when it had a real good beat, but this stuff didn't. It had a sort of tricky beat that you had to jump to get, and she couldn't quite catch it: TAdada TAdada TAdada something—somebody called it a *polka*; they all started singing suddenly: *stodela-stodela-stodela pompa, stodela pompa stodela pompa!* Anna couldn't tell if they were all talking to her, or what they were saying— kicking and jumping around her, mouthing something crazy. The man on her left was breaking her arm and the one on the right was drooling on her shoulder. She probably could have danced real well but she looked confused and stupid. The attendants always think these things are funny, which just shows you. I couldn't stand to look at her when she looked so old and stupid and not dignified. I had to look away from her. But there's no place for dignity. That I would know.

And so we socialize:

> Two Dianes and one of our Shirleys are flanked in front of two chairs which are exactly in one corner with the flag pole just behind them; and in one of the two chairs is Weird Diane, and you can see her shoulder just past Spacey Shirley. And then the Dianes lean forward a little to look at Earl-From-G with a spoon up his nose and you see (for the flash of a second) old Weird Diane with back ward Ugly Harry. The bare thighs clasping Harry's green pants-leg; and then it's gone. The Shirleys and the Dianes block the view again (they're laughing, nudge each other). All you see is feet below and one of Diane's arms across his shoulder (he is past her). Then Tall Diane bends down because she's snickering and you get a real good view of what she's doing with the guy. And then it's blocked again.

So much for the attention of attendants.

In the hall on the ward, old Weird Diane shoves me up against the wall. And says: *Them eyes. One of these days I'm going to put them big eyes out sugarbabe!*

And the gym was so filthy, so torn and yellowed and brown that it made me want to stick my fingers down my throat I felt so dirty. Just to be in it made me want to throw up all the air I breathed inside it.

I would go directly when I got back to the ward to the shower room and breathe in the clean greensoap smell and feel cleaner. The gym floor they waxed right over the chewing gum and pop and ice cream and spit from cud tobacco; but you looked down in the shower room at the grey tile floor and it wasn't perfect maybe but it wasn't shiny over dirt, it was even dull wherever the soap could reach (and shiny where it didn't reach) and even the grease spots bleached clean and matte and something like medicinal. And hot water.

Though you have to leave it sometimes. So I'd play solitaire, the double kind, with Anna, till lights out at eleven o'clock. Or we'd play euchre. But we were so good at euchre we made lots of people mad, which made me nervous. Don't make people jealous. That won't win.

I dreamed, sometimes; I went through times when I dreamed continually of lifeoutside. I seemed most to dream when I first fell asleep, and after the dances, often dreamed of Tina. Tina's the one who took me off the street when I ran away. I only dreamed of the way I thought she was when I first met her.

I hate to remember before I knew everything.

8

IT IS true that people like me are just no good. When my head's in a certain place, I just come on to you. Straight at you like a skinny cat who even knows you'll only go and kick it; a cat will come because that's all a cat will know to do—but that's not me, of course. There's no excuse for me.

Brian was never any good either, but I'm not sure that was his fault originally. He was just one of those kids born faggot, so they hated him. It doesn't matter really how you try if you're like him—it's in your body. He is made wrong, like a girl. His stepdad always called him things like *chickenshit* and *goddamn little pansy* when he was only maybe six years old. When his mom got married.

Life grants every person at least one blessing: that you never have to be a child again. No one can make you.

There were foster homes and children's homes and various kinds of assault he doesn't like to think about at all. And never does. One time, after he was beaten up real bad, he cut himself. Got religion and decided that God had sort of just screwed up and made him wrong. He managed to cut one ball off but went into shock before he got the other. He doesn't remember what happened after that except a lot of foster parents and some shrinks and a real nice man from State Patrol that they put in prison, some time later, as a pederast. Finally he tried to geld himself completely and they made his court commitment, meant to last until majority. Then if he still was queer, they could convict him of a felony and send him up the river, where someone would surely volunteer to kill him. Naturally.

It's natural to hate what isn't potent.

He had an average of three shock treatments a week for several years, and on and off till they finally gave it up as a waste of money. These were hard on him. He said that he'd figured out that he'd had about 500 ECT, give or take a couple hundred thousand; but his memory wasn't really very good, so I kind of doubt it. He had aversion therapy and various other foolings-with his organs. And then he grew up and got a job, and staff pretended like it hadn't happened. Which was fine. A rotten memory can be a blessing.

Well, I had nothing like that kind of misery. I brought mine on myself.

They picked me up off the street about the third week in October after I had run away in early summer. You can't put stuff like me in with the kids in Juvenile Hall, because we're catching, like venereal disease. You can't put stuff like me in four-man (woman) cells when we are juveniles because that is illegal. You're supposed to be eighteen. So what they did was, they handcuffed me to a wall outside the cell blocks, and that is where I started through withdrawal. And I hadn't known that I couldn't just stop with jazz anytime I wanted to; it was just that I hadn't ever wanted to. So the shakes and gut cramps were a big surprise. I was addicted. I'd never thought that I might be addicted to that stuff. I was a mess.

They cleaned me up and moved me to a window in the hall outside a courtroom in Juvenile Chambers. They carried out this trial for me that nobody invited me to attend. I was busy with gut cramps, anyway. In '64 a juvenile didn't have the right to even be present in the courtroom. So I stood handcuffed to the wire grill inside this big white milkglass window. Right outside the courtroom, by myself. Hours and hours.

Please don't tie me up like that.

Maybe they were deciding what was wrong with me—I was supposed to be lesbian, but I hustled. Maybe they were in there just deciding what to do; how mad to be at me. But I don't know that. I just knew that I felt rotten.

The panes on the milkglass window were enormous, bumpled like with big white welts making a pattern, very white. Next to where my hand was fastened one of the panes was broken, lots of pie-shaped pieces shattered out. Wind was blowing sleet through this and the naked cold enwrapping, like enfolding me, freezing all the guts in me, which were shaking anyway. The hand that was cuffed to the broken window started turning blue. Not very fast. The cold was working up to my trembling guts deliberately and almost peacefully. Some misery is peaceful.

There was nobody in the hall, and it was quiet there; with the sounds of voices from the snack bar far below me down the stairs, many flights, falling and rising, echoing. Public buildings echo and they have this funny smell: cleaning wax, human pee, duplicator fluid, burning coffee.

I had to turn my mind away from being hooked like that and so I thought about the cold and that was peaceful. The icy handcuff metal scalding the skin around my wrist; I thought of helping it, helping that intensity of cold by not resisting it. As if the cold would be more endurable if all the warmth I had were driven out—or somehow quieted; like hunger that you cure by sticking your fingers down your throat until you vomit. As with any of your urges.

65

I strip my denim sleeves above the elbow and I watch the cold invade me, the fish-white skin turn blue and shrink and bead with blue-and-cream until I almost cannot feel it anymore. Is that my arm?

And I pull my jacket open and my blouse out of my jeans and work its buttons loose; the acid smell of days-old perspiration from my skin; the little lines of wave that shimmer up and stream away and take my heat; I stare at the scars around my navel, curliqued and maggotlike and shaped like the Hebrides. Let it be cold.

I stare from the metal cuff down to my scars again. You have to keep your head from knowing when they've tied you up, or you will lose yourself. Nothing will be free in you. Never think they've tied you. . . .

How easy it can be; let it be cold.

So hard to see till later, when they find me. I pry out a thick pentagonal slice of blunt white milkglass. I push the edge against the scars till it makes a ditch which gleams at first—dark red and then pours thickly, heavily, and very quietly. Little quiet, dark, heated rivers of myself. Flows too slowly so I saw much harder. The hair on my neck stands up and water flows into my mouth but not my eyes because I never am that cowardly; family trained it out of me. Dizzy and sick and I have to work quite hard since it cuts real lousy, not like metal does. . . .

I tucked my shirt back in but the blood leaked out around my tennis shoes and they changed the stitches and bandages all that fall and into spring. Which isn't peaceful.

That, said Diane Brown to me, *was a crazy thing to do. There are better ways than that to croak yourself. Good God!*

Which wasn't it at all; it never crossed my mind to make a suicide attempt. This was something different: something from inside me. Something about don't make me fast like

66

that. But they were committing me anyway so what the hell's the difference. So I'm crazy. What of it.

They did not interfere with me like they did with Anna; and I lucked out about the stuff they did to Brian. In part because the times had changed and suddenly fewer patients were getting ECT'd every Monday after breakfast; in part because there were lawyers unemployed from Civil Rights who paid attention, and we sometimes got ahold of them. Anyway—Diane Brown did. And in part because the pills they gave us took the place of staff, and this was cheaper than those older forms of therapy had been, which were more personal.

Aversion therapy is really personal. And Brian had a lot of it. He laughs.

This is where they've figured out the way you like to screw, and make you hate it. Brian said they used two different kinds when he first came. One kind is real technical and lots of the male attendants then had liked to mess around with the equipment. What they'd do is, they'd paste these wires on his balls and nipples and show him sexy pictures of young men. One set of wires would tell them when he'd gotten good and stiff, and then they'd shock him. This can really be discouraging. What happened from that is when he got stiff, he'd panic. The other type of aversion they tried was somewhat more exotic; he tended to like it more because it had a pleasant part. And somebody made them stop it.

In fact, the state stepped in and actually made them give the good type up. They kept the first kind, which only really hurt. In the second type they would show him other pictures (not just queer stuff)—pictures that they wanted him to really learn to like. Filthy pictures of women where they hold the sex parts open—they paint the sex parts bloody-looking carmine. Meanwhile, Brian's own sex parts were cased up in a lot of rubber tubing. They had his arms trussed up in leather cuffs, up in the air, where they could reach them.

When they showed him ladies, they would run warm water through the tubing. They had him wired up so they could tell when he was stiff, and then they'd dim the lights and play this music. He told me that the music is what kept the thing from working somewhat better; he is tone-deaf and he just likes a good beat. This was Muzak, which will lose it for anybody.

When they showed him similar pictures of young sexy-looking men, they gave him shots so he'd vomit. One time this got out of hand; I think they gave him much too big a dose—he vomited clear into dehydration. Choking and gagging. They had to knock him out to stop his heaving. And he snorted in his sleep and got some fluid in his lungs and got pneumonia. This was summer and the dehydration plus how sick he was meant off he goes again to Mercy General. He got real good at helping hallucinations hang around. That's like you do when you're tripping and it starts to bum you out. What you do is, you dream again and try to change the ending of your dreaming. . . . But he had to come out of it, some time.

Both of the great Aversion Therapies must have worked real well, he always told me, but he always said it laughing. Now every time he has sex with a man, he vomits; but he's learned to heave. Life is hard.

It was Miss Wykowski who always changed my bandages. Except when it was weekends, when the Nursing Supervisor had to do it, and I liked the supervisor. The only wards with weekend nurses were the front ones, A and B, and you can't make front ward staff do slum duty by coming back to our ward. The Nursing Supervisor was this sweet old gray-haired lady who was nice to me. She told me I was smart and I'd get out of there if I'd only keep my mouth shut. She said when she first started working there that the average *short-term patient commitment* lasted something like thirty years and I didn't want that, did I? She said that this was maybe changing though, what with these wonder drugs, and I could probably really leave unless I actually lost my mind; which of course I wouldn't. Who would do a thing like that?

But anyway it was mostly Miss Wykowski changed the stitches:

> (I sit on the table as Wykowski scrubs the red mass on my stomach. Very professional, very much the nurse. She looks at my face from time to time to see how much I'm lying; but not often, since she doesn't really usually want to know.)

"Not still picking at this scab now?"

She doesn't want an answer. I don't give one.

"You shouldn't get it wet; you know your Doc wouldn't want to hear about you doing that. . . . Well, I saw you and that Rec Therapy guy down at the dance last night. He is kind of cute. *I* think so. You were over dancing by the stage but then I looked up and I didn't see you anyplace. Tisha, where'd you go?"

> (Pulls on the thread; snip-snip-snip.)

"Where'd you go with him?"

> (Look hard at her.)

"Kind of like him, huh?"

" 'S okay. He's just like everybody else."

"Except he's a hunk." (Slaps my thigh.) "Be a fool if you didn't. He sure likes you."

"Unh."

"Well anyway, where'd you go with him? I know you weren't over there by the Snack Bar, I was looking for you . . . and no, I did *not* miss you—you're not invisible yet, although I don't know, if you don't start gaining some

weight. Look at these ribs! What is it—you're not eating
again? I think your Doc will put a stop to—"
"What do you mean he likes me? How do you know he
likes me?"
"... *Well*. ..."
      (Pulls tight; hurts.)
I *like* my bones.

They harassed Brian about the way he stood when he was
resting. He was supposed to naturally stand with his hip
bones perfectly even; supposed to have his shoulders
slouched and weight put on both feet, exactly evenly. But
he was walking with a swinging rhythm which is faggot stuff,
or maybe womanlike, or anyhow, perversity. That he was
meant to make his shoulders swing when he walked (or to
hold his arms real stiff) and in no case should he swing his
wrists or elbows. That is only for a girl.
    I had never known how busy other people are with staring
at your gestures until Brian started telling me, but it saved
him a little trouble in the long run. Though he never got
very good at looking masculine (the way they kept on bul-
lying him, every waking minute), when later he started to
camp it up, he didn't have to concentrate, all he did was
screw up all their instructions. And he really was *Miss Brian*.
    Some people take him for a woman anyway even when he
isn't being campy. On the street they'd sneer *that guy is more
like a woman than my wife*, which is really a very terrible
thing to say about a man; but somehow he'd turned insults
into compliments. Or it might have been those brain treatments had done him much more damage than he knew
about. The way you look is really only everything, otherwise
people have to know you, which is just a waste of time. How
you got that way can't really matter. But if all a woman is
is just a bunch of wimpy gestures, then people are even

dumber than I thought they were. Close-fingered gestures do not get you children.

What if everybody has to work at looking right? What if everybody's mostly faking it? That everybody's checking on their gestures every minute, taking just the right length steps so nobody will notice them; all that effort just to stay unseen. . . .

They sideroomed me once for sitting on the floor, which ladies don't, I guess; and I naturally walked more femininely than half my attendants did (I mean the women) since I had already learned that on the street; and once I denied I was gay they left that pretty much alone (I was *outgrowing* it)—so I thought I was pretty clever. That they deserve any lie you tell them since they want to change the truth; or at least the look of it.

(And women are not sexual anyway.)

(And Miss Hart says about Anna: It doesn't matter about that handicap—only don't let on and can't nobody see it.)

Deaf is wrong. Odd is wrong.

I asked my Social Worker—the one that looked like Sandy Dennis—why you can't be weird if you don't hurt anybody. She looked up past my head like she was reading something printed on the ceiling. And said: *Our job is for society, not for the actual patients you will work with; we do not adjust society for the patient. We are here to adjust the patients for society. . . .*

Brian said I was pretty much adjusted up to suit them—anyway normal women hate sex, so that was fine. (Only bat my eyes—*bat-bat-bat.*) I don't have to get anything to rise to prove to them I'm cured; all a woman has to do is lie there. Which I do. All I have to do is be unnoticed.

By the time I would leave Wykowski and the examination room, the central lights would be dimming in the hallway. At the end of the hall, black windows with the curious blue-white glow from the snow beneath them.

71

I'd look out into the very black night and see the snow only, blue under the moon, and a few black blocks of buildings set against it. And the soft glow of the hospital, the squares of smiling light. I had come to feel a kind of comfort in it, but that made me feel ashamed. I had used to resist that comfort more completely.

And when I'd waked up frequently in the night when I was first committed and had found the constant lighting in the hallways an intrusion, an invasion of the privacy of sleep. Our ward door would be shut and the light glowing off the waxed grey tile beneath it, shooting up and into the room and making a warm bar on the wall; you could see somebody's pale pink slippers, part of a pale blue robe; feel the pitch of sleep. . . .

And at first that had invaded me, that lighting. That I didn't have the privacy of nighttime any more than in my parents' house. But then I began to find it kind of nice. I began to think of it as protecting. That I was awake in a nightmare but then I had always been. Only before, I was by myself. That lights were on meant people were somewhere close to me, maybe people I could talk to, although that's a lot to ask in this life. And there were guys close by who were playing cards and talking on the phone and reading magazines, the night attendants, men, who were bored enough to notice me. You had to play their way or they'd get rough with you. But at least there were lights at night and that erases some of the loneliness. And anyway, there is no unmixed blessing.

9

I AM *taking some of my family through a crowd. It seems to be a circus. Sometimes I am a circus person and sometimes I am just leading my family. There's my mother and my sister Billie, who is holding one of the babies in her arms. I lead them by the hands but they seem to wander. Bright sounds, too much light, you can't make anything out. They seem very little and the crowd is very thick; I try to see my way but every time I turn around, my mother is smaller. She's very little, smaller than my sister is, already. But sometimes I am just a circus person and I'm watching them go by and they're not my problem. Don't let go, it'll get you lost/but it's not my problem. . . . Come on Mama, don't let go; the lights too bright and loud but it's not my problem. . . . Don't let go, you can't make anything out, and they're all so little. They're not my problem since I don't even know them now . . . Don't let go, but you can't make anything out, and I let them go. And they're not mine. . . .*

I dreamed more there than I can remember doing before or since, and the second time I heard Anna try to say any-

73

thing aloud was in sleep, so that may be a general thing, to dream so much in a nut ward. Her room was down from mine and across the hallway. But even with doors shut between us, I heard her. Half a scream; an animal's sound. Maybe it was supposed to have been a person's name. One of her children. Maybe her husband—she'd caught him as he fell, when he had his heart attack:

(Hands parallel to the table, one palm up, one palm down; turn them over smoothly; now repeat.)

—Don't understand.

(Hands parallel to the table, one palm up, one palm down; turn them smoothly.) She writes on her pad: DEDANG.

—What?

Writes on her pad: DEADING.

—Oh . . .

The hands can be *person*. Stand the *person* on first two fingertips, other digits folded back like modest arms. She signs *person* for her husband, who is digging.

Tree, she signs to me. *Dig-dig-tree* (underneath part).

Person stand (digging vigorously); *me, I watch* (maybe she will help him); *person dig, hard* (s-t-r-a-i-n-i-n-g hard; wipes off brow): *whew!* (Suddenly stricken—hands to chest): *pain here* (grimacing, agonized); *pain, heart* (person wilts): *pain, fear* (person sags): *fall. Flat. Hugs-to-chest; hug-like-baby; pain; heart; fear; dying . . .*

Oh.

I do know that sometimes she dreamed about her family. She had a sign for "dream," I think, but I never got it right and I never recognized it, so she'd say *see-with-eyes-closed* to mean "dreaming." I think she said this most around the holidays. But holidays there would give anybody nightmares. I learned to hate them really thoroughly in there. And weekends with them.

You learned fast to hate any holidays in there, not just

because of the sentimental stuff—crazy people, funny enough, are not, as a matter of course, very sentimental. We hated it most because of staff reductions. On weekends you would have three-quarters staff. On holidays they scheduled about two-thirds of that. And holiday weekends, nobody wanted to fool with us at all, and they mostly didn't. Back wards are not interesting to anyone.

The percentage of reduction, and the way this was accommodated, varied. It was related to the normal routine of staffing on the wards, which was unequal, in conjunction with the patients.

On the front A and B wards there are eighteen and twenty patients, respectively. There are two fixed nurses, one for each, and one that they share back and forth between them. Each ward has about four attendants but not all of them all the time, and lots of doctors—since they all get up there sometime (and this makes them somewhat happier). But then you have the staffing at our level. D and E and F have twenty-five to thirty patients: we get so much medication they don't need to fool with us, so it's cost-efficient. We share a medications nurse and each ward has its own two or three attendants; mostly, two. And some of the docs have offices here, but except for Dr. Kim, they stay away from them and that is fine with us. Except for the signing of privilege passes, shrinks are not much use to us up here.

The staffing you explain by patients treated.

On the A ward there are nine women and nine men living on opposite sides of the hallway. The mixture is a sign they're Getting Better. They are all white-looking and rather docile; and some of the ladies wear jewelry, some of the guys wear watches, most of them shine their shoes—for this place, that's pretty chic. On B ward they're all men; they're Getting Better, but still weird. Staff want to show them girls, but not too closely. These guys are pretty white except for one who wears this hat and sounds real Jewish; and this other guy who looks Chinese and a third who is half-black or maybe Indian.

Brian's ward is half black and half white, and so is he. This gives them an equal chance to hate him.

All the staff on A and B are white and real Professional—uniforms with tops and bottoms matching; shiny shoes and name tags that are carefully arranged, as if they're wanting somebody to read them. I think they must be paid a little better on those wards—they've even got some men who work the daytime. Mostly men just work the male back wards or in the nighttime—in both of which they draw a differential and not just women's pay. On Brian's ward there are two old white-haired rednecks—guys, of course—one with an anchor on his arm and the other spits tobacco out the window. Everyone else who works that ward is black and somewhat younger. Except the docs—but they don't come around.

And then there are our attendants. Women's D.

Miss Hart is a very muscular woman. She (she's told me), first in her family clear back to the boat, had forced herself ahead and finished high school. What's more she took some typing courses and a lot of LPN work at a night school but she had to finally drop that kind of thing. Couldn't find someone to take the kids—and she had plenty: ten kids by five marriages, but it wasn't two by each but something else so complicated I never got it right and stopped attempting to—one guy making none at all and another one who said that he was sterile, but he wasn't.

Miss Hart's been an unusual woman.

I would have been the first one in my family, too—and clear back to the boat. And we'd each have been in the holds of our separate boats (and hers beat mine), but I'd have been able to walk around and they kept her kind chained up. How times do change. Of course, they only jacket you, not chain you, here. She is bitter to find herself up here—a back ward after all that education. After all that work and all those kids to feed. Every time they send a new patient up to D it just enrages her: that after all that work she's stuck with colored.

How have the mighty fallen.

Mrs. Pratt's an old snot of a redneck from Kentucky.

Well, holidays they cut the permanent staff on all the wards. On back wards they increased the medication.

What can you do when you have about five hundred people, not all in our section of course, and you have to watch them, for which you generally have about one hundred staff, but sometimes you only have thirty of them? And with a lot of patients who are vegetables and have to be changed and turned over so they don't get bedsores. Well, first you can sort them all out to separate wards, the vegetables and the catatonics and the actively maniacal, and the hospital did do this to a great extent, but then you have the ordinarily crazy and the lumped-in, like me—something the court just sent you—so you have to just put them any old where. Somebody once told me that on the veggie wards they just washed you up and changed you nice and dry and kissed you goodbye till Tuesday morning after a three-day weekend, but that may not have been quite true. Think what a mess they'd find. But probably the truth was something like that.

Some of the things you can do are: no visitors, no mail, no laundry, no walking in the hallways with or without passes—after all you have no place to go: cancel the Snack Bar, the dances, the movies in the gym which we have on a totally random basis anyway, depending on whether anybody here can run the projector; cancel Recreation Therapy, Occupational Therapy, Rehabilitation Therapy and Music Therapy.

These last are anyway not therapeutic at all. They make nobody more tractable, but they do give you something to do and a place to do it, and that way you see your attendants for fewer hours a day; and they feel that way about you, too.

Us ladies got Rec Therapy less than once a week because we were ladies, not supposed to move around, but I once argued that since I was a kid I had ought to have it more than once a week and almost got my point across. And Dr. Kim had actually listened to that one and had made these faces for days as he thought about Bending The Rules, but decided against it. No use drawing attention to himself for an exception. My age has never been to my advantage.

You lock up all of the fire exits and double up the wards. You close the cafeterias on most floors and just delay the losers' mealtimes. Sideroom the most difficult patients, tie them up or knock them out, be more efficient as you allocate your staff.

I spent my holidays hoping for a fire which is why they light your cigarettes for you.

Well, the front wards had the most room, of course, but when they squawked the staff would have to listen. These were future funding voters. Well it can happen. The front ones naturally were not enthused to be wall-to-wall in borrowed lunatics. Since they objected to us, they got each other most of the time; and so did we, which was all right I guess.

Or mostly.

Most of the time, we got the vegetable wards. Like G and H and F.

The vegetables are all right since most won't hurt you, but when I first came I didn't want them touching me. Lots of people feel that way but most will not admit it. It's like the roaches that get in all the food here—they don't do much, and processing has probably got them sterile—harmless enough, but the sight still nauseates you. These guys will drool on you and pick at themselves and worry their scabs into festering, like an animal will; and they aren't washed enough, so they smell bad. A lot were sent from lifetime residence where there were only feeble-minded. Permanent Custodials you call them. They were sent to us so they could be near the downtown Medical Center. These had developed cancer, and they had that rotting blood stench cancer gives you. My mother's mother had that smell and I had still loved her. She had lived with us till I was twelve and sort of like protected us, and maybe that meant that I didn't mind that smell as much as other people did. And I wouldn't steal from them either—everybody steals their penny candies. I despise to do the helpless ones that way. Which tells you I won't get ahead in life.

Sometimes we'd get the varmint wards—with nobody to help you. And that's how Old Diane got pregnant, which they wrote a paper on. A big deal that a senile woman on heavy medication managed to get that pregnant by immaculate conception. Somebody got his name in a fancy journal over that.

Not immaculate.

But I couldn't fight them off myself, so I just ran away. And that still shames me.

I didn't mind the retarded ones at all, compared to them. There were Permanent Custodial types like Chris and Oscar from ward G. They were at least as smart as dogs, and acted kind of cute. At least, I thought so. They liked to try to run and play, like they'd done for fifty years; but they were doped heavily, especially on the holidays. They never caught on to the way our hospital differed from their old one: all the cosmetic differences like calling doctors "Doc" and attendants "Mister"—at least when there were visitors to hear them. They wanted to call everybody "Daddy" and "Mama." Those were names they actually could remember pretty well. They couldn't grasp that the doctors want you to act like little troopers. They wanted to hug everybody they saw, and hoped that you'd hug them back. They wanted to hug their doctors, and that shows you just how dumb they really had to be. And they looked so hurt when you shoved them away and started screaming at them. I think they hoped that some-day they would wake up small, and we'd pick them up and hold them.

I always like Little Margot-with-the-yo-yo from the way-back lady ward. She was about Anna's age and small and wrinkly and had this little yo-yo she was always playing with. She'd stand and flip it and fiddle and almost never get it right; she enjoyed this though, or at least I think she did. And so one holiday when she was stuck with us (I think Thanksgiving) I noticed that all she was playing with was string. I said, "Margot, what have you done to that thing!" and tried to look at it, but she would only say, "No, that's me! That's me!"—and wouldn't let me see it. But for sure, all she had was that string, a loop of it around her middle finger, and flipping the string up and down like she thought there was an invisible yo-yo on it. Well she was crazy after all, I guess, and not just plain retarded. Next time I saw her, at a dance, she had a little plastic bottle cap on the end of it, and was playing with it like it was a yo-yo. I figured some-body took her only toy and I didn't like that. She was about as smart as half a sandwich.

So then when I was down in the Snack Bar just before Christmas I saw all these boxes some charity had given us, and some of them were toys, so I swiped this yo-yo. A little green wooden thing with a flower decal. I gave this to old Margot, which was something.

She didn't seem to remember what it was you had to do. Her hands were used to playing, not her memory. I had to put it on her hand and jig it up and down, and then she had it. Yo-yoing that thing to beat the band. Up on the stage and showing her attendants how you do it, but then I saw her next time and again I saw that all she had was string. I went up to her attendant and I asked about the toy and she said *get out of here it's none of your goddamn business.* But then finally she told me they had taken both the toys away from Margot. She took it to meals with her and it was just too much of a bore for them to clean it.

Looks are everything.

Many of the vegetables were randomly violent, but they were not smart and they weren't coordinated, so you could usually see it coming. You could predict the bad behavior and stay the hell away, or try to do that. Though the crowding was a problem, naturally. It was up to you, you were really on your own on holidays. For you it was not much of a celebration.

Of course, patients were shown what holidays did. For Thanksgiving, we got meals one hour later than usual. And we had orange-pumpkin gunk and cranberry-red gunk, and leather turkey, and pictures of cornstalks on the walls with talking birds. For Christmas, there was a big fake plastic tree with tin plates on it. We got some sort of presents that richer people had got rid of, mostly perfume—which was pretty good, if you chased it down with Coke.

Mostly the attendants' holiday:

They'd lock up everything (*god I hate to work a holiday!*); that's how you'd know it was you moving; gather up their purses and magazines and needlepoint; sometimes they'd yell at us "bring something you want to do" though they never did say what—I would have liked to bring the dog-cage. And then suddenly they're yelling, "Okay ladies, please!" and herding us, and tying up the loony ones; or if we were on the receiving end, suddenly there'd be a whole ward emptying into ours, maybe women, maybe men, maybe dangerous; two-by-two like off the ark and carrying things to do. The retarded ones things like hats and paper airplanes and spoons and bottles of orange juice, spilling over into the ward rooms and starting to go through our things. Such as they were. Hands all over the things you've managed to give yourself. The attendants screeching at each other from the

81

opposite ends of the hall: "Why Miss Hart, you've gone and got married *again!*" and "Wait till I give you this recipe, Mrs. Pratt, it puts yours com-*plete*-ly in the *shade*."

And if you were stuck on somebody else's ward until evening shift came on, you were just stuck, that's all. You couldn't lie down, couldn't take a shower, couldn't be alone (and don't get cornered off or you'll really be in trouble), couldn't go out on the porch because there were only porches on wards that were facing west and there were few of them; and the damn card games and the damn TV and the goddamn Muzak, all going like Roller Derby to drown out the fighting—

Goddamn it—don't eat that! Them's my cigarettes, you fool!

The attendants brought in holiday food and gifts and decorations, and managed to console themselves a little. A little party inside the nurses' station—locked up tight away from us.

Anna had just come at Christmas, and the nurses' station had this tiny tree, with blinking lights. There was this other one in the lounge but I think she didn't like it. I sure didn't. It was ugly and it reminded me I was stuck in there and my grandmother was dead. This little tree in the station had these tiny colored lights that were fascinating. Anna stood and looked through the window at it till they pulled the big shade down. She made them nervous. Anyway, they couldn't talk to her.

You were generally luckier if others came to you. Although not always. With Old Diane it was right here on this ward (the attendants watching New Year's football). Sometimes they sent the front ward patients by little groups to every open ward.

Anna and I play with front ward patients.

Can she understand us?

—No.

Well how can we play, then?

—Just deal the cards. She plays cards.

I knew a deaf man once.

—Well! Pin a rose on you.

Anna signs the front wards: *fancy bugs.*

I did go out on the porch a lot. It was so cold that winter that it wasn't too hard to chase other patients out of there, at least patients from other wards.

I liked to look at the kids downstairs when they were airing out, or whatever they called it. And up in that cage, I thought about walking a lot.

When I first took off, I walked for miles. I mean miles and miles, as much as I could put behind me without falling in the street. And the first night I found this church that was always open and I slept there. Or rather, not to sleep in, just to rest because I didn't sleep much then. And the next day, and the day after that, I walked and walked. Used to be I could do that when I still had some fat on me; it was useful. I could just walk, and after a while it's just your head taking a ride up on your shoulders, looking around. Don't slow down and don't you stop and what you can't see won't get you, just keep going; and you get to a point where you're going so smooth with the world going by and you can't even feel your legs. But then I got back to the church, which was filled with people; so I went down to the bus station and that's where I met Tina, and she took me in. That was too long ago.

On the street I found this little radio in somebody's garbage, and I got a battery for it. Not easy to do. It had a little earpiece and everything and it kept me company. Listening to Chicago in my ear. But then I was walking down the street with the earpiece in, and it was kind of a nice fall day, a little nippy, not too many people out, and I was down in the alleys around the canning factories on my way to try to get a job at the Stokely plant, and suddenly slam! I'm down on my face with my breasts and elbows hurting like they're broken. He banged my mouth down hard, on the cement walk. He took my radio, which I really wanted, which is stupid. You never should love what someone else can take away from you.

On holidays I also went into my room a lot, to keep an eye on visitors and on Vivian-who-doesn't-ever-talk. She'd go through your drawers the second you weren't looking.

She'd go through our things carefully, but not with care; if she found what could be eaten, she would eat it; cigarettes she tasted cautiously and spit back out. She liked your photographs and she would taste the little faces. I came in once and she had a picture of my little sister and my grandmother and I screamed at her, which pissed off the attendants. You're not supposed to scream if you're a lady, and especially on a holiday.

Well. Go in your room, lie on your bed; listen to the fighting. To the Muzak: *We Three Kings; Jingle Bells; Silent Night; O Holy Night; White Christmas.*

I think maybe I'd like to be a Jew someday.

Lie on my bed and look up at the ceiling. I first learned to sleep only on my back at home; it's harder to be taken by surprise that way. And when I did turn over onto one side, it would be so that I could wrap my hand and arm over my throat to hide the back of my neck. This is hard to get used to at first, but it does protect the back of your neck—it's hard for people to get their hands around it. But mostly I lay on my back.

There are things to look at on the ceiling. There are the cracks, from which you can make out pictures. And the wildlife of course, other than the spiders which are somewhat overwhelmed with competition. You wouldn't think you could make out the bugs as well as you can, since the ceilings are maybe twenty feet. Maybe only twelve feet. Anyway, they're high. But from wherever you are down near the floor, you can tell which are the roaches. That's because of the way they run. Like millions of tiny balls in a pinball machine; waves of them; a little zig, a little zag, a slow careering which from below looks like a little ballet; little feet doing ninety miles an hour (but you can't see that); what you see is the thick drunken lines of them up on the ceiling, especially in the morning before the sun is up when they bring up the lights. Waves of scuttling drunken lines, the only creatures dancing to the Muzak. I really hate them. Millions of them; trillions of them. They drop off the ceilings with a little *tack!* sound; *tack!* they go in the darkness all around you. Little light paratroopers all around you, rustling in the dark around your bed.

They are always falling on your bed; when you have a cold you sleep with a towel on your face. I'm not very squeamish, you go nuts faster that way, but I don't like to be touched or fallen-on when I'm asleep. Which is unreasonable, I guess, since it's inevitable.

But I did sometimes sleep well enough to dream, around the holidays. Something about the pressure of a memory; I'd dream about knowing that my family did not want me. Dreaming about Tina, the way I thought I knew her, before I really did.

Dreaming about Tina.

Very small with a body very wise; still, she was larger than I was. And much older—20, I think. I dream of her pushing my clothes, pulling the buttons; criticizing everything I'm doing; she'd call me *baby* and dress me like a boy; together we're the yin and yang of girldom. Taking snapshots of her in my memory. Every angle as she holds her head. Every attitude she gives her body; always posing. All I am wanting to do is worship; keep me at your feet.

And always posing.

Whenever she went to touch me, I'd go rigid. She'd come and kiss me lightly on the cheek, like an older sister. And if she'd put her hands on me, I'd freeze. That was not something I remember wanting, but I think no one believes you when you say a thing like that, if you are gay. Freeze like a statue—absolutely nothing.

It is summer and we hit a drive-in movie, some kind of sad, dumb story. Sitting next to her. And it is a warm night, and warm in the car, and very warm against her and it breaks in me, all that hesitation. Hot confusion bubbling up, luxurious, into joy and all the fear is gone. Extravagantly happy.

Which just shows you.

I hate to remember before I knew everything.

10

I GOT a pink pass in March so that I could finally walk inside the grounds around the hospital; winning the privileges of a five-year-old was evidence of great improvement for a lady from my ward. We were all equal under the laws that governed our vicinity; Weird Diane and I were on completely equal footing for advancement. I got my pass entirely due to help I got from Brian; it was Brian who explained to me Get Better Scheduling.

Get Better Scheduling is sometimes written. If you get hold of your chart you see the notes they take are really quite revealing of the view they take of you. Like:

Some signifgignt interactin in the Day Room. Manic perods more freqent. Sugest medicatins check.

—Translation:

I went into the Day Room and played cards with Anna most of the afternoon. It was snowing so hard that it almost blocked the door to the dog run shut. The wire walls admitted that much drifting, even that high off the ground. What snow that winter. Wykowski came on and jumped right in and ruined our conversation; I got up and walked around the halls and out onto the porch. Which took some doing, and I had to get some help to open the door against the snow, and that is "manic." Any time you use more motion than attendants do, you're known as "manic." That's just shy of "maniac," and they want to drug you up. "Medications check" means having your doctor come and drug you up some more. But I palm the pills.

Seems to be adapting more better and not combatant.

—That is, I let Weird Diane just knock me flat. I crawled behind a table where she couldn't kick my teeth in (till she went away) and then I crawled back out and had some coffee.

Adjusting good now. Better jugment; demonstrats better williness to acsept responsibility.

—This is a quote from the chart of this guy named Frederick, who was stuck on Brian's ward. What he had done was to ask for a pink pass (this was his third day).

Inaproprite adaption prosesses. Erratic jugment; unrelistic and iresponsable demands.

—As above, except the timing was about three weeks; and except the patient happened to be a woman (Diane Brown). Diane Brown was a case in point from any way you look at it, thanks to our amazing commitment laws (in '64). She'd wanted a divorce but happened to be a Catholic. And married to a lawyer. All it took was her horrified parents' signature that she was acting crazily (I mean, to want *divorce* and embarrass your *family* like that). The court got letters from her priest and her husband and family, and that was all it took to be an inmate for six months. An education.

There's a balance they expect from every patient, though it varies; you're supposed to have the proper blend of passivity and aggressiveness appropriate for the role you fill in life. Not equal treatment or responsibility, of course; your proper role depends on what they have divined you are. Or what you should be.

Some things you're given; some things they watch for you to ask for and they time you as you ask; if you mix these up, you are regressing.

You are given:

Food	An account in the
Linen	Snack Bar
Medicine	Lots and lots of
Coffee	*Time* (but not
Cigarettes	alone)

You must ask for:

Mail	Privileges (like
Visitors	passes)
Permission to	Privileges (like
bathe	talking to a
Medicine	minister)
reduction	

When you ask for privileges, this gives them an opportunity to deny you something they now know you're wanting. This tells them about how vulnerable to *therapy* you are, so they're on top of you.

An entry on my chart, the last of February (big change from November):

Seems to demonstrate much healthier attitude toward authority. . . .

—Miss Wykowski likes me. Very nice. You can tell the nurses' entries—they can spell them.

If only you could always get your timing right for them—that sure would help you. It would benefit everybody. Even staff. It can't be any picnic trying to figure out what lunatics are doing. There's always the chance you'll be drawn down into looking at them personally. Not likely, though—seeing so much of them anesthetizes you. You're not like patients.

Dr. Kim was really good at figuring out your scheduling, but major deviations were anathema to him. Books had told him things that motivated us. He had to read those books

89

just to imagine what a life was like that wasn't blessed of Christ and very orderly. To imagine disobedient wives, kids who were not grateful—rank pathology. This was a crazy country—at least they were good with *order* in Korea.

Brian told me when to ask my doctor for the pink grounds pass. My problem was attracting Kim's attention from the chart.

"Tell him anything," Brian had told me. "Especially you should tell him how you want to meet more men." But a "conference" with your doctor only lasts for fifteen minutes. You'd better hope he doesn't have some questions of his own:

(Keep your eye on the clock; you know that *he* will.)

—Dr. Kim, I got a yellow pass in January . . .

I look at your medical history, I see some questions.

—Questions?

The examine questions, it is not complete.

—Oh. Well I'd like to get a pink pass, now. You see, I really don't like being around only women that much, and—

You have the feminine exam before to come to the hospital?

—The how much?

(*Checking little boxes on a yellow dittoed form with smudged blue printing.*) The feminine examine? The doctor, the . . . ?

(*Low, opening motions, very strange ones.*) The gynecological?

—Is that where they stick their hands—

Yes.

—The police did a—

Not the strip search, no; but the doctor examine.

—I don't think I—

(*Scribble, scribble, scribble, scribble, scribble.*) We have to now renew the testings.

90

—Which tests?

You have the gonorrhea. We have now to check and see that it is all gone now.

—I had the *clap*?

You have the gynecological examine. We schedule that.

—Why didn't anybody tell me that? Which pill was that? (*Scribble.*) I think next week, then . . .

—Is that another one downtown at the Medical Center?

Please to not interrupt. This must need to be complete now. Have you ever have to take berscontrapeel? (*He's looking at the wall clock.*)

—Beg your pardon?

(*Looks at his watch and shakes it against his ear.*) Have you ever to take berscontrapeel?

—I don't know what you're saying. What are you asking me?

(*Scribble. Scribble. Scribble—with his eye fixed on the clock. He sells his time to the state. That's all he has, you know.*)

—Dr. Kim, I've been here since six months ago and I'd like to know if I could have a—

What?

—I'd like to know if I could have one of the pink—

(*I've distracted him—absolute amazement.*) Have you take the berscontrapeel?

—The what?

Berscontrapeel.

—What is that? What are you saying?

Berscontrapeel. Have you take berscontrapeel?

—I don't know what you mean. What are you saying? Look, I'd like to know if—

Berscontrapeel! Have you take berscontrapeel! Please not changing the subject; have you take berscontrapeel?

—Have I take *what*? Look, I don't know what you're asking me. Could you maybe write it down?

91

Berscontrapeel!

—Right, but could you maybe write it down for me?

(*Looks at his watch. Scribbling on another piece of paper. He is mad at me.*) Here! Please answer. Have you take berscontrapeel?

(*It's just my life, to me. Be very calm, collected. Read the note.*)

—Oh. Right. No. I never have taken birth control pills.

(*Sags. Irritated. This is not cooperation, please.*)

Wykowski told me that this had been a pet theory of his. Birth control pills—which are, after all, female hormones—that birth control pills made rash young women lunatics (like me). Ladies who would hang around a guy like the one who ran our Recreation Therapy—but it's not that I liked him, it's just he was available to me. And you could always find change in his pockets. Never did take hormone pills—another wonderful theory shot to hell.

I've tried to imagine what Kim thought American lives should be, and I concluded that he got it all from reading. And Wykowski added something that I hadn't understood until she told me. That Dr. Kim had never studied any kind of social work; likewise, he had never had psychology. In our state a psychiatrist didn't need to know such stuff. A shrink was a neurosurgeon with an internship and residency with lunatics. But degrees in social work don't mean you're right on top of everything. People will still be weird to you if you don't look at them right. As in Bill Mullinger. My friendly social worker.

Mullinger is the guy they replaced my Sandy Dennis lookalike with—full-time social worker, part-time Nazi. By that I mean he looked like a newsreel Nazi—right after the *Deutschland Uber Alles*; all those shaven-headed blonds with funny scars.

The stubble on his head looked real unnatural. Like somebody'd gone and glued sand on a billiard ball. White blond, big shoulders, absolutely nothing so effeminate as spectacles—eyes like somebody maybe training snipers. Big on religion; fortunately I can't remember which of them. They loaned him from the Department of Corrections to the hospital; he scans his narrow eyes at me and I grasp his whole approach to young offenders—like the Indian fighters'—*nits make lice . . .* You make no play for this one; that is clear to me.

He's showing his scorn of precious little lady social workers. The record is *inaccurate* he says accusingly:

(Jerks the typing table to him, anxious to impress himself with diligence.)

Your middle name is NOT "Estelle"?

—No . . .

FULL name?

(Quotes himself, typing furiously.)

—Latisha Earl Prentiss.

Earl?

(Typitty-tap.)

Well. Father's full name?

—Earl LeFleure Prentiss.

(He types like an ape in mittens. Spell "LeFleure" for him.)

Mother's full name?

—Mama.

(Hard look: *We'll fix what ails you.*)

—Lorraine Jolene Predewski Prentiss.

How do you spell that?

—LO—

The maiden name.

—P-R-E-D-E-W-S-K-I.

(Accusingly): This record is completely inaccurate.

—? . . . ? (I've never seen my record.)

Polish?

—What?

93

Is she Polish?

—She's from Pennsylvania . . .

(*Know what we do with brats like you?*) Religion?

—I don't have any—

(*THIS is not NEGOTIABLE.*)

What is your family religion! (Hands poised. . . .)

—Well uh, it changes. Mama is usually a Baptist about this time of year. Around Christmas, she's Episcopalian.

(He pauses.)

(He re-reads carefully.)

(He'll die of apoplexy with a temper like that.) Well.

(Tap. Tap. Tappitty-tappitty. Someone is whistling *Popeye* in the corridor. How icky unprofessional.)

And your father's religion. Is it the . . . same?

—He just laughs.

Listen here.

(Type.)

Listen.

Type . . . (*Bears have a look like that.*)

I can make things very rough on you. What is your father's religion?

—Mr. Mullinger, I swear to you that I have heard my father say that he doesn't think much of religion.

(*And now we share one common opinion: Father.*)

Place of birth?

—I think he was born in—

Yours!

—Uh . . . Wright-Patterson Air Force Base, Fairborn, Ohio.

(*Interest.*)

You were born on an air force base?

(*He thinks maybe Mama was a B-52.*)

—November 11, 1948.

This says 1938.

(*Accuses me . . .*)

—Well? I didn't write it. It says I'm crazy, too; and that's a bunch of baloney.

(Type.)

(Type.)

(Type.)

(Typitty-typitty type tap-tap-tap. Glares like a searchlight. Turning back and typing: Type-type-tap. . . .)

He thinks that, if they'd whipped me more, I wouldn't have turned out like this. He's far too dumb to realize that's how I got this way.

When I was first out on the street I felt so free that I just revelled in that freedom. But then, of course, remembered I was a woman. Or a girl, I guess. I think a woman has much bigger knockers. When I was first out there I tried to fight back sometimes; and later, because of Tina, when they'd get too rough, I'd try to fight back sometimes but you know how furious that makes a man, they just go crazy. Like if they're mad and they kick a dog but it bites them, they'll just kick the thing to pieces; kick it to death. God how they hate you, even if you fight them just a little. They'll just destroy you. I mean the men I know and the men that Tina attracted—not the type you find on television. Never do meet those.

Just cry, Tina tells me. Make believe he's hurt you before he really does hurt you. Don't be stupid.

—But I can't. . . .

Whattayou think—he's going to think you're noble? Girls aren't noble, honey-bun—just CHALLENGES.

I hate to remember being such a precious little sissy. But it wasn't the pain, so much; though I remember the pain. You get through it. It's the part afterward when you hurt and hurt for days and you can't eat and people laugh at the way your face looks. That makes it worse; you get dizzy and sick from pure hate: your head pounding . . . Don't let it show so they laugh more; so what I'd do was be just like a

95

rag except I'd try to cover my face and protect my teeth, but I'd learned that at home, anyway. I would try to keep my body from fighting back by clenching like a fist—holding my breath—it will be over . . . but I always thought even if I didn't fight—how you have those fantasies where you can make everybody eat dirt (big and strong—*BLAM!* like a hand grenade—) even if I couldn't fight back, someday I'd bite through your throat, like a rat will.

(And what would it be if you told your doctor this—*looks grave; scribble, scribble, scribble; isn't ladylike.* But that's the trouble with acting like a lady does: you have to rely on other people's liking to be nice. And they *don't act that way.*)

With the pink pass I could go all over the hospital and out onto the grounds. It was cold and snowy and rather boring, without Anna. She was not allowed to go where I did now, and maybe she resented that. She'd stand up in the dog run looking out at me and that would make me hate her. Holding me back; making things *so difficult:*

Play-card now?

—*No, Go-out, me.*

She looks: *oh.* Turns abruptly. Does not look at me again. So what do I care.

Down in the Snack Bar, I would speak with Brian about *progress.* Someday they would let me get a job. (*Like yours? I ask him. Ha, ha, ha. . . .*) Just don't crack up and we'll get you out of here.

Like how.

First, we'll get you a little trip to town with me.

For what.

To see how well you handle it, he tells me. You know, it can be harder than you think. Then if you want to, we'll get you away from here.

To where. Of course I want to go. You think I'm crazy? I've got a surprise, he tells me.

Which he did.

A letter.

See you can't get letters unless they've read the contents first. And you can't send them out unless they're counter-signed, but Brian smuggles letters. Brian the postman. Brian is the one who got a lawyer for Diane Brown, and she got out of there. Except it took three months. And also they don't let certain people send you letters, since they won't be *therapeutic*. (Like if you're queer, this means your lover.)

It's from Tina.

And all of a sudden, lifeoutside is real again to me. I am forgetting how I had resented her. *Get out and come with me to California. . . .*

And how do I repay him.

Not to worry, he tells me; I've got friends I'm sure would like to meet you . . .

Yup, he does.

So what do you want. There is no unmixed blessing.

In the main bathroom, Anna and some other ladies washing up for bed. Anna, in the mirror, staring at me.

You—blackbird—eyes—you (makes smaller-and-smaller-and-smaller motion)—*disappear!*

—Hah.

That!

(She points to my ribs—now with counting motions.)

That!

(She points to my pelvis.)

What/kind of/basket? For carry. . . . (and now she's carrying the market basket of my bones, slung over her forearm;

picking up egg) *here, chick-chick* (picking-from-a-tree . . .).

And now she looks at herself.

Down at herself, accusingly at her belly. Beneath her flaccid breasts, her fingers gather up a wad of flesh. Remembering.

—(What's the) *matter?*

That!

(She squeezes the flesh-wad.)

That!

(She's plainly angry. . . .)

That—thick (growing-growing-growing; puffing out her cheeks, out her ribcage)—*fat—pork-like—ugliness!* (Furious, she whirls toward me): *never/before/this-place/never!*

Inactivity, greasy, sweetish food has simply got to you. Now you fit; now you're like a lady. . . .

—*You look okay!*—I tell her—

Keep-shut!—she tells me—*Liar!*

Hurt my feelings. . . .

And so I ask old Dr. Kim for permission for the trip to town.

Dr. Kim reading from a ditto sheet.

(Businesslike; like Tojo in one of those bomb-the-Japs-to-hell warflicks; glasses down on nose—scribble, scribble. Asks a question. Waits. I answer him):

—Well, it got so I wasn't sleeping good. I couldn't sleep.

(Scribble, scribble. His eyes jump around a lot behind his lenses. Me. Page. Me. Page. Me.—Beginning then when? (Pen poised. Mouse eyes.)

—Maybe a couple years ago. After I hit thirteen. I guess three years ago.

At puberty then you could not sleep. (Scribble.) This sleepless to begin at thirteen? (Scribble.) It is the daydream? The daydream in the night, you cannot sleep, the sex thoughts . . . ? (Bright mouse; peek-behind-the lenses. . . .)

—Nervous. It is just that I was nervous being there.

You are nervous. (Scribble. Scribble.) You are having the girl thoughts then? This is when you start to have the thoughts?

—I don't remember. All I remember is being like real nervous so it was kind of hard to sleep. I'd go to sleep and I'd wake up. You know. It's like I couldn't stay asleep, that's all; and that will make you nervous.

Nervous. (Wise mouse.)

—It made me nervous, sleeping in that house. My parents' house. I didn't like it.

(Scribble. Scribble. Scribble. Scratches nose.) And you waken. And you do not go to the washroom, get the drink of water, go back to sleep?

—I never got up. I never even moved.

Very nervous.

—Yeah. Really very nervous, do you see? I used to take one of the babies to bed with me, like one of my littlest brothers. That sort of helped. I mean even though they wet on you . . . I didn't like it, see, waking up and having that staring all the time—having him looking at me, standing there in the doorway. . . .

. . . Your father?

—Yes.

(Droop mouse. He hates to hear the bestial, the incestuous. What an awful job he has. Scribble, scribble, scribble.)

He touch you then? He touch the sexual way?

I never answer.

(Scribble, scribble. Staring at the paper.) Well. And so. (Looks up at the ceiling, trying to see what he should read up there): So. Well. Did you ask God to help you with this temptation?

Stupid mouse.

*   *   *

I think his trouble was, he got all his ideas out of books. The kind they put in high school reading rooms, from which I'm missing. I've seen those books; I used to read a couple now and then. Sometimes I even loved to think about the world they showed you: people are nice to you if you just don't hurt them; they get all sniffled-up if you raise your voice. If there's something that's gone wrong for you they fix it. Or they try to. And you think, from the book, that's how things are; but then you look around you. For the kindly white-haired gentleman who helps the little girl get home. Don't give me that. Old Daddy, who's so kind and good; Old Mama, in the kitchen baking cookies. The big clean house and the big clean lawn, where your uncle doesn't pour lighter fluid on your dog and set her afire because he feels like it sometime. I'm going to kill that son of a bitch someday.

School was all right. You learned things that other people already knew, so you didn't feel too stupid. It wasn't really so bad a place to be. The other kids. Indoors, nobody's allowed to torment you, and you can rest. And I didn't mind the reading about *real things* I didn't know about, like how you get your butter and eggs from farming or whatever; how they change a kettle to a steam engine; that's kind of interesting. But I hated to read about the stuff in Reading Books and Children's Books: Daddy's so nice; Mommy's so understanding. Life is *clean*. It was pretty and it was fair; and it was absolutely horrible: I wanted to carve my guts out just for wanting it so much.

11

ALSO IN March we had a run of movies. There had been movies every two or three weeks since I had arrived; that is, whenever the Rec Therapy guy happened to go downtown to the library and check a few of them out. We had seen *Going My Way* and *Miracle on 34th Street* just before Thanksgiving (but of course I'd seen those forty times on television anyway); and usually we had cartoons and a Laurel and Hardy film, or some kind of mystery type with dubbed-in English, very blurred. Like the Mexican one with this kid who got bit—stung?—by a scorpion and rolls around on the ground for a while but the English didn't really fit the action and maybe belonged to some other movie. But anyway.

In March, however, Rec Therapy ran into two good deals for us all. One had something to do with syndication, so that we were able to get some good second-run films; then he found these newsreels and a bunch of World War II training films in one of the storage rooms one day when he was so bored he decided to clean something. A few of them had *historical value*, which meant that there was fairly good money in finding them. That must have been his good luck for the year.

We got to see the ones he didn't sell, the rah-rah war effort stuff from the middle forties. The reason I will not sit through a newsreel.

That night, which was toward the end of the month, we had a series of Prepare for the Coming Invasion films. Anna, of course, did not want to see them. Anna never cared to go to films: big flapping mouths and vague gestures; though she didn't usually mind travelogues. However, that night the attendants made her drag along with the rest of us; they wanted to lock the ward. The only staff that was left up there was Mrs. Pratt, to watch someone locked in the sideroom. (She didn't want to fool with someone who could move around the ward. She probably slept.) The rest of our staff had a hot date with other staff, their form of socializing, so off we all went to the movies.

We could sit anywhere we wanted to (the staff went off immediately by themselves). Anna and I paired off to the right and sat in the middle of one of the long, empty rows in the huge, empty auditorium; it was made that big for back when you had to attend church services to be a Good Mental Patient. We slumped down in the seats and stuck our shoes on the back of the seats of the row in front of us. Which was kind of nice. You could kind of imagine that you were Out for the Evening. You could almost imagine it was your idea.

But as soon as we got to our seats, there was this big commotion down in front and to the left of us—a lot of fighting and screaming:

"TAKE IT OFF ME!" this gangly kid was screaming at his attendants. They were dragging him down the aisle toward the movie screen.

"I DON'T WANT TO SEE ANY COCKSUCKING MOVIE ANYWAY—GET ME OUT OF THIS COCK-SUCKING THING!"

102

He was wearing a camisole—a straitjacket—and he didn't want to wear that kind of evening dress.

Who that-person? Anna signs to me; but I wasn't certain who he was. Everyone was staring with great interest, like they do when there's a fight. The kid was an interesting preview to the movies.

What I had heard about him, and I certainly had not heard much—they had been locking him up like you do a bad dog—was that he was of course a shock-head, pretty well out of it. He had had a truly remarkable number of volts through his head, like Frankenstein. They were also, ran the report, doing some rather exotic kinds of *therapy* to him, the nature of which nobody seemed to know, even Brian. Brian said that he had been caught out doing something strange, by his religious parents. The kid had also been religious. He had cried, and they had cried—and they came over on Sundays to sit in the lounge and cry over him, bringing their minister—and he had consented to this experimental whatever-it-was. Whatever it was, it had certainly not made him very much smarter. It had also not made him attractive: he was red-haired, acned, his jaw hung loose and he drooled. But he may have been that way before they fixed him.

At the moment he didn't seem very cooperative. I turned to Anna and went to sign—*don't know*; but Anna had obviously given up on the answer and was trying to take a nap. That was the way she dealt with movies as a general thing. She was trying to sleep with the lights still turned way up.

For everybody else in the audience, movies were a big deal. They were absolutely the main social affair. Here was a chance to sit in the dark with anyone who would have you. Even who wouldn't.

"Get your GODDAMN HANDS OFF ME!" the kid starts yelling. Some patients off to our left begin to clap and yell encouragement to him. His attendants were going to buckle him down in the seat, but then they decided against it. They take the jacket off of him and push him into a front row seat and leave him there; and exit attendants, laughing. He's staring around and the lights go down and the cartoon credits, up.

And it's Bugs Bunny.

Running around with a lot of cutesy stuff, and then the film breaks. The lights go up; some of the dumber patients start in yelling *where'd the pitcher go?* The lights go down. Rec Therapy starts a newsreel, circa 1942, but it breaks immediately and the lights come right back up. When the lights are down it's as black as pitch; when they come back up, the lights are absolutely blinding. The constant change in lighting frustrates Anna. It wakes her up so often that she can't quite settle in.

In the back of the room, Rec Therapy is fiddling with equipment. Anna signs some things uncomplimentary to him. And the lights go off.

And now we have the Coming Invasion films: Life In Your Own Bomb Shelter; Bandage Rolling (why don't you fold the damn things, anyway?); I glance at Anna, who has gone to sleep again. How To Survive (—eating Government-Issue rations: Soak the biscuits. Stick them in milk or water—dig a well or make yourself a cow). The lights go down and up as he changes reels; he's only got the one projector. Each time the focus changes, so the effect is not quite real.

When the lights are up, everybody looks around. Looking to find the Prince or Cinderella. People thinking to change their seats to start another ward-to-ward romance—just holding hands, real kiddie honeystuff. Lots of kiddie-style love affairs are born and die before the main attraction. Lights go down.

And Anna is awake and decides to hell with it. With the lighting shifts she cannot stay asleep.

She sticks out her hands and nods to me—

One, two—scissors cut paper.

Sure, I don't mind playing that. Who wants to roll bandages.

This is a kid's game: you hold your fist out, nodding to a count of two, then you make a hand sign. There are only three: *scissors* (first two fingers); *rock* (fist); *paper* (open hand).

One, two—

(Anna's fist to my first two fingers): *rock breaks scissors.*

One, two—

(My palm flat; Anna's first two fingers): *scissors cut paper.*

Rec Therapy had started to bring the lights down but they're going right back up again. My hand's a fist—Anna's palm is downward, which says *paper covers the rock.*

I say:—*why you win, win always?*

Taps the side of her head: *thinking, thinking.*

Lights go down but we continue playing. She beats me most of the time—I really think she reads my mind. Or maybe my face.

Scissors cut through paper—Anna wins.

Newsreels now, very patriotic. And in the middle of all these Army-issue documentaries (*there go the boys in blue, ladies and gentlemen*—yes but it's khaki—*and let's give them a great big hand!*) along comes this film on Aliens Among the Population—the Japs and how they are neither Chinese nor Koreans (how you tell the Nips from Chinks, who are *our friends*); that Japs're ugly and short and fat and wear funny sandals; you can find *geta* calluses right between the first two toes . . . Pictures of Washington and Northern California where the patriots are bidding on their relocated neighbors' property . . . an honor to inform on funny neighbors and it's pretty damned rewarding . . . And the lights go on again and the B ward guys scream at their Asian-looking member *take your shoes off!* so I guess he's Japanese. He's grinning like an idiot as everyone is staring at him—blameless and he knows that doesn't matter.

Lights go down.

And now he finally shows the Main Attraction: *The Five Races of Russia—Our Allies in the East.*

I notice Our Friends in Need have turned around about the way that mine do.

The credits flying *(Courtesy, War Department);* and there we see five children holding hands, who certainly look like different races; a white blond and a gypsy type, a Mongol-Asian and a couple of others. Grinning in the camera with a curtsy (ripple of giggles from us lunatics); when the screen shines brightly enough, we still play *Scissors, Paper, Rock.*

Rock breaks scissors. . . .

On the screen, they wave from twenty years ago.

Scissors cut paper. . . .

Either I'm getting better at this or she likes this kind of film—

Rock breaks scissors (again!).

But not terribly good . . . Nice lady skirts that billow out like carousels; stripes and bright embroidery; strong little peasant boys, who dress more pretti-ly than U.S. ladies. . . . Rousing folksongs, bright accordions—happy peasants smiling, singing and dancing. . . .

A tap on my shoulder breaks my concentration. (*Rock breaks scissors*); up in the light from the movie screen, blond and precious, it is Nurse Wykowski. Shoving in, wants to sit between us (which we don't quite seem to catch . . .). There are lots of seats to the left of us and she sits down next to me. HI! she's waving in Anna's face—who doesn't see her. Anna seems to be both deaf and blind.

The happy factory workers wave to the camera crew (some patients waving back . . .). And now How To Put a Lugnut on the Turret of a Tank . . .

Scissors cut paper—

"Oh—me too! Let me play, too!" says Wykowski. Well, well. Must be *therapeutic.*

I know that she will demand that I play up to her—be a kid, giggle when she wants me to. She feels her best when others act like fools. I play up to her, since it usually works to help me; however, I only try when I can stand it.

Up on the screen the tanks are rolling, hundreds at a time. Russian flags, handsome people waving (there's a U.S. flag . . .).

Wykowski reaches across to play, so her hand is on my knee. Since only two people can play at a time, when she butts in either Anna or I can't play this. Nurse makes *rock*, as I am making *paper.* . . .

A bear is dancing on the screen, his flat black feet turning round and round, a red scarf on his neck with Russian writing; the kids around him are dancing too, laughing, clapping, also wearing scarves. . . .

And Wykowski wants to start in with her jokes. She likes to tell the vicious kind that teenage kids are supposed to think hilarious. And she wants to add that slapping part to the game that guys will have. If you lose, the winner slaps your hand (and usually, pretty nastily); naturally she makes it *two for flinching.*

I lose, this time; she slaps me—

. . . All these pictures of these Russian-looking buildings. . . .

She wants to tell these nigger jokes because she knows Miss Hart has never liked me, much. She thinks I am just like herself and will hit with any weapon I can find.

Anna beats her (doesn't slap).

107

I don't really want to act the way Wykowski wants me to; right now I just want to be dull in the dark and stare up at that screen and through the scenery. You can get lost in a movie because the skyline is so big, not like the teeny skyline on a TV screen—you can hardly see that. I like the skyline, I really like this Russian skyline—wide and flat above us.

She asks me did I hear about the cave-coons.

Falling back to the dancing peasants of twenty years ago

—(let her talk, you can giggle every now and then . . .).

But there's a commotion. It's the shock kid, who has been down in front but now is running around the room, sitting here and there and acting very crazy. People yell at him. Somebody right now yells, "Get off me you idiot!"—people laugh.

Wykowski has ended a joke and I giggle for her; then she suddenly slaps my hand because I have lost to her, making *paper* to her winning *scissors*; and I jump (two for flinching, I had forgot); she slaps again, she wants to hurt. Little slaps, little hits; she wants to hurt but doesn't quite dare let herself, someone might find out. She wants to nick but can't stand the sight of bleeding.

Anna's really looking very irritable. She sits with crossed arms, looks away from me; what's the matter with you? You know I didn't plan it this way, you know I don't really like her; what's with you? But I can't say this because she can't hear me; and I won't sign, don't dare, in front of Super-nurse. Suit yourself, stare at the wall, don't even look at the screen. See if I care.

Lost in that skyline's where I'd like to be.

Over in the middle of the room there's a lot of carrying-on. It seems to be the kid again, jumping up, sitting down. Acting pretty crazy. Patients are laughing.

Now there are white rings in the corners of the movie frame; we're coming to the end; goodbye Russia. There are the kiddies back again, all the races dancing in a circle. Very happy. The races mixing as happily as the ones that were in my block. Which is only when you face them with a camera. Very nice. Very convincing.

And Nurse slaps Anna's hand, and Anna jumps. For an instant I'm afraid that Anna will hit her: I grab her arm; I am smiling in a very loud *calm down, dammit!*—smiling my ears off—*that's not therapeutic*—but Anna has had enough of me—not just irritable, she is angry. She's red clear to her collar, you can see it in the ending light from the screen; and then the lights are up (really very angry) and she jumps up; I grab for her arm—*wait*—she flips my hand away and she's stalking up the aisle—*wait*—I wave; she just waves *get lost!* at me. Then she won't look back.

Well who needs you anyway. She goes clear to the back of the room, to my right, sits down, slides way down in her seat, time for a nap; well who needs you anyway.

Since the lights are up, here's Wykowski as Professional again: sitting stiffly, she smooths her skirt and makes her face like a teacher's when she talks to me (*all this talk is therapy . . .*) And the shock kid's up again and closer to us, walking very loose like Howdy Doody, only you don't quite see the strings. His fingers dangle, his arms hang, his mouth gapes loose, like maybe the catch is busted; you imagine that his eyes and ears hang open too—hoping to grab up anything his small singed mind can grasp. Runs up an aisle, plops himself next to a lady who pops straight up, and I see that it's Diane Brown: up and running; she's across the aisle and several rows down and flounces in with a group, and people are laughing, it looks pretty funny; the kid slides down in his seat and looks pretty well disgusted.

To our surprise, Rec Therapy's going to show another film. Apparently there's a newsreel he's forgotten, and the lights in the house go down again. Something about the Scotch. Wykowski's arm finds itself across my shoulders, very chummy, starts the jokes again. The one about the cripple with the suit that doesn't fit. Of course, I've heard it. On the screen are these guys with skinny legs jumping up and down, in skirts. Patients hoot: *looka that guy? Come 'ere, honey!*

Nurse tells me a joke that ends with *you got lockjaw and I'm going to break your face.*

And up in the light from the screen is the shock kid, right next to Wykowski, seems to want to sit between us. He looks really tall against the picture, grey-and-white Scotchmen marching through his head. He shoves by Wykowski, sitting next to me, and she moves her arm from around my shoulders. Very discreet, very Nurse. "HI!" he says in my ear, but I don't know him. I take my cue from Wykowski: we don't know him. She's a lady; I'm a lady, too.

"HI!"—he taps on my shoulder; and I mumble "hi," but I'm not looking at him. If I just ignore him, there's a chance he'll take himself away.

On the screen are these scowling soldiers with hairy legs; a marching band, colorful insignias; a tank with a man in a plaid skirt giving a speech to it. . . .

"HEY!" says the guy, again; "MY NAME IS DANNY."

Wykowski has sort of slid away from me; she somehow gives the impression that we are people who have never met each other. The guy leans on the armrest which is between his seat and mine. His face takes up a little of the space I'm breathing in. I turn my head and shoulders toward Wykowski but she's taken with the newsreel, like *nothing is wrong, everything's fine; everybody see that I am not aware of the people to my left.* I ask her a question about the crabby Scotchmen.

"Little ladies from hell," she says you call then.

The guy to my left is trying to get my attention. He is hitched down in his seat and has spread his knees apart, almost touching me. I see in a minute that he intends to reach them to me, but I'm too far away for him, he can't quite make contact. "YOUR NAME'S LATISHA, ISN'T IT?" says Danny.

"Which side were they on?" I ask Wykowski. And he grabs my arm: "TALK TO *ME* NOW," he orders. I pull my arm away from him and I notice that he has the funniest smell, an odd smell like paraldehyde, which some junkies use, and sweat. And his hands are hot and wet and his nails are jagged; as I pull away, he scratches me, mostly because he's clumsy. His hands hover over my skin, and I feel his heat. I lean far away from him over toward Wykowski; I am almost in her lap.

His hands grab for my hand, but I cross my arms.

"My gosh, it's almost nine o'clock; I've got to get back and get the meds ready—"

"Wait a minute—"

"Well, I'll see you—"

"Wait—." But she's standing, bright in the light from the film on the screen, which is now ending. The reel is over; the lights are coming up, but I can't stand up because this guy's in front of me, his face hanging over in front of mine, right in my way. "HEY I WANT TO TALK TO YOU," he tells me, and he's standing over me, leaning into my face. "DON'T YOU WANT TO TALK TO ME? WHAT'S THE MATTER WITH YOU, DON'T YOU LIKE ME?"

In the narrow row, he stands between my shoes. "Move back, would you? I want to get up"; but he doesn't. "HEY I WANT TO TALK TO YOU, WHAT'S THE MATTER WITH YOU, DON'T YOU WANT TO TALK TO ME?" He puts his hands on my shoulders; I can't get up. I seem to be in an awkward position; it's hard to keep my legs away from touching him: he takes up all the room.

Somebody cheers: "Hey DANNY, got you a GIRL-

FRIEND?" His body's so big that I can't see around it and his face is like a flat and oily wall; he aims it down at me, leaning on my shoulders. I push up against him and suddenly I am streaming sweat: the familiar terror of his iron strength; "let me up!" I say: but I should have said *please*; I should have said *I tell you what, I'll talk to you later.* I should be thinking of things that I should say to him but I don't want to think; all I want to do is get away from him, and I can't see around him.

"Hey DANNY!" somebody yells; and as he's distracted I try to duck under his arm; he doesn't like this, he grabs my wrists. "Please let go of me," I say; and somebody cheers at us. His whole ward's having a wonderful time: there's got to be a way to do this gracefully.

His iron fingers are crushing me; "get back!" I say, but he jams his face down at me. He wants to kiss, he slobbers; I duck him and he hurts my hand and I say *"you get away from me!"*—and he doesn't like that; he doesn't like to be talked to that way—I should have said *no I really like you but there's not room here*; I should have said *honey, why don't I meet you someplace else?* And really make up to him, acting like a lover, rubbing up to him, maybe grab his pants—except I can't, he's just so horrible—

"DON'T PUSH ME!" He shoves me, hard. Everybody's looking at us; someone is yelling sexual suggestions. I twist my wrists against his thumbs but he gets a better grip and now he's pinning me, his knee between my knees and pressing my skirt against the seat and he really hurts, jamming his knee hard between my legs; "DON'T YOU LIKE ME?"—he says this over and over again. "WHAT'S THE MATTER WITH YOU? DON'T YOU LIKE ME?" And his wet mouth over my mouth and I'm tangled with him, and it suddenly comes to me—what it is they're doing. The exotic treatment everybody talked about, it had to be aversion therapy: this was what they wanted; all these people staring at us; his hands are on my legs and I grab for his hands; and Miss Hart shouts from the back of the room: *Now Latisha don't you let him hurt you*; men are hooting, offer to help him; wet lips like a fat fish, I keep ducking, I keep shoving; and I'm not going to get out of this, gracefully or not; he can't really move, he hasn't the room, but he's stiff against my leg and if he's impotent I know he'll really hurt me. He's one of the kind, if he can't come he will butcher you. My clothing rips and I push at his face and suddenly, he's swinging. Slaps my cheek so hard my ears ring; and finally I'm screaming, I never scream: *"Get this creep off of me! Come and get him off!"*

And there's more laughter but now his attendants are yelling at him *easy Danny, easy—now don't hurt that girl* and we're all tangled up, he hardly can move and so he shoves; I won't tilt toward him—he can't get in; he tears my skirt and it frees my leg so I get a knee up into him and he shoves right into the knee and hurts himself—he slaps again. My lip is bleeding; I shove as hard as I can and then it's his fist, my teeth explode and my head snaps back, cracking hard against the seat; instant nausea, I can hardly think; and suddenly they've got him up under the arms and they're standing on the seats on either side of us, twisting his arm—there they are, much too late as usual, his attendants. I am sick, dizzy and sick, and he's furious, squirming and kicking; he tries to kick between my legs but I quickly curl and he slightly misses aim and they've got him off me. Both attendants look down as I quickly grab my skirt; they've both looked down and one of them actually flushes.

So many people around us; most of the room. People the furthest away still hooting and yelling at us. My head is pounding and my mouth is very sensitive; *hot stuff!* somebody yells; *kiss her for me*. I stumble out to the center aisle

113

and the people who are close to me won't look at me, especially the women. Across the room men still hollering at me.

And the carpet blurs and my face is flaming; fumbling up the center aisle spitting tiny white bits of tooth and somebody shouts at me *hey honey, give me a kiss.*

He has broken one of my teeth, for which I go to see the Nursing Supervisor, whom I like. I tell her that another patient hit me. Not much of a concussion, she tells me, although I *could* go to Mercy General if I'd like; no thanks. She's sorry about the tooth, she says; she's sorry that she can't treat the pain with anything stronger than ice, but it's on my chart—I.V. use of heroin. I know. That at bedtime they could double (almost) my evening dose which would maybe help me sleep.

No thank you.

We pin my skirt and she pats my arm as I leave her. *Now take care,* she says; *you're a smart girl,* she says; *and you'll be all right; you just take care of yourself.*

Oh I will. I'm doing such a great job.

I am calmer as I'm walking up the stairways. Half an hour has passed, which I have needed. But I'm dizzy and nauseated as I'm banging on the door, and they unbolt it. "Thought you wasn't coming back," says Mrs. Pratt. She is fascinated.

I know that my face is a sight, and somebody giggles. The ring of them look at me, blocking my way. What do they think they see. I think I am blushing and I tell myself to stop.

Almost clear of them all and I step around Wykowski, *don't you speak to me you bitch,* and then a low voice comes,

114

Diane Brown's, and several of them giggle, one of them saying *well I don't know, do you really think that . . . ?*

Under the shower spray, letting it beat against me, letting it pound into the skin, I go over plans I'd made up months and months ago. These are things I have thought of *just in case.* As things I will do if I can't take this any longer. If I can't stand this *therapy,* what I'll do. They make a litany, I sing it for myself to help me think. Help me quiet; not very often. Turn up the shower HOT and make this litany.

. . . There's a lady here who had tried to hang herself and it didn't work. They have almost shocked her brains out, so I know I won't try that. Sometimes it takes a long time to hang yourself and they find you at that: *what's the matter with you? How on earth could you do a thing like that to yourself?* (why not? joining everybody else—) and boy do they try to make you sorry you screwed it up.

I've given up the idea of the razor blade. The official ward razor is a bent-up blade in a dirty holder which has been screwed shut. There's a little set-screw in it so that you cannot get the blade out of it in order to croak yourself. And besides, that is so primitive that it's easy to blow it and then they're onto you, you're a troublemaker, do you have any idea how many reports follow a murder or a suicide around here? You'll be sorry you found out, sorry you missed your only chance.

And anyway, who says you have to be colorful. Be creative.

Next to my bed, in my six-bed room, is this ugly three-way lamp with a colored lampshade. There are these great big purple pansies on it. There's no plug on the lamp, the cord sticks into the wall; it is connected to the current directly, just like the overhead lights. The lamp is on the table between my bed and the one against the window. You can't see the space between the beds from the doorway to the hall.

Bring in a glass of water and pour it on the floor. There's a little dip in the wood between the bedsteads, a little place where the floor is sagging, nothing shores it up, and this holds water. I know because I've tried this. You bring in lots of glasses, lots of water. You fill up the space between the beds. Good and wet.

You tell them you've got the cramps and you *think you'll go lie down.*

Take off your shoes, stand in the water; take a glass of water and pour it over your head (down your hair, down your blouse); nobody will come in with the television going, so you set your teeth to the cold—

(Turn the shower up. . . .)

—standing in the cold water; reach into the purple flowers and lift off the lampshade and turn the bulb on, as bright as it goes, and lift the lamp and smash the thing bulb-down into the water—.

(And one use of having a father who thinks he is every kind of a handyman is all the stories he tells you about electricity, ugly little stories.)

> I like the water pounding on me. This much com-
> motion on the surface of me makes it quieter in my
> head; it helps my thinking. A little calmer, a little
> peace; a little calm.

Then there's this shower which leaks all over the floor in here. It makes a big pool, even when you tuck the curtain in all around you. What you do is, you bring two coat-hangers in here with you and straighten them out. You can find coat-hangers if you look around. Turn on the shower but leave the curtain open and the spray directed at the floor; flood the stone floor. Now you have to do this in daylight because you have to be able to see what you are doing when

116

you turn the lights out. You turn off the wall lights, over the lavatory, by pulling on the chaincord. There's a chair in here for you to drape your clothes on. Stand on this chair and unscrew the lightbulb; toss it in the sink.

Hook the end of one hanger in the metal cuff of the light where the bulb screws in; mash one end of the other one into the middle part of the cuff where the base of the bulb touches when the bulb is screwed all the way in. Keep the two hangers apart, don't let them touch. Stand down on the floor in the water, holding your wires by the free ends. Put one wire in one hand, put the end of the other wire in your mouth and pull the light cord—(*flash* . . .).

If this doesn't work, please don't anybody tell me.

Think of that sudden flash. . . . What if it fails you . . . No, think of the flash and the blankness, isn't that peace? I think that might be a great freedom, you break out of this and like a great butterfly . . . Or of course, exactly not that. What if it is that you do go on, but you go on knowing nothing directly, nothing by sense. No memories (*that's* freeing). Alone, abandoned with yourself (*nobody here* . . .). And you spread out, are sucked out into nothing until there is none of you, even the question. Cold, my god it must be cold there: no sense of warmth, or no sense, period. Sucked out, vast and entirely ignorant, utterly abandoned with yourself, sucked out into nothing.

Is that likely? I have always wondered if the secret of religion is that it's all a lie and that every person knows this; knows that when the power's cut, the lights go out forever: that it's *nothing*. I really wish I had religion; it must be so easy to just let everything go if you think that the *I* goes right on thinking—except it doesn't and you know that in your heart if you've ever seen a person or even an animal die; power's gone and the lights go out, goodbye. You know *this*, and then you know *nothing*.

Nothing, nothing, nothing.

117

And think of that flash. And you really don't want it to fail.

Weeks of pain. Weeks of restraint. Years of Them.

Warmth of the water is really marvelous, and I direct it at my face.

Do you know that I have never driven a really nice car? I did drive my father's a little, more than he knew about. I have never seen an ocean. I have never seen the kind of mountains they put on book jackets; I wonder if there really are any. And a good job. I keep thinking that someday I'll have a nice place, and having a good job I'll pay for it and have food in it, you know where everything is; I'd like to go to a drive-in movie again—you're in a car where nobody can bother you and you put your feet up and eat fried chicken and drink Southern Comfort, always like that, and if you don't like the movie. . . .

Why didn't I get up the minute he sat down. I do know better than that. Maybe you can't always know, but I ought to know better than that.

No memories. That's free.

I know what my parents would do if I kill myself. I can see myself in the water with my eyes open; maybe there's blood. I don't like my mother to turn away like that, at least *look*; and my father looking around to see if anyone is looking and if they are he's grief-stricken—disgusted (but it is a relief); disgusted (but thank god that's over, nobody really knew and *anyway* there are other girls, daughters, he has his pick, goddamn you anyway). People you hate go right on living. A funny fact. You've done the one thing that would please them most. And how they all love suicides, I can see my father: tell each other nasty little suicides they once knew, like the attendants do in the Snack Bar: *did you hear about . . . and blood all over the floor . . .* (Anna's face); they tell about somebody they once knew, maybe it was

118

puppy love and better dead than socially unsuitable and then you're a story, and then you're nothing. Maybe a marker (maybe not . . .). Maybe a photograph. *Nothing.*

I saw a zoo once. I really liked that. Maybe there's not a lot of people who like that work. I could do that. I'd like to try.

The picture left, and then they lose the photograph. *Nothing.*

There's a picture of me that I found one time in my mother's purse: a starting-school picture, me with a frizz of brown hair and one tooth out, I look *little.* I stuck the eyes out with a thumb-tack when I found the thing. And Mom goes *what is the matter with you anyway? You used to be the sweetest little thing.* . . . It's magic, Mama. Don't wonder— thinking makes you crazy; (*flash* . . .) and if I did, God would just tell her it was okay. It would be on *Love of Life.*

Why on earth did I not move. I actually screamed; I never scream. How they loved that; they really ate it up. Wouldn't they love the rest of this if I do it. God knows. . . .

We had a neighbor when I was about twelve, and his wife died so he killed himself. I think he gassed himself. Before that nobody knew him, nobody talked to him, nobody had a thing to say about him but after he did it, after he pleased them like that, he was the only thing that anybody talked about, it was like they loved him (for a while). Nothing he could have done would have made them happier; everyone saying *isn't that awful*—my god you have to listen to the way people say things or you will never have any damned idea what on earth they are talking about. How they love that. After, of course, you're dead.

People who hate you sucking up details of you, now that they love you, now that they know the ending. Damn them all. People who hate you flow on past you; they have light and you have all that *nothing.*

Hugging my bones, standing in the water-stream;
count my ribs, holding them into my body. . . .

I actually screamed. . . . (*I thought you were supposed to be the cool one, Latisha . . . I thought you were supposed to be the sexy one, Latisha. . . .*)

God, why didn't I know better.

(Turn up the water, aim it at my eyes . . .)

Catch on sooner—my thumbnails in his eyes; break his little fingers, rip his throat out with my teeth . . . and his attendants, the blond one—I explode all over all of them like a hand grenade *BAM!*

And I'm so tired. . . . Somebody in the back kept yelling *hey Danny, you need any help with that*—

Imagine them hearing all about you, all the juicy details, wouldn't they love that.

What I really want is out of here, let me out, but I'm so tired I'm half-crazy, and I hurt. My mouth hurts. My teeth hurt; all these bruises . . . on my wrists, on my legs. . . .

Hate may be your strength but it still sucks on you, really sucks you dry. I want out, but not *nothing*. Let me be free, let me have sleep; sleep would be so delicious. Turn the lights out knowing they come on again, think of the lamp, my grandmother had a lamp like that; I wish that religion was right, I wish I could see her; I hate death, I hate that slammed-shut door; I want *out*, I don't want *nothing*.

Let me out.

And let me live. . . .

12

About the end of March, they were writing things on my chart about Rehabilitation. This meant that perhaps I could go off the grounds to job interviews. Of course Interview People don't actually give jobs to us, not after they check our address, but this is what the Rehab people are employed to do, get you interviews. Nobody thinks that anything else will happen. You are not going to be Rehabilitated out of what you are or what you've done, only out of what you could have been. The best of my Progress Notes were in Wykowski's cramped script, not in my doctor's. And Rec Therapy wrote me some lovely ones: masterpieces, almost little essays.

He is sensitive and is going to write a book someday. He says.

With the pink pass I can go to the night Rec programs private citizens sometimes give us. Their programs are tax-deductible as donations.

There was the little man who came in and blew up balloons into these animal shapes, mostly little doggies. But he didn't really like our stupid ones, and those were, unfortunately, by far his best audience; and when Earl from G jumped up on the stage to grab a pink and green dog-balloon this guy fell right off the stage backwards. He wasn't hurt, but he said he was *humiliated*. I think that's funny; I think he meant his pride was hurt. There was the Makeup Lady from Blaisdell's and this Priest who gave us talks on All the Miracles that Make Up Daily Life, but he was pretty much misinformed.

The one who came most often was the Photo Man, who knew how to run the enlarger in Occupational Therapy. That's because he gave it to us and nobody else could make the damn thing out. I practiced my best smiling at him: *bat-bat-bat*. He told me I had this talent for enlarging. . . .

There was this attendant that Brian wanted but the attendant wanted a woman, so Brian introduced us. Brian looking hard at me, so I smile and bat my eyes real ladylike at this guy, who's a gorilla. We are behind the curtain on the stage in the gym. It's private and there are piles of curtains and sacks and old costumes lying around. I don't know why. Somebody must have put on a play, once.

The Camera Man fixes the camera: fix, fix. On the enlarger he twists and switches: fiddle, fiddle. In the Occupational Therapy Department in the basement it is cold. Usually patients stay with this guy till after 9:00 and watch him enlarging noses, teeth, baby behinds; tonight the photo stuff has broken down and everybody left by eight. Except me. He looks at his watch, now the door. Nobody comes. Fiddling with the lenses; fiddle, fix. Two of his teeth are gold, and one is broken completely off. It gapes as he beams at me, then wipes his mouth with the back of his hand. After this he fits that smile back on again. Purple lines on his nose, like an aging drunk. Tiny eyes squint shut behind his glasses. Then he beams. We're such good friends. . . . Looks at his watch; blinking, twitching, wipes his palms on his shiny trousers, eager like a dog: "You know . . ." (he wipes his palms) "you're rea-lly a very . . . very . . . attractive . . . girl . . . ?"

(I'm not.)

(Wipes his lips, hitches up his trousers so his butt won't show.)

"You think?" I say, as he jingles the coins in his pockets. *Bat-bat-bat.* . . .

Brian goes away as the attendant puts his hands on me. He's rough, and he smells like men's cologne on the back end of a horse.

I say, "You're a hunk." I bat my eyes.

He likes that stuff (unzipping white duck pants).

"You maybe . . . You maybe . . ." (now smile). "Got any spare change?"

Wrong number.

Red patches on his jaw; red past his collar. This one is a stud. The broads pay him.

I grab his fists. I whine. I smile too hard. "Don't be mad."

Wrong number.

Wykowski sorting towels onto the carts out in the hallway; they're bleached too white, with thin and tatty edges. "What have you been doing to yourself? Look at your mouth."

"Nothing."

"Well, do it more carefully or I'll have to file an incident report. Sweetie-pie."

My lips hurt, my eye hurts. Every time I get hit in the head, my eye hurts. My nose hurts. Amazing how many nerves a person has.

I am walking away and she snaps a towel and hits me on the butt—it really stings. For maybe half a second I am furious. For maybe half a second I can't breathe—hold on, hold on. I have that feeling of something trying to blow out through my head; hold on.

Cutey-pie! she says.

And I really almost hit her. For an instant I think I see I've got my nails stuck in her eyes and I can't breathe; hold on, hold on. This is sex-talk. Smile nice at the lady like she wants. I kind of smile. I go and take a shower.

On Wednesday afternoons the Charity Ladies come and talk to each other in our presence. Sometimes they bring us jigsaw puzzles and Projects for the Mentally Ill like printing leaf veins. Like in Occupational Therapy. Only duller. They seat us around them and never see our faces. You tell them lots, but they never remember your name. If you want to get rid of them, tell them what you're in here for—but that always makes me feel bad, so I don't. I haven't got used to reactions. Unlike Brian.

A round lady, giving out cookies, runs into Ajax from ward G (which is for vegetables):

Ajax: "Oh my, Mama! I like them things!"

Lady: "Wellofcourse. Here—" (*with a help! help! look—*)

Ajax: (stuffing in many, mostly sideways): "Why I thank you. I thank you, Mama. I like them things!"

Lady: "... Yes...."

Don't worry none, lady. He won't bite you.... You ain't sweet enough.

And they sure did always bring us sweet stuff. Charity is food. Sugar's cheap, so most people use it; but I lost my taste for sugar, shooting jazz (which you cut with some kind of sugar, usually). Of all the stuff they could have brought, they brought us sugar. Pies, cakes, doughnuts, rolls—bakery third or fourth day stuff, cheaper than for retail. For holidays they put up little signs to tell us which one we're to celebrate

124

by eating. To eat is *social*, so they could *socialize* with us without ever seeing us.

Brian's charity is his useful information. I listen to his advice. I don't take all of it. Handing me some of the visitor's frosty glazed stuff:

"No thanks."

"This?" He stares at my hips. I make a face. "No matter what you look like you're never going to be a boy, honey."

Easter, when they throw this picnic with candy bunnies:

"What," he says, *"a spread.* 'Tisha, aren't you going to eat some of this here? You don't want to waste *donations."*

(Ick).

"What about one of these stuffed eggs here? Got deviled ham. . . . Or some of this here whatever-it-is. . . ."

(Potato salad? Got little peas in it.)

"Look, they have given it in here to *eat.* So how much in this life have *you* got that's free?"

"Oh. . . ." (Pick up a carrot; break it into eensy, teensy pieces.)

"Look here. You can keep this up. You can just clean disappear and nobody will give a damn, honey, except your old Mama, here."

(He means himself. A way he has about him.)

"You go right on down to nothing, honey, but you'll still have a little girl's bones, that's your problem. Get clear down to a skeleton and your leg bones will stick out past your ass and there's just nothing you can do about it, period. Maybe ladies don't look like old coat-hangers but little boys don't neither. So eat a little something. You look awful."

"Well I'm not hungry—"

"In a place where all there is to do is eat? Look. Now *look—I know* it's none of my business."

"Right you are."

"None of my business but I think you ought to want to look the best you *can*, I mean in case you—now what? I mean, what are you mad at *me* for? You look like, you look like a . . . a bird cage."

"What do you care, you fuck canaries?"

" 'Course I care. We got to stick together. And anyway, I was going to introduce you to—"

"I knew it!"

"Let me finish! I was going to introduce you to this guy for when you leave here. You know you're going to leave; I mean unless you want to go on twiddling your tits in here until you are twenty-one, I mean."

"A pimp!"

"If you was to leave you know you're going to need protection, but he's picking me up for work last week and we see you down there in the yard, stomping around in the snow like you do, and we get one good look—even in all of that wrapping—"

"He's a pimp, isn't he!"

"AND he says to me, 'save your breath'; that you looked like something smoked up out of a gravehouse, and he didn't need to know no sick bitch he'd have to go and bury."

"Sounds like one fine, southern-style gentleman."

"You got to be a little *realistic*, for god's sake."

"I *am*, Miss Brian, I *am*."

"As is, you are not sellable. Now how on earth you going to protect yourself? Pretty soon the only way you *can* live is in the nut house. You don't know that yet, honey. You don't know how you *slip*—you're going to be too bony for a prick, and too goddamn *ugly*. You think they're going to give you a job, out there? Hell no—you're *crazy*, now. There won't be no job, and you're too goddamn ugly to sell."

. . . Sounds like roses to me . . .

How people love to give you good advice: good for them; give you charity and good advice. Actually, I like my bones

126

like this; makes your whole body something like Geography. Rec Therapy says I'm like a porcupine. Which is okay. It does feel weird to shrink like this, though.

You have this twisting feeling in your guts. The funny thing is, you can find it rather nice. In the long run, you could say that all intensity is kind of interesting. It doesn't surprise me with hunger, like it does with when I've had sex feelings I liked. That's a surprise that's almost rage—you know you'll trap yourself with that. Usually those feelings just come when I'm asleep. They leave the instant somebody touches me.

When the hunger twists, it's working on you. That makes it good: it's taking apart your breasts and little handles. Bones stick out, guts sink in, more of the one to see but less to touch. Maybe freeing. None of the nasty woman things: no blood, no cramps, no nausea where your jugs swell up (and anyway, they're gone). But you still pretend that happens every month (and keep account in case); you ask for Kotex (because you're supposed to be a virgin at your age, you don't need everyone to know).

13

THIS BODY does work okay, Nurse Wykowski tells them in her little cramped-up script: *Progressing & no sign active disease process. Neisseria spp. therapy (—).*

I had, from chopping on myself, four separate surgeries. Three of these were very minor and I had them because something in there was rotting and they kept having to drain that part and sew everything back up. They said I wasn't healing right, to eat more meat. About the end of March, the very last stitches came out, and healed my *social life.* This was Progress, which is fairly close to Employable, depending on the definitions of employment, which is what you are to be Rehabilitated *toward.*

Wykowski is taking out the final stitches. I sit on the examination table, and she talks.

"You know, you used to talk about Whatsisface all the time. Down in the gym. You know who I mean. I came down that one time, and you were sitting on his lap. Look at me.

You were following him around like a poodle before Christmas and now I never see either one of you. How come you don't say anything about him now. . . . Have you got a crush on him?"

"He's okay . . . ow, don't pull."

"You did this to yourself. It can't hurt any more *now*. . . . Well, he was saying that you were going out for a job interview. What was it, I think to the Libby plant. From *your* ward—what did you do to him? I mean the men do that, but . . . he got the order signed for you, didn't he?"

"Who?"

Slap on my thigh, lightly. "Whatsisname. Recreation. He went over everybody's head and guaranteed you a pass *out*."

"It's recreation," I shrug. "I don't know."

Tiny scissors cutting tiny stitches. "You jerking him off?"

"Nobody has to jerk him, he's already—"

"Now that I think of it, look at your hand. Look. You bite the back of your hand. . . . Where does he take you, up on the stage? Look at me—aren't you going to ask me how I know? The stage, right, up behind the curtain in the gym. Like with that *foul* attendant—*how did you touch*—Roadan, Rowman, whatever his name is . . . aren't you going to ask me how I know? *Aw, don't say all the guys are lying, Mary Sue* . . . Look at your hand. You bite your hand, don't you?"

Rust patches on the ceiling where it leaked once.

"Well, if I've heard about it, everybody has. Nobody talks to *me*. What do you think your doctor's going to say. You know he's going to hear about it. Well, I suppose he could say it's *improvement*, given that *girlfriend* of yours."

"Not a man alive won't lie about a woman."

"Poor little innocent thing." (Slap on the thigh.) "Of course, she's in prison. You're lucky *that man*" (she means the doctor) "doesn't believe girls can ever like girls or your own mother wouldn't know you. That's the kind of thinking that is truly helpful. . . . Say, aren't you eating anything?"

(Slaps my thigh.) "My God, look at these ribs—"That man, I can never understand him. Can you make him out?—Oh, that's ugly."

Ugly scars. Actually kind of interesting. "Is it over now? Do I just look this way, or get any more stitches?"

"No, that's it. . . . I guess this is the last time I get to handle your little body." Compresses her lips. "I mean, we've had all this time. . . ." (See what she wants.) "You, of course, you're not going to say a thing. Are you." Pulls last stitch. "Well . . . let's get you up on these scales. Your doctor ought to *see* these—."

"He doesn't even like me! You know he doesn't—the Rec Therapy guy. I mean, I kind of thought he did for a while but—" *(I don't move).* "He just puts up with me. I mean, it's like I'm his *sister*—"

"Let's see, you were ninety-eight pounds—"

"How come it still hurts?"

"What hurts?"

"Here . . . right there . . . close to the dimple. . . . In my guts. Right there. You see where the—"

"Oh, here. Lie down. I'll take a look—"

Usually I will not meet her eyes. Funny, but now she's the one avoiding mine. Her long blue fingernail is dinting my belly, very much the nurse. Her face is close, her long hair almost brushes me. See how the bright gold hair is rabbit brown against the scalp.

She notices my skirt. It hangs from a peg on the table, and she lifts it.

"Is this a pocket?" she says. "What have you got—well."

A five. Patients are forbidden to have money.

"If you press here, see. I sort of feel sick."

"Did he give you that?" She waves the five. Money.

"Here," I say, pointing below the dimple.

She bends again. Casual, but professional. "I suppose

130

there could still be infection. God. What are you doing, spitting in it?"

Long hair like a cheerleader. Bent over me.

"You know I've got to report that. . . ." Touches me. "Let me get some Phisohex."

"Take it."

Touch: she places a finger. Touch, touch. It makes her sweat.

"I had that when I came in here. I just keep it for luck."

"That's a pretty serious violation. . . ." Touch, touch. "Look at these ribs. You look like a xylophone. Yes you do—oh, *smile*. Now we've got to get a weight on you. . . . Did you hear the one about the moron priest who wore shorts every time he took a shower? Didn't want to look down on the unemployed, get it?" *Touch.*

"That's a Polack joke, Miss Wykowski." I move her fingers, squeeze them a little bit.

"Phisohex. . . . No it's not. Not the way I told it it isn't." She reaches across for the bottle—

And my hands are up under her arms, behind her head. I place my lips on her mouth, and we are lovers.

It's not so hard. You crawl out the back of your head. . . .

When Tina first made me sell myself, I wasn't very good at all. I had to take a sort of mental roll-call. I had to tell each part of me to give. Sometimes your body fights when it's not convenient. If you can't relax when you hustle, sex will hurt you—which is where jazz comes in. If you're high enough your mind can take a walk and you don't care what they do to the rest of you. Very much. If they don't like the look on your face they mark you up, so if you're smacked-up you have a better chance of keeping your teeth. Most of your teeth (and you don't hear what they say.) I didn't have all mine anyway.

Nobody fancy ever came to Tina or me. Nobody like you see on television. We were just small potatoes, baby-kiss, small change and everybody knew it.

We were just on the street and hungry, by ourselves, without a pimp (and you need a pimp, a man to crush other men, but he'll make you want to kill him). And what proves I'm no good is that sometimes I was happy on the street. Bad things happen, but none of it is personal. There's an uncertain feeling that's sometimes very nice. You didn't know for absolute fact that everything that happened to you would end up miserable, no matter what way it started. It's not the emotional obstacle course of family life. It doesn't take a part of your heart that was beautiful and twist it through your face.

Sometimes things would get better as the day wore on; that never happened at home. Sometimes we'd have money—drive-in movies—southern-fried chicken and jazz, and Southern Comfort. Not too bad. I mean, there's still the fact that you had to hunt up the next trick when the money ran low, but what's perfect. At best he doesn't hit you, maybe he just smells, but he still just pumps up and down on you and doesn't care if there's anybody in there and besides you never feel like *you* are anymore. With jazz especially. But anyway.

And knowing men like that, knowing the ones at home, what do you say to a guy like Rec Therapy? If you've met one, I mean, and I hadn't before they locked me up. Or maybe I had in school, but how would I know it? When you're in school you think most people live like you do—that they just disguise it better.

I did follow him around, there wasn't anything else to do. Playing Games in Therapy:

Blint-blint-blint—raps three bumpers and the cueball

makes a kiss against the 8-ball: Anna wins. Our gals versus Recreation Therapy; he sighs and rolls his eyes. The six of us are jammed in this little room just off the gym, next to his office. Anna picks up the rack to set up again. I'm across the table from her.

"Okay," he says, resigned. "Okay, tell her to rack them up."

I say, "Tell her yourself." But just as he nods to her, we're invaded.

Suddenly there's an entire ward of goons. A big one shoves Anna back from the table, grabs the rack away and starts to rack the balls.

"Hey! What are you doing!" I yell.

"We've had the table for a while; peace in the family." (Rec Therapy: Dignified Guy.)

I'm disgusted, though it always works this way here. Anna doesn't like to be shoved around and isn't used to it yet. Therapy is obviously planning to slide off into his office, whistling a tune, thumbs in his pants pockets. I stop him. "Look!" I yell. "You're the boss around here! Why don't you stop it! You think—" I use Anna for guilt. I'm angry. "You think that's supposed to help her want to interact or something? You've got an alarm—you could get every Security in this loony bin in here! I mean, why not—"

"Back off, girlie," snarls a goon, and grabs my cuestick.

"Let's go have a Coke," says Therapy. "Let's head out to the gym—" which he is doing.

"Right," says Diane Brown, who is following him. "It is certainly not worth a fight."

"Nothing ever is, is it!" I yell.

The man who has taken my cuestick starts in singing. It's something with lots of cunt and bitch and tits in it. I start to leave, but suddenly he slams me back into the frame of the office door—and Anna's got a chair and swings—*crack!* into his skull but it just makes him mad. It really doesn't

133

slow him and he's right after her; on the way through the gym door she grabs up a pool cue and *slam*! across his throat—knocks him back. Definitely not ladylike to act like that. I was thrilled but they sideroomed her three days.

I pretended I hadn't seen her there, which I hope must have helped her pride at least a little bit. But she never got used to the fact that people could treat you like that. Neither did I. Whether the staff or whatever.

Rec Therapy of course was not like that man. He was above the abuse of physical strength and into the use of mental strength, because he believed that he was mentally superior. Many people believe that because they are bigger they are much better than you, but not him. He is *smarter* than you, which has to do with his hormones, or something. He has the right to anything he really thinks he wants. He's *sensitive*, so you have to do what he wants.

I think the guy would never have hit a woman. Probably. This guy wasn't supposed to have to force you:

Brian and the cigarette butt: oh God (and turns his face).

One of the vegetable ladies throws herself around him: *"Now Evelyn"* (pushes her off), "act like a lady, dammit!"

On evaluations he writes things like:

> Regression continues but demonstrates positive attitude toward group and group activities and static nonaggressive peer involvement within the general context of sufficient ego-enhancement . . . (Weird Diane).

Which is like:
1) If you don't include her, she'll slug you.
2) Cheer her way and she'll peel you the tiles off the ceiling with her teeth.

Self-determinative style coupled with impressive motor skills. Egocentric and subject to lapses in self-control. However cognitive skills may lag far behind her ability which appears generally adequate for low level interpersonal contact unless undue stresses appear in her otherwise controllable environment . . . (Anna Robeson).

Of this evaluation, the Head Shrink, Dr. Falgus, yelled at him *who the hell do you think you are, anyway? What we want out of you is does this patient play badminton or try to punch everybody out or just sit and bang her goddamn head on the wall?*

To quote Miss Hart.

Falgus was not impressed, but I certainly was. I was interested in the shrinklike way this guy twisted ordinary things—I figured that the knack of making specific things so general that they are almost untraceable to meaning ought to go with a certain type of mind. If I could make this out, maybe I would understand why this guy was the nicest person I have actually hated.

One time when he was out sick and some jerk from Corrections came over and knocked us all down with medicine balls, telling us what slobs we were, one of us bumped into the office window and broke it. Of course the jerk wrote up his version of the story, like I figured, but I didn't want Rec Therapy to brood forever on why Tall Diane didn't love him or something, so I left him a note tucked up under the edge of his desk blotter. All it said was that I had seen Tall D. doing her usual sweeping craziness while Der Field Marshall was bellowing at everybody, and then he decided to grab her broom away. Which broke the damn window. Signed, Me.

But of course, so what? It's not like I expected my testimony would be so important. It's just that Rec Therapy wanted us all to Act Right, and if a lady disliked him, he would brood. If he went into one of his two-week snits we couldn't shoot any pool and me, I wouldn't have any money. But who am I?

So I wasn't surprised when they started up revenge on Tall Diane's life, such as it was: locking her up, dragging her out, screaming at her night and day and yanking away her broom. It was safe to do this, so everybody felt that A Problem Was Being Dealt With. What had happened though was that he never got the note. It had got shoved under the blotter and he only discovered it the next time I happened to be in his office. He saw it at the same time as me, following my eyes.

"A note from you?" he said; and I could see that he was totally confident that he would soon need to Let Me Down Gently. But then, when he reads it, he mopes.

"Your handwriting surprises me." He coughs; holds the paper up to the light. I think he's trying to look like Sherlock Holmes. Coughs. "It's very nice."

I just sit.

". . . What I mean is, it's nice. I mean it looks nice, neat. I could do something for you. Look. It's all lined up on the edges, you have these neat little curls here. It lays on the paper like a good business letter. Maybe . . . I think that's something you should study. Maybe you should pick up some secretarial skills. We have an agreement with Illinois Business College. I could take care of getting you in."

He waits. Studies the paper. Like a will.

"It's clearly expressed. Grammar seems good enough."

I haven't answered him, and he's turning red. I think hard: "That's great. I mean, glad you like it."

Wrong guess. "Well," he pouts. "You could use better spelling anyway."

I couldn't miss a word, because the picture stays in my head. "Like what?"

136

He looks even madder. "There: correctional. It's only got one 'r.' "

"Two."

Even madder.

"Really. Just look it up. Bet you . . ."

When he finally checks, he just plain sulks. "Hey, it doesn't matter," I say. "I mean, you spell your stuff real good. It looks good. I mean they're in all the Day rooms and Activities boards and your stuff looks a heckuva lot better than those kind that say *Notice, Effective Immediately!*—"

"*That's* Falgus."

"Right, and they're just scribbled and not spelled right and yours are so—so typed and—"

"Those aren't worth his *secretary's* time. He just puts out this *crap*, but you should see what he sends out to the court and County Medical and the State Board. I mean it's beautiful—and you know why? I mean, you know why it's not this lousy crap he sends out to us little—slobs?"

"You're upset."

"I tell you why. I'll tell you. You know what? I work over that stuff I send out. I mean, it's perfect. I work over every one—you know the movie announcements? I work them over an hour or more and then I go down to the shop and get it lithoed. None of this ditto crap. There's some *pride*."

Crap is such a heavy word, he shakes.

"I'll tell you why, I mean you don't get fifty-thousand bucks to write your own goddamn letters. He has this little hotshot secretary with nothing to do but—wipe up his— mess. The guy's an illiterate. He's simple-minded. Anna the deaf-mute knows more about the wards than, than—"

"You're upset, doll, let me make you easy."

"A gem. Every memo, every little evaluation, it's a gem; I mean the *restroom supplies* for God's sake. I work my fanny off. That's what we're supposed to be *doing*, for God's sake, *documenting*—for the court, the docs, the families—if I had a goddamn secretary—all this *crap*. . . . Oh . . . well . . ."

"I'll close the door, okay?"

"Well . . . anyway. But you know what? Like half the time I end up taking this crap home to my mom. She works hours . . . easy, honey, it slides down easier than that. . . . What am I going to do with you? . . . I mean."

Drawing a curtain. Because I don't want to say it. But then he has to go and say:

"You're a smart kid, Latisha, and I mean that. You're too bright to go back to the street, and I'd like to see you somewhere. A secretary maybe. I mean that. Now we could get you into Business School and—now what's the matter. What's the matter, you ready for your period or something?"

"You got any spare change? I want to sneak out to the Staff-Student lounge and get a Coke—"

Such a handsome man.

What is funny about that was that I was offended, and it is funny that anyone like me could be offended about anything, but his saying "secretary" to me offended me. I knew I was not the secretary type, to stand behind and hold everybody up—not lady enough—although there was a time when I thought that was just a job you got, like being a cook. I thought it was just one kind of job, and I said that real casual to Tina one time: It was out of the rain, anyway, and with clean hands.

We were down on this low part of Main street; guys think they're cool down there, bumping arms with bums and kids like us. And guys would turn to look at her, she'd strut for them: hands to hips, showing off her knockers; thumbs in her belt loops, showing everything. How they'd look at her.

She kept telling me that there was a way to do this right. There was a way to stay on top of each situation on the street; that you could learn to tell each guy and each situation, it was only a matter of time, a way you'd know. What you needed to know to tell was who was trouble, whose idea of a screw meant he grabbed you by the throat; it was only a matter of time to train yourself and you got it. She was always saying how smart she was—and you see her on the street and you believe her. And we were just walking this one time, and she asks me where was I that afternoon, and I tell her trying for this job as a secretary-trainee, but they wouldn't even listen to me, not even take an application—and she laughs at me.

She says:

Here you don't want to sell a piece of yourself, you want to sell everything. Sweet Baby! to the kind who would tell you what you can wear and how you can look and when you can come and when you can go and what you do when you leave, if your friends are moral, and have you smile whatever you're thinking, whatsamatter sourpuss; don't talk to them because they don't hire you to think and you do stuff that would stupify a cockroach but when you're bored and there's nothing to do you have to keep this damn smile on your face and you can't even read a magazine. And you can't move around, this is a lady job and it's freezing outside, you wear this rag almost to your crotch and you can't wear pants but the boss wears this thick suit; and don't always keep your skirt down whatsamatter with you and you can't afford the clothes anyway on the shit they pay you. And you can't have any hooks on your personality that they might accidentally notice, something besides your ass—not a voice so ugly they hang right up or so gorgeous they forget what they called for; if you can just keep dull enough without hooks enough to smile like a sick fish without them catching you back in the file room tanking yourself up maybe you'd just do great at that. If you don't have any pride at all. But you never can go anywhere or do anything cause what they pay you is shit, and you got to do babydoll clothes and hose and shit. And you don't have money, what can you do? But listen, Babycakes, you listen to me, I'm doing the big stuff, we're going to Lake Tahoe— maybe Hollywood—end of next summer. You get me? Hollywood . . . ! She was talking this way and eyeing the guys we passed.

And you watch the way she moves, and you believe her. You watch them look and her flash on them, and you think she could grease through you-name-it. Except that it's all a mirage and you both know it. Except if you say *well, yes but what about*—she'll try to knock your teeth down your throat. That you've seen her cry with her face so you couldn't recognize it. That she most believes her deal with a hustle when she's absolutely slack-jawed on jazz.

So what do you want.

Tina's wrong about me. Sometimes your body won't act right and that includes your mouth. Sometimes your mouth won't fool anybody and the truth just spits on out. Like (this to Rec):

You sure you're up? . . . Oh, come on. I was kidding. . . .

Wow. (Smile like a mannequin) *That's all you got? Wow. This is me, being impressed.*

You got a bicycle pump?

You're too insecure.

Here we go again, and—

What else did the Good Fairy bring you?

He amazes me: he only wrings his hands.

I did hate that in myself, I really did—how you begin to get hateful that way, but that's what happens with pride. See, there's not much you can do with pride.

What the nice guys demand is the illusion that it's all voluntary, just what you needed . . . you need a dentist for this cavity. And I do act like that, but things just slip out:

Tell you what, let me sit on the desk . . . because this hurts my knees for God's sake . . . Oh for God's sake get higher. Can't you get any higher?

You have to watch that or you won't be worth his time: he'll remember he's Catholic; watch that because of how easily you break.

Don't go away . . . here. Now that's better . . . see? Better . . . Mmmm—whoopsie—spaghetti!

You do have to watch yourself. Nobody needs you.

And.

I do get ashamed; he looks so hurt. And then I feel a little pity, which is stupid because it's not my mind he wants; it's not my heart. Guess what it is.

And the same ones give me good advice, all of them. Brian out of self-interest, Wykowski out of screwed-up boredom. Therapy because on the one side he feels guilty, but that wouldn't ever stop him. And they say: Why don't you dress better—better make-up, better hair (*Look at her, whatever possessed you to smear that stuff under your eyes, Latisha*): You get better and we'll get you better. (*You're a wo-min now,* says my dad. . . .)

Well but if you look awful. Otherwise it's okay for everybody to be horrible to you, lean out of their cars and yell *Gawd, looga the wo-mern there,* and if you look nice, then guess what. And on the street I had the body of a kid, which is what most of them want. But then there was my face. It scared them off. Though they don't look at that because somebody might be home, and my face spooked them anyway. Get real mad, knock me around.

I don't like blow jobs. That makes me vomit, but when I have to do it to keep from getting hurt, that's okay. What's wrong is a matter of the dice of who you are. Guys like Rec Therapy make me sick, but you need them.

He was careless though, and I always picked his pocket.

They have what you need, but you have to whine for it. The ones who make you say you want them to shit on you make you want to kill yourself, but pride isn't worth that, you'll take what you need and things will be okay for you, it's like you're a fortune teller: they'll get mugged, broken somehow. And something like that did happen around the first of April.

Rec was hanging around in his little office (with the blinds shut into the gym, he didn't want to see) and some guys outside were bouncing the medicine ball WHUMP! against his wall, and one of the upstairs secretaries ran in with this letter. It was a cablegram or aerogram or something, and he stared at the thing like horrified.

"Hey, what happened? Did somebody die?"

"... My God."

"Not your mom I hope—"

"My God. They turned me down. I can't believe it. They didn't believe me. They actually didn't believe me. What in God's name did they want?"

"WHO didn't? Let me see that—"

"No—I. . . ." (Puts the message down. Picks it up again.) "I'm . . . drafted."

I guess my face doesn't have the right expression.

"You don't know," he says, bitter. "You can't even imagine what that means. Two years of my life. Can you believe that. A free country. They turned it down—I've got to get a lawyer. Yeah, a lawyer, that's—"

"I had a mouthpiece, and that's how I got *here*."

He says, "You could not" (sour face) "possibly understand" (and bites his lip—says something, slavery).

"Do you know how much a lawyer *costs*? Why don't you just skip out, there are lots of—"

142

"It's not that simple, they can put you in prison. You can't just not go—do that and you give up your family, your home; everybody hates you. Your dad says you're gutless. Everybody thinks you're a coward."

I laugh, but he's not joking.

"You can't get a job." He wrings his hands. "You can't, you can't get into a decent—I had the papers into Harvard. They liked the stuff. Maybe even any school, and here I've been working at all this *crap* and I—now it's absolutely no damn use. . . . Geez. I could go to prison. . . ."

"You're a big strong guy, you could get by—go West, change your name—a big strong guy like you, you could swing a pick someplace. . . ."

His head jerks. Clenching his teeth, he sneers: "What," he crumples the paper, "am I talking to you for? You could not possibly . . . know what I am talking about. . . ."

He almost forgot about sex.

I guess I felt a little sorry for him, more sorry than he ever was for us. But when you watch him hyperventilate, you know that he's thinking about the army—but why worry. You think of things that might happen and you think you know you'd die, but the misery is that you won't. People don't die of humiliation, they just hope they will.

The draft notice would take effect maybe ten days later. At work he went on coming on to me: against the wall or against the window over his desk he'd inch forward, pump by pump, until it was banging my head on the one or the other and I hated that. So I handled him, said I was on the rag, and starting blowing him. It was so freeing—I got to where I could do that without gagging and when you can do that, you can kill if you want to. You're free. You can do whatever you need to do . . . except Anna doesn't ever understand.

But.

Come to in the night, suddenly awake. Ask yourself how. Play back the details; you put this here, this is the way you act to him; this is how you look. This you take in your mouth, and how do you do it. I don't know.

You live, and you just shove how, out of your mind.

14

Spring had come, but the snow stayed with us. That was the longest, coldest spring I can remember, partly because it was as if a Dr. Kim was running the building heat—going by the calendar and shutting off all the radiators. But the weather stayed cold; and fat, wet snow kept falling, freezing on the bars and the floor of our porch. Anna and I would freeze out there, sometimes too cold to play kicking snowballs at each other. We'd come in cold, and it was hard to warm back up. Or I'd come back in from running around in the yard downstairs and have to run hot water on my fingers. The only time they'd turn on the damned heat was when one of the docs got cold, but docs wore suitcoats. And white coats, and undershirts (which are not ladylike). If the cold got through all that (and it sometimes did) then immediately the heat would go up to about 80° (and Dr. Falgus yelling *what makes it so all-fired hot in here? Turn down that damn radiator*—) and then down it goes, back to a high of 40°; I had one cold right after another.

The weather was so miserable that sometimes they kept

in the kids downstairs; the porch got a little more boring. The sky was white, the light was dull, the air was dully cold and somehow wetted you. Far away, the roads were grey and glossy, melting and freezing, wet and filthy. The snow around turned black and brown from smoke in the air and mud thrown up by buses and trucks, automobiles and cycles. Down below in the yard hectic mud lines: shoe-prints, dog-prints, bird-prints and papers, spit and piles of snow and spatters of coal bounced out of the trucks, like deer shot; blots of oil—an ugly modern painting or a dog's breakfast, horrid to look at. And too, walking in that yard was uglify-ing; you sank through three to five inches of dirty crust snow into that much mud, and it sucked on you; your feet got blue and stiff and the mud exhausted you, sticking to you; you never quite got clean. And you almost stopped the pac-ing, the circles you made of yourself around that yard. It was too ugly, it was too catching; it was too hard. But I didn't stop. I didn't quite stop. Though I did slow down.

There is a time when you switch from being bored by your surroundings to boring yourself; you don't have to be like Diane Brown—you don't have to think that the world is here to entertain you. But I just let myself think a lot, and imagine things, and poke and pry and get to know every-body. I was, I told myself, very aggressively sane. And I am sure that was at least half right.

But the person hit hardest by this change was Anna, even though I had thought she had been adapting fairly well. She had been as busy as could be: weaving on a loom in Occu-pational, shooting pool in Recreational, volunteering to wash the windows on the Nurses' Station (but the janitors made her stop it). It is not interesting to be there, but you can develop some interesting projects; that was probably the rea-son Weird Diane liked to sneak up behind new medical stu-dents and junior nurses and then suddenly screech *YOO-hoo—whatchu DOING HERE!* and one time one of them was so jumpy he started to run, and after that every time she saw the guy, she pointed him out and went *HEE-HEE, HEE-HEE-HEE!* which was kind of fun. But Anna wouldn't have done that if she could have. And if she'd wanted to, she couldn't have made herself very clearly understood—not in English. They insisted she use English, that she babble.

Anna had been adapting—she did what they made her do, and stayed to herself a lot; she didn't get her pink pass, but that was because of her pride. She wouldn't bug them about it; she hated to see the effect her voice had on attendants, and her writing wasn't much. But she was, I think, really adapting when she got this letter from her daughter down in Louisville, Kentucky.

It was this letter folded up with a card that said *Happy Birthday* with this picture of a bunny rabbit in a straw hat. I guess she must have had other birthday cards, but I hadn't seen them; I hadn't even known it was her birthday. And maybe she hadn't either before that card or the other cards came; days in there look pretty much alike. The letter folded out into this big sheet of newsprint with bright-colored snapshots taped on it and some big scrawled simple words and drawn arrows, done with a red china marker. Like one pointed to a big building, maybe a barn, that said RED MAN on the side and was painted yellow. From what Anna motioned and scribbled to me, I figured out that this thing had just been painted. She didn't like it, signing something like *ugh* that ended in *piss*.

—*You live there?*

No.

—*Oh. . . .*

The daughter obviously knew her mom was illiterate and had tried her best to communicate. A picture of a standing lady, smiling, face like Anna's; a picture of two kids about three and five and the lady again with a squinting hunk that must have been a husband: she was holding these two very tiny little babies. These babies looked almost exactly like; I guess they were twins. Anna jabbed her thumb down, hard, on that picture. Agitated, almost crazy-looking; tried to talk to me; pointing to the picture, signing something over and over; taps on the faces, points to herself; many motions I could not make sense of:

(Taps on face): *to me.*

—*What to you? . . . Something yours here?*

No, no. . . . That, that. To me.

I never did get sign language very well. When it baffled me, it really baffled me. Maybe she hadn't known the girl was pregnant.

—*Surprise you?*

No . . .

I shrug.

Brian is outside the ward door; he waits for me, waving through the cage wire; I'm supposed to go to the Snack Bar with him.

—*Daughter you*, I begin again—

"What do you think you're doing!" yells Mrs. Pratt. "Don't you go talking dummy talk to her, she don't learn that way!"

—Sorry (to Anna).

I leave with Brian.

I didn't turn around; I didn't usually when I left her any-more, no sense seeing what you don't like; and part of the reason was that I hated to see that look on her face, that stubborn look. She was so damn stubborn looking. And the stubborn ones who are holding themselves back so hard always hate to see the ones who do not do that. I don't know how she ever stood the sight of me:

Anna comes suddenly around the corner of the hall and Wykowski jerks her arm back like I've bitten her. Certainly revealing.

148

Anna stares at me.

Turns abruptly.

And why didn't her family come more often? Well, there was the staff's asking them not to—that she was morose when they left, unreasonable for days, insisting on talking no other way than manually. Her people didn't want to make her *sicker* (and what could they make of those stories she told them about this place; such things; none of that could be true . . . all of us made the mistake of trying to tell about this place, which proved we were nuts). And if the doctors said that Mom was nuts from sign language, what were they to answer to that? It's like when the docs tell you newborn babies can't see anything, even as you watch them turn toward faces. Contradict with what you see and it's your imagination: what do you know? But the main reason they didn't come was adaptation, which is natural; this happens to most everybody's family, even good ones. Like this was a song and they heard it on the radio; it goes: there is nothing for her here or for us, there. She is better off to be where she can't hurt herself. They are fixing her there and we can't fix her; everyone is better off this way. Send a postcard, send a sweater (forget to sign the card inside, and maybe it was just an old one anyway, why waste it . . .); the songs you learn the fastest are like this one, those which drown out counterthought.

And Anna was so proud. She could surprise you though. Like one time after one of those How To Be A Good Lady talks, one of the Dress Yourself To Be Luscious type, she disappeared into the john and then out she comes, fingertips so light on a wing of hair; dressed in a Hannah-the-Vamp-of-Savannah way; she walks, god how she walks. . . . And she did just deadly imitations of the doctor and especially Mrs. Pratt. About Mrs. Pratt, Diane Brown once said she looked like a penguin with a thyroid condition. She meant, I guess, the pop-eyes.

But Anna played cards with us, she did socialize; she played cards with us almost incessantly and that was sometimes kind of comforting. It is comforting to have to be around people who have to put up with you; even if they're lunatics, you need that.

And to play cards, Anna was around us, and we had some interesting things happen; of course lunatics are so interesting they can wear you out, but I mean tame things, nice times. Like this one time everyone was sitting around, smoking, the TV on but it had a lot of singing so nobody was noticing except Spacey Shirley (and she did love to dance, holding her skirt out girl-fashion like she wasn't maybe eighty years old and arthritic); and Shirley was dancing around with this cigarette, one eye shut trying to keep the smoke out, dipping this way and that way, partners with the television set. The rest of us cuddled up in sweaters, mostly pink ones out of the charity bag, tossing cards on the table at Crazy 8's which was something even Weird Diane could play, when she was coherent and sociable, which wasn't too terribly often. It was pretty cold, and it was going to stay cold, Mrs. Pratt said, because the day before it had been warm and there weren't enough doctors around to get cold, so they wouldn't turn up the heat anytime soon. Mrs. Pratt was losing (which didn't make her in any better mood about heat or us) but she was almost by herself, Miss Hart wasn't there, so she either had to talk to us or herself. She would have bored to death even herself, so she was tolerable.

And she tells us Miss Hart is late, and Anna tosses an eight on the pile and wins that hand. *And she better get her fanny in here quick too. I can't do all this watching and reports too and all of that reading* Mrs. Pratt preaches: and here comes Miss Hart with a rattle and slam! of the hall door, dressed like blazes and singing away—waving this little guitar.

When you see too much of people, you forget to look at them.

About Miss Hart. There is more of Miss Hart than of a movie star: she has breasts and hips, still luscious after all those kids (*5500 members of the Marines and the Green Bay Packers can't be wrong says Diane Brown, who is flat-chested*). She wears it right, I guess from chasing crazy people and kids, but then she was born in the deep south. I think to different work. She has this amazing smile but she seldom aims it at us. *Ladies! Ladies! You guess where I've been!* she belts out, and she means look, no uniform. *WHY MISS HART!* yells Spacey Shirley: *She's gone got married aGIN* she tells Mrs. Pratt.

You gone got married agin! OOH you GONE GOT MARRIED AGIN—I WANNA DANCE screams Weird Diane— and she's up on the table with her skirts up over her hips. *Well who is it this time!* says Mrs. Pratt and Weird Diane screams: *OOOH you wanna hear a song?* and shaking her buns she's going:

Grey! Squir'l! Grey! Squir'l
Boo-shee Boo-shee
Tail!!!

Now you COVER yourself! yells Pratt but everybody's laughing fit to die, and Weird Diane is pleased with herself, and even Vivian-who-never-talks almost got it. *Why, you got you a gy-tar*, says Old Diane; *Why no, that's a uke, ain't it honey?* Spacey Shirley says; *hey, let's sing a song* shouts Miss Hart, real loud and all of a sudden it's *A Good Man—Is Hard to Find*—with her twanging away on that little ukelele, and I even sang two notes. Anna is beating time on the table, everybody up.

But then there was this phone call and Miss Hart went to answer it and something better came on the TV, so they turned it up. Miss Hart stayed Miss Hart, the way she always

151

did when she married, basically because half of her patients couldn't have figured her name out. Anyway she married much too often to change her working name. Professionally, so to speak, she'd die Miss Hart.

But every time we had a good day like that, every time she was a part of us, afterward, Anna would completely retreat. Back away, too proud. What will pride get you, that's what I wanted to tell her. Cooperate; make them think you're part of them, that's what I wanted to say, and usually I was really cooperative, but then sometimes I'd catch myself out at the opposite. You can't always know yourself and when they've really pissed you off . . . but you do try to catch yourself. Sometimes you don't catch it fast enough, though.

Like one time Mrs. Pratt had done something I didn't like, I don't remember what it was, and she came over to play cards with us and I didn't want her there. There was Anna and Diane Brown and me, and we needed a fourth for euchre, but I didn't want her. She's this old hick, real motherly until you cross her—and find out what she's like.

"You shut your face," Mrs. Pratt says to me. And I start to shut my face, but Pratt won't stop it.

"I bet you think this is some easy job, don't you! I bet you think this some easy job I got to do in this place, putting up with crazy girls that can't even wash theirselves and ugly-natured little snot-nosed whores that is never—"

"Don't you call me that!"

"—Got a decent thing to say and—"

"Don't you ever dare to call me that—you hear me!"

"You talk to me you keep civil! Who do you think you are! Ugly-natured little—you think anybody in their right mind would work in a place like—"

"Boy I sure am sorry for you!"

Miss Wykowski's coming in for a Medications Check. Miss Wykowski stands, arms folded, watching.

"You SHUT YOUR FACE!" yells Mrs. Pratt.

"You sure are right!" I scream. "Whyn't you just quit! Maybe you're crazy! Why don't you just commit yourself!"

—And she slaps me.

"Don't you shout at me," she's shouting and I'm furious, absolutely furious, hanging onto control with my fingernails; I whirl, scream at Wykowski: *"Did you see that?* She slapped me! She is not supposed to lay a hand on me! Did you see that?"

"Hysterical," sniffs Mrs. Pratt. "Anyone could see that."

But I usually got along okay; I was adapting. Anna wasn't. And maybe it's true that you can't always see the right way to change yourself, the corners you have to file so you won't catch on anybody who's above you; maybe you can't always know that the pressure in your head is up too high, but you can ignore it most of the time, that's what I think. It's just that maybe she didn't try enough. It could have been words, of course; she only had her eyes and her ideas. She didn't recognize many words on paper, and it's possible that all the ideas in the world were in her head, but the words—words I would know, words in English—were not there. And words would have helped her, that's what I think; words for ideas help you misinterpret things and that makes life much easier. I decided this, looking at her—thinking. All the time.

What was she thinking. Watching us all. Registers everything going on, but can't pretend (with words) to take this philosophically. Words prettify ideas, screen events for you; help you stand your life.

When you have a lot of words in your head, you can pick among them to describe to yourself what you see; this works for you, it helps you to protect yourself—suppose you are walking down the street and ahead of you this female person of about fourteen is leaning on a building. Two men walk

153

by her and she walks up to the one and puts her hands on him. This is what you see.

Well, you could tell yourself exactly what you see and then ignore it. But maybe you're feeling really good, and you want to tell yourself nice things are happening all around you— like if you see a dog with a part of a rope on his neck in the street, instead of thinking somebody might be worrying about him, instead of *wow, somebody might have been being mean to him, making him want to go and break away like this* (that could like depress you)—you tell yourself: *ah freedom. He's got free; he must be happy*; and you let it go at that. But with the guys and the girl you don't just cover-over—after all, you've got to keep an eye on other people, you have to make sure what they do won't spill on you— with them you choose words as interpretations.

If you like sex, or you don't care much what's happening, you can tell yourself: kids are so *free*; that was some *come-on she gave that kid*!—but if you hate whores, or you hate sex, you go: *hustlers* on this street, this very street! And they come so young, now *throwing herself* on that *boy* like that it's *shameless!* And if you hate sex and you hate men, you spit out words like *little girls* and *young punks* and *social deviants* and *prostitution.* You have all these words to fit your ideas through; and what actually happened you won't remember; you'll remember your words. Not whether one of the guys looked like her brother, but what you chose for what you saw. How you filtered it.

And that mesh of words is what Anna did not have; not words for the same thing that feel different. For her, *girl, chick, bobby-soxer, missie, maid, babe, cherry, baby-kiss, virg', filly, gal, broad,* and *debutante* could all be said as woman, young or woman, child—and then she'd act out the way she wanted you to see this—hand on the hip, or blushing and embarrassed—never exactly the same twice; but in her head

154

it wasn't different words, it wasn't different signs but different actions. Not as easy to remember; not as easily misleading like remembering all these different words. She had to see, then she had to remember what happened. Not adaptable with words. She could not blunt the way she saw, with words. I would have blunted things by reexplaining them for her so she'd have hope.

I wanted her to shield herself, protect herself. I wanted her to be subtle, to adapt. This was because I really cared what they did to her. People will tell you that you shouldn't care what happens to anybody else, only yourself (you hear this all the time now) but if you look behind their words you'll find some shrink has told them this, or wrote a book they read that told them this. And you can see, if you've been in a place like this, why a shrink might want to think that way—there is almost nothing he can do. That he can't make crazy people well (or any smarter) and that terrible things can happen and make people crazy. Maybe he could stop some things, I mean maybe stop the gas company from cutting off gas so this lady burns coal in a bucket and she wakes up and her kids are dead, period. And she goes nuts. I mean maybe he could stop preventable things, but it won't make him anybody and he won't get a cushy practice. And who wants to think about all this so they say *don't care;* so they say no *guilt.* That guilt will make you sick instead of protecting everybody else from you.

This is easier, and people are a lot happier doing nothing. Unless they're in pain, of course, or unless they're like Anna is. But I was not the shrink type either: I cared about Anna. I wanted her to act as if she was better, as if she were really adapting to that place. Because I did care. And there was absolutely no way I could talk myself out of that fact.

And the awful thing is, how well she could have adapted. Acting was so natural to her; you're supposed to look sooo nice for the guys—love BOYS! love MAKEUP! and etc. and she could have done all that so much better than I did. I had never learned to give the look and not the fact—I had not yet had any opportunity to—but I kept learning, and I wanted Anna to learn everything too.

Hey I ought to be on stage, I learned so much.

And it sank into my head that she thought the worst thing that could happen had happened. Don't ever think that—that's what I would have told her. If we had had the words for it, I could have told her that the worst things that could ever happen you do to yourself. It wasn't just people sticking electrodes into your head; that hadn't happened to me. I hadn't had aversion therapy or ECT, but there had been that time when I first came. I think if I could have told her about that maybe she would have tried harder. I would have, if anyone had told me. But nobody had. I had to figure out everything myself. Everyone lies in there when they tell you to cooperate. Except for me. I only meant: just look it. Don't really do it. Or you may find you cooperate too much and you lose yourself. And when you know that you've done that, you hate yourself.

You see when I had first come there, I really cooperated. That's I guess because I was ashamed of the way I had become. Being hooked; going through withdrawal like that, crying and shaking and heaving.

Of course that was when I had first come, in the fall; in fact during the first week I was told that I was going to this *interview* at the downtown Medical Center (and I didn't want to go, I had this feeling about it) and I was a kid so there wasn't any chance I had anything to say about this; I was going. I only wish I had some way to tell Anna: look cooperation. Don't cooperate.

They put me in a straitjacket to leave the grounds; of course then I didn't have any kind of privilege pass. I was in this very passive state, I was really being very cooperative. I thought that my life was either over or that everything that had ever happened to me had probably been my fault. What did I know, anyway? So I was real cooperative. After all, maybe they could fix me here, that's what I thought. It wasn't that I even wanted to be much different from the way I was, but that I thought what I was certainly wasn't much; why not try something else? Maybe I could learn to live like people you see on television: have houses, reasonable neighbors, no fights, no blood. Sounded all right—I was tired. I could maybe learn to be like other ladies were; maybe there's a trick to liking sex with men. Or at least to learn to stand it without junk. After all, I hadn't ever met any woman who liked sex except Tina. No decent woman did. I could learn to act like a decent woman and lie there like a rock. That's all you needed. Maybe I could learn those tricks like that. And maybe I could finish high school. And live decently. It's not like so many of the people I had known had been so decent—I didn't really want much to be like them. Maybe there was a trick to living any other way—that the love I had for ladies would just fade, fade away. So I was passive. I was passive but they stuck me in this straitjacket.

So I say, you don't have to do that, I'm not going to run off or anything; and this attendant they have stuck with me, Fletcher, says *Last time I did that, I got to chase this guy fourteen blocks and then he goes and tries to kick my teeth down my throat*; and I'm five-feet-four and 98 pounds soaking wet, but I stay in this jacket. And they, he and this lady attendant, walked me across the grounds under the windows of the front wards, out past the guard houses, holding me up under one arm because when your arms are fastened like that, you can't catch yourself if you start to fall. We get into a white van with lights like an ambulance and *Eastern Central State Hospital* on the side; and Fletcher goes: *Hey, you want to have some fun?* and starts to turn on the siren, but the other attendant, the woman from B, says *No, not really*. Fletcher sulks and tells her: *Aw, you're no fun*; and people are already staring at us anyway, every time we slow or stop for traffic, so I say that I really don't want him to turn that on either, and he turns and stares at me like part of the back seat has just said something. So I shut up.

And then he reaches down and turns the siren on, and we go like bats out of hell down the middle of downtown streets and around the corners at an angle of 30°, scattering people and dogs and cars; and then we come to the Medical Center, stopping in front of a large brick building in the middle of a flat green square of grass with tiny maple trees like broomsticks set around it.

Around the entrance are all these young men, smoking. Stethoscopes and pockets full of pens; some with name tags, their hair exactly alike. Even the bald ones. I smile at one. He looks away.

Miss Hart once told me that Fletcher had wanted to be a Medical Student, but he was too stupid. Well here was his chance.

Fletcher gets out and helps out the lady attendant onto the curbing. Then he turns and takes hold of me—jerking so that I fall forward and he has to catch me: into his arms; every eye is fixed on us.

He shoves me ahead of him into the pack of them and they fall back, making white coat walls—enameled coffee cups, cigarettes posed—all identical faces; and then up the stairs and into a crush of people drinking coffee and eating doughnuts; the smell of burned coffee and cinnamon; steamy windows; and here there are women in lovely clothes and smelling sweet, many in white coats and none can see me; and then I get yanked into an elevator and we go way up.

We walk by an enormous room into a connected teeny room with control panels and chairs in it. This was where this doctor tells me what is going to happen. There is a connecting door that opens into the big room we have passed; as he tells me this big room is filling up. With white coats.

That I am going to talk to this man in that room. About girls. About being attracted to girls, whatever made a person do that? About my sisters, about my mother, about my grandmother, about my father; have I ever screwed with my father?

Those things are mine. Even the bad parts; so I just say no, I have nothing to say, even though until this moment it has not occurred to me that I could really care what happened to me. But I see that I still care. A little. So then the doctor leaves the room and Fletcher starts to tell me what they ought to do to me, he is the kind that talks like that to women: he excites himself; he's like my father is. And then the doctor comes back in with those little capsules and says take these, they'll relax you. But I won't take them, even though I had wanted to act right. I don't want to take the pills, and when I refuse them, I feel how they have changed the way they treat me: *we are not friends; you do what we tell you.* Fletcher wants to shove them down my throat, he has this intricate way, but the doctor won't let him. Not that way.

If I could say what that was like.

The doctor says something, very low, to Fletcher. And the lady attendant says something like I wouldn't give them any trouble now, would I? And then I see the needle. And I think no, I can't handle this; not without jazz, not if I'm still in my head; and I was going to tell them I would take the pills but the words stuck in my throat.

I didn't want to talk to any roomful of people, and I didn't want them to give me any shot. So I wrapped my legs around the chair I was sitting in, and Fletcher and the woman start to grab at me but the doctor makes them stop. He doesn't like the way that outside force looks; he wants me to be forced from the inside, either by the dope or by my liking to cooperate, but I've already blown that part. I should have pushed harder on myself to lie, to pretend, but I hadn't had enough experience. He tells them to unbuckle the jacket, which they do, and they twist my arm out and he jams the needle into it. Into the bone, I think; it makes me bite my tongue. Bruised for weeks.

And then as I was getting high, I was almost grateful. Almost.

Imagine the drunkest you've ever gotten, drunker than when you start throwing it all back up. Only there was no getting dizzy or nauseated, just blurry and extremely high. I got higher and higher and higher until I had to make sure I wasn't looking at Fletcher or I would never have been able to get rid of that son of a bitch. I hated him and didn't want him to know how drunk I was. High like jazz.

So then, high as a house, I was in this roomful of faces and the doctor took me in there by the hand and I had to lean on his arm, I was so drunk; I couldn't stand up. I guess it was some kind of reds that they gave me; I always like reds, where you're drunker than drunk. And I sat down and looked up; it was a lecture room with the rows ascending; and all I could see were the white identical faces of the boys and the high-crossed legs of the girls who would not meet my eyes. And I answered everything.

But not truthfully. It's that I thought maybe I could make those blank eyes open and I answered everything. I told them things that happened to me, and things that happened to people I knew, and things that never happened to anybody. I looked hard at the boys and some of them blushed (and all of the girls) until they were leaning forward. And I saw the equipment but I was too high to stop.

And then later, when I was coming back to myself, after I had slept off all that junk, I thought about it and realized that they had put the whole thing on film, that that equip-

160

ment I saw had been camera equipment. That they had me on a TV camera telling unknown smug faces about sex and the way it wasn't. Recorded forever.

That's one thing about men like Brian, they don't remind you of those men; women like Anna, they don't remind you of those women. The ones who blushed. The ones who *aren't like you.*

So when I would see Anna not cooperating, not looking, not being right for them I almost hated her: I wanted her to act right. If I could just have told her there's no end to what they can do to you.

Please adapt, I wanted to tell her; don't hold me back.

I had my ways of adapting. I remember them:

It's dark in my six-bed room as I lie on my bedspread. Stare at the ceiling, hiding from the television programs. Light pours in from the hall in a white cold slab, oblong— part on the bed, part on the floor, part on the wall.

Wykowski suddenly blocks the light; a spider cut-out shape against the light.

"You asleep, 'Tisha?"

"Yes."

But she comes right into my room like I invite her.

"I thought you were going to play cards with us. Why didn't you stay? I was going to join you. . . . Nothing is the matter, is it? You feel alright?"

(Stands by my bedside, blocking off my light.)

"Nothing's the matter. I just didn't feel like it."

"You're depressed."

"Oh. . . ."

"You shouldn't be alone if you're depressed. Maybe I

161

should make a note for your chart. Maybe they should increase your medica—"

"I'm fine. Everything is fine with me. It's just that I don't
always want to play cards. Sometimes I—"

"—Didn't he increase your thorazine any—"

"I'm fine. Everything is fine with me."

"Well. Good."

    (Leaning close; blocking the lighting.)

"Well . . . would you like some company . . . ?"

"S'okay with me."

"That's not very—"

"Sure I want company. I like your company."

"You're not just saying that."

"Oh, no. No, I really like your company."

> As I lie on my back, my hands are spread at my sides
> and she almost touches one; almost, with her hip.
> She will stand like that till I make some kind of sign
> for her.

"Yeah," I say. "Maybe I want company."

> She will wait for me, leaning over, hinting. I must
> be the one to make some kind of sign. I'm the wan-
> ton one, it says so on that chart they made.

". . . Just company?"

"Maybe more than . . . company."

> I lift my hand and my fingers begin to trace a tiny
> pattern. From the tight white waist to the hem of her
> loose, white skirt.
>
> I feel I'm a machine I'm operating. Click goes the
> section turning on the stroking. Click goes the sec-
> tion switching off the mind.
>
> But something's wrong and the mind's still operat-
> ing.
>
> Not pulling back; it's like it wants to stay in there.
> Click, I go, and the fingers moving, smoothly. And
> I look for escape but I'm still inside my head. Hold

162

on; hold on. Not pulling back; all wrong, and it wants to stay in there; not pulling back, it's almost like I'm wanting her. How good some arms might feel; I want to feel them. It's like I want to stay in my head and be inside these arms no matter whose . . . *stop.*

God. Not me.

Get away; don't touch; not till I can back away right; hold on, hold on; not till I can back away, get gone, hide right—not someone who would leave me like that—*someone I hate.*

"Now what's the matter? Here, don't turn away like that; don't be rude; look at me. Latisha, look at me. What's the matter. No, look up. That's better. Don't be rude to me or I'll smack you one."

She seats herself on the bed and takes this hand and rests it on her body.

"People come through here. People come through here all the time. You don't want them to know."

"Don't be rude. . . ."

And I'm not rude; how your body can surprise you.

I'm embracing her till I hear the gasp and I open my eyes on Diane Brown and Someone.

"God!" says Diane Brown and takes off running down the hallway. Omygod. That leaves the Someone standing there; half in the dark; white eyes reflecting light; almost seems to focus on us: Vivian-who-doesn't-ever-talk. Eyes like ice.

Wykowski talked to Diane Brown. I don't know what she said, but it all blew over. Which is fine.

Minor setbacks. Put them out of your mind.

All in all I was adapting; even my body was adapting. Adapting so much it was joining the other side. A curious sense of relief and of great betrayal; betrayal like you feel when you start to menstruate. Like you thought somehow that would pass you by (and every disgusting thing that was connected with it) if only you absolutely never let that cross your mind, let sex cross your mind, let any of the real horror of womanadulthood get into your head; if you did, then you would never get it out again: a lifetime with the lively paranoia of a bored target; never a verb, never a who, always a whom; the done-to; the object of the race but not a half of it. A lifetime as a dirty joke—dirtier once a month. But you get used to it; you get so you can exploit that. Leave a drop of blood on the toilet seat and good old Dad throws up, can't stand the sight of you. This has its points.

I say you can adapt to anything; if everybody hates you, so can you and there you are, on the same side—no reason to feel left out. What's the problem. If I could only have said such clever things to Anna; but then it would have been a two-way street. Then I would have had to hear what she had to say, and I don't think I wanted that. I saw that in her eyes.

And I didn't want to be maladaptive with her. I would not have ever let her disapproval hold me back. Leave me alone. Even though I cared, but I didn't want to. Even though I no longer knew what, exactly, I was going to do about things, how I was going to act. Even though I sometimes confused myself. Very confused, because it was getting so I always seemed to be lying; that seemed to be the first thing to do. That there was nothing sincere, I decided, left inside me; I kept looking in a mirror at myself to see if I could catch it in my eyes; it's bound to show there; but I was never quite sure where it was in my face, if it was in my face; maybe I was too good at it. Sometimes I thought I'd caught it out. And Anna didn't have that look; she was far too kinesthetic; she was madder and more frustrated and she showed it; not like me; not an adaptive one. And I cared because when she'd suddenly turn away from me I was sure it was because she could read *I lie* in my face; she read how my eyes were changing.

And I couldn't see how she could stand the sight of me.

15

Though from where we were you couldn't tell it—outside, things were changing pretty rapidly. Even in the ways to handle lunatics. We went on with the same green walls from day to day to day, but how we were supposed to progress was changed for us, changed by definition of our "illnesses"—some of us got *better*. And it's true; some kinds of crazy get better with pills. Even I saw that.

I saw miracles happen. Sometimes. People who take lithium—and suddenly they stop running around, sit down and make some sense. I saw that. And some of the schizophrenics with the wild hallucinations, sometimes when they were heavily doped, stopped suffering—not so badly frightened and so violent. Really living easier. And then, at my level, I was glad for the side effects on the really crazy patients: with the dope they had a lot less strength to slug you with. But that I think wasn't what really interested the people who run hospitals. Not the proven miracles—there were still too few of them; it was that they perhaps thought a real miracle was in sight. That someday we would all just disappear. A real humanitarian effect; think of the inconvenience this eliminates.

There were a lot of us who were hold-overs; people who had come in under other styles, other wonderful experiments, and like laboratory rats, what do you do with the survivors?

Like—

> Case History: Diane-with-the-glasses (she has cataracts). In 1934, she is thirteen, and she's expecting; that would mean she's Sexually Precocious, and that's a definition of *incorrigible* in 1934. (*"Just like you!"* says Miss Hart.) Said it was her father's, which of course just made things worse—you're supposed to *die*, resisting incest.

I was really surprised when Miss Hart told me she was incorrigible—I looked around for that old fart with her milky eyes and that vague way she cringes away from you; I said—HER? Yes, committed until her majority and now you see what might just happen to you if you don't act right, so act right, Miss Hart tells me. Yes ma'am.

> So what happens to her is she goes to this Farm, a Mental Hygiene place. The idea was that lunatics should work to earn their keep, which is less boring. So she goes to school and learns to keep records on cows and goats, they were raising cows and goats, and then the experiment's over, the funding's gone, so they break it up and she ends up in East Central. They were doing insulin shock research, so she gets a lot of those; they then do ECT, so she gets that stuff and that must have proved something-or-other. Time passes and she develops diabetes. Nobody notices this until she's lost a lot of weight and both her eyes. Life is hard. Nobody's job to investigate; so every treatment coming in the mail with the medical journals has been done to her. Now it's all these pills.

By now I guess she's cured of promiscuity. Anyway, she's not knocked-up.

Like—

Case History: Lloyd from G. Passive and a vegetable; he drools. Rec Therapy told me that there hadn't been originally anything wrong with this guy, it was that he was epileptic. They found this out suddenly right after he fell forty feet out of a tree. He was ten years old. The whole thing must have been a big coincidence. But, bad luck: he lives in Indiana. To be an epileptic is illegal, and you have to be locked up (although there are nice farms you can go to). You have to live only in a State Hospital there, but maybe Illinois has the same law because that's where he ends up. They sterilize him and commit him for his lifetime. He doesn't like this; this is dull and depressing. They keep him doped on barbital but every now and then he has a seizure.

His family moves away and never writes. He grows up fighting and surly, really hostile, so they tie him up a lot, but this doesn't really seem to sweeten him. Every time you turn your back this guy goes over the hill, and so they're sick of him. Give him a lobotomy. Now he's so much pleasanter. Also all those shock treatments. Not too bright, though.

Treatments come and treatments go; where do you bury the survivors? Those are the kinds of interesting things you learn just because your attendants are bored—so bored that they'll even read the *beginnings* of your chart (those charts are *thick*). Usually staff just read the top page in order to know special instructions and medication changes. And you know, that kind of thing really held me up at first. I didn't understand how it was that nobody cares how you got the way you are (except for when they publish something); only stop it, that's all. Take a pill. I think I had had these great ideas about psychiatrists, how you babble at them and they like you and they say these real wise things (and this takes forever) but then I saw real ones. Of course, nobody paid these guys by the hour to listen to anything; and that would have affected *me*. You pay *me* fifty dollars an hour (or more!) and I'll listen to your nasty little childhood until sometime the middle of next year. And more than listen.

But you know Diane Brown had had a shrink from when she was a little girl (she was rich then) to when she got married, and she just loved him. Invented things to tell him and then really got depressed when he believed her. *These*, she says, *are not really psychiatrists*. But then she's one of these people who never changes a *definition*, only makes sheets of *exceptions* in her head.

What inconvenience.

Well I looked around me and I saw a lot of craziness. It seemed that there are some people who become crazy, who knows why that is; and some people who always seem to have been crazy, collect pancakes or try to put your eyes out; and some people that if you treat them bad enough for long enough will look crazy, maybe they'll become crazy. And the beauty of each new *treatment program* is, these are all alike. Treat these lunatics exactly equally.

And I was benefitting from this attitude (don't look too close—I'll give you the right answer); most of the staff don't look too close and the ones who did—I tried to keep those occupied. For the rest of it, the pills really were a miracle cure for me. Now there was talk of job training, there was talk of even real job interviews for ladies. Even us. That was because of the *getting rid of us* part of this therapy. That was because we were all going to be cured, or at least controlled so that no one would notice.

They were going to take the Dianes-with-the-glasses and dope them up and turn them out after fifty years in stir, no more fooling with them. Not that this would be soon, but that it would be possible after the next new kind of dope. Medications that dissolve in our blood and will keep us in disguise—society would not know that we are lunatics. Close the wards; fire the lower staff; find the important people better jobs.

And if there is anything wrong with this, anything suspicious or inefficient or savagely cruel, this could be minimized, this could be ignored (how much do you know about butchering?). The Lloyds and the Dianes and the senile ones would be wandering on the streets, helping all the muggers make a living. Staff couldn't see them. Close the records (*cured*).

And whether they'd take their drugs or not (and whether or not these worked) wasn't a question with any statistics in it, so there wasn't any funding in the asking, so nobody asked. No one important. When Brian told me that's what they were aiming for—doping people up and getting rid of them—I didn't believe him. I didn't even realize the benefits to me.

He said they were going to release the retardos, and I said *how?* And he said they were going to be put in these nice homes with these nice people who would be paid to help them deal with stuff. And I felt sarcastic, so I said *great, just great. I can see it all right now. I can see it's in style to talk that way, so maybe we'll put everybody in these nice houses with these nice people to watch them live and everything will be lovely till the state gets tired of paying for all these nice people and the nice houses. Then they fire the one and close the other but they've already replaced the morons with other morons or closed the place entirely, and what a great benefit that is. You get rid of the people who were a drag to have around in the first place—no back ward retardos, no nice homes on the street—no more dingbats. They just burn themselves out and down, get raped, get mugged, fall in the river*

*and drown and everyone's rid of them. A two-step process
everybody can benefit from. After all, all they had was the
right to live, not a way to.*

But I actually didn't believe any of what I said. I really
thought that it had to be written down somewhere that you
have to take care of people, especially the ones you've made
the way they are. Like children. You make them—you take
care of them. Or someone does. Or anyway, someone
should. If this isn't written down somewhere, it should be.
(And there is nothing wrong with the people who think it
shouldn't be that a hand grenade wouldn't care). I knew that
anyone who looked at us all couldn't really be that cruel.
And I think it was my inability to understand, that made me
not understand, exactly, that I might get out. I was careful
to take advice, however.

> *You're a smart girl. You take care of yourself and
> you'll be all right.*

Osure.

> *Committed until her majority and you see what might
> happen to you if you don't act right, so act right . . .*

Yes, ma'am.

> *Just don't crack up and we'll get you out of here. . . .
> We'll get you a little trip to town, to see how well
> you handle it. There's this gentleman would like to
> meet you . . .*

Yeah, I know.

And from the point of view of our ward, the biggest
change of all was in the fact that I got my brown pass, the
one you need to go to job interviews. Brian was going with
me for the first time—just maybe I'd need a little help, he
said. Except I didn't believe him. Then.

Mrs. Pratt said, I never heard of such. Miss Hart said, you
just mind yourself; remember, it's the court sent you here,
and you violate that and the next time they get hold of you,

you have had it. And they always do get you, we always get you back, only this time no privileges for you—straight away they shock your head off. You won't go nowheres again. And Wykowski says, oh isn't that just lovely; you know maybe we could go to a movie in town some night, there's a theater about three blocks from my apartment. . . . And the Nursing Supervisor says, how wonderful. I told you you'd do all right, dear. Take care of yourself. . . .

And Dr. Kim is pleased to grant these *privileges* (maybe toward job training). With all these good reports he sees he's curing me of homosexualism (or sexualism)—and this was the basis for calling me *incorrigible*. Not the prostitution. Or the dope. That was the one real thing that the court had listened to. Something real exotic. It was a feather in his cap to cure my *sociopathy*.

Boredom therapy.

Lots of good advice.

But—

> Asleep and dreaming, right time of the month: I am this famous performer (of something) and the performance is over, the audience loves it; and I'm coming backstage over the clatter of applause and I see this lady, half behind the curtain—baby-faced where I am hard-faced, and I see her and it's just *wow. Gee.* Just look at her and say that, dreamily. And everyone else is leaving and I say: *look honey, do you play around?* And she swallows hard; she has this gorgeous deerlike throat; and she *says oh* . . . and I say, *look you want to go somewhere for a drink?* And she says *sure*; and we're at the restaurant of the hotel where I am staying as this really famous person. And I just sit there, looking at her white filly throat and the open collar that frames it, the black mane of hair

down the slight, boyish shoulders, the black eyes dropping so often (catching them painfully delicious, both of us tasting) and then we go upstairs and I don't think I finish locking the door when I have my hands on that strong waist, I stand on my toes to catch that sweet wide mouth; she bends to me, arms even stronger than I thought they were (still containable), wrapping around me, turns my heart to butter; chills, fire. Utterly rash a thing to do; never feel so fine and fiery a desire, never so dying in the arms of anyone. Passion is so treacherous. . . .

Treacherous. Always gone by morning.

And I had always resisted the feelings like that, afraid they would trap me (who wants to hand them the strings of your heart to choke you with?). But now all the trapping part was gone. The happily-ever-after thoughts were fading out, and this was slowly freeing me. Sex thoughts were much more welcome. Much more an appetite without a pause. Without a pain. And without memory; very much like food.

You have to eat.

You don't remember it: it simply pleasures you and you go on and on.

They were right of course.

I was cured of sexuality.

16

After all that good advice, after all the good and plain examples, there I was—outside the gates, actually waiting to leave. Coming in that way I'd been in handcuffs (*just in case* they said) without thinking, holding my mind tight shut like stubborn teeth (*don't think about this; never think about you'll never leave again*); temporarily leaving, of course, but still actually leaving there, and only seventeen. Only months. Not the years like all the Shirleys, all the other ones.

Though of course this wasn't the end of it. What the court says, the court sees through. Pride like a doctor. Even with mistakes.

"You remember," Brian told me, "now you're going with me to Hook's while I pick me up some gin. Now you'll be fine. I'm going to be right there with you, and all you got to do is call that friend of yours. Now won't that be nice. Got that? You'll be fine. Make sure you got you a dime."

Don't talk down to me.

This was succeeding; I had never succeeded. It's a real strange feeling.

It was cold and blowy, very hard to believe it was already April. Time kept passing for life outside. So I would guess. Our breath was white in the air and white snow patches lay on the mud across the grounds, and water in ruts, water on sidewalks. Air very heavy and wet. My day of freedom.

"You'll be fine," he said.

We waited by the guard houses at a little-used stop by the edge of the big brick gates, traffic crazy in front of us and around us; and all around us clung the smell of snow in the air and days-old diesel fuel, slightly suffocating; jammed up automobiles and trucks sprayed a constant spattering of gray slush—very wet, very chilly, thick and blurring the roadbed. And out of this wet haze a huge gray bus forms itself out, and chingling its gears, forcing and squealing its brakes begins to tack toward us, forcing slowly across two lanes and rolls down to a crawl and then a throbbing halt; squawks and yawns open. And as we climb the wet metal steps, what is it that's happened. So dim, so wet, the grill floor wetly filthy right in front of us. And everybody on the bus moves way back to let us halfway down the aisle, elbowing up against the doors and windows, jamming against the seats and making way for us. Just remember freedom.

And the red gates pull by. And telephone poles, and several other buildings but much faster as the dim bus picks up speed—you can't quite see them. The steamy windows make the seeing difficult; it's very close, but cold here since a window near is broken.

A three o'clock bus and it's crowded, early rush hour on a busy street in the industrial part of a compact little city; very compact here, and very uglified. I stand in this crowd and can't quite make the faces out, they look too much alike; bus goes faster; Brian beside me. Though I've been through these streets before, I still can't seem to know exactly where I am, with the windows steamed. Faster now. The posters over the seats are colored brightly and have ads I've never

175

heard of. Different products; different companies—one of them with black people grinning *Pepsodent* and I've never seen black models; not on a bus, only in alleys. Only in places like I sell myself.

Curious to be feeling like there's nobody on this bus when all around you're jammed by hats and raincoats; smelling raincoats and wet leather. Outside the windows passing little trees, slightly greened, you can't see any buds, I guess it's spring; their greenish haze looks like a damping mold, something rotting; passing buildings dark from wetness, can't see any features. And around us pressing bodies just like sticks on shoes, and so many of them; so many feet. When I actually see a face it looks so strange to me I can't believe it's human.

The gray floor pitches upward like a trampoline and I am breathing faster. There's a window broken next to us and the wind blows in my face and shows my breath to me and other people notice. Breathing faster, heart beats quicker; now I'm breathing even faster.

The bus has stopped a time or two and now is stopped at a noisy bunch of factories—gray high walls and pipes and fire escapes—filmy windows blurring tiny lines. People climb on and the floor is tilting, groaning; and they crowd behind us. spilling up the aisle clear to the driver; all around us. So many of them. Almost touching me.

An old woman's nose comes over Brian's shoulder and my eyes go quick to him and he steps in front of her face as her nose is about to smell me, about to invade me; and somebody stuffs some cloth in the broken window and it's suddenly stuffy in here, very close; heavy. People pushing at us and Brian steps in front of me, placing his hands on my shoulders and turning my full face to him, placing me exact to him, both hands on my shoulders; and we're folded together, the top of his coat in the space beneath my chin and his knees against me and it's getting really stuffy; people pushing; breathing faster and a ringing in my ears. And he suddenly pulls me to him, into the fox fur collar on his jacket; wet fur in my face. The wet floor pulsing, swaying us. The people. And he smells like sweet cologne and cigarettes; he smells like clean dark body and old wet dogfur. I stand rigid, getting warmer; warm because of the press of bodies; rigid, keeping one and one-half hairwidths between my coat and the coats in back of me and beside me; rigid smelling the wet dead fox, trying not to breathe so hard and trying not to feel this rising pressure in my head. A lot like panic.

I keep starting to jump.

I keep starting to start to draw that one superpowerful breath to scream and maybe blow out the sides of the bus. I keep starting to start but suppress it. I keep starting the breath but not letting it start and the strength to keep me away from that is dizzying. They have to back up. They have to back up from me, get back from me, get away and they are taking all my oxygen. They have to back up. If I can't make them back up, what will I do? I keep starting to jump.

Each time I do not jump I jerk like electric-shocked. A lot like panic. And Brian gets closer. And now he pulls me even closer into his coat, and people are looking. And for a while I hide like this, seeing only the little narrow stiff and separate hairs of the dead dog on the lining, beaded water clinging to the stiff tips, iridescent with the thin lights under the posters with the teeth and all that *Pepsodent*. But then I start to jerk again and Brian wraps his thin arms completely around my shoulders forcing me into the foxfur collar, crushing it into my mouth like we are lovers.

Warm like that. Almost suffocating.

I do not catch on when he starts in counting stops. I can't seem to register exactly what he's doing. Swaying; hot.

Around us the city is rising up aggressively from the flat dirty railyards and the truck stops. Actually rising. The tops of buildings headed for the universe.

And then he's shoving me toward the driver making pressure between my shoulders with his knuckles saying, " 'scuse us please . . .'scuse us pretty-please . . . there's a love, let us get by. . . ." A blank young girl with her butch boyfriend are blocking off our exiting in the aisle; they stare at Brian. Showing this hatred, not even seeing me—but he's black, of course, and faggoty so it's normal. Brian nips my wrist with the hard bones of his fingers. "Let us by," he tells them, "pretty-please? This is our stop."

"Hey, come ON!" bawls the driver. "I ain't got all—"

"Pretty-please? We've got to get off." He's businesslike; his voice is girlish.

"You . . ." says the guy.

"Now you see this little girl here got on back there at East Central, and if you want her to have a seizure right here in the middle of the aisle you just keep her right here, blocking our way. And I hope she heaves right on those pretty cowboy boots—"

And then we're off the bus in the black snow-melting street.

Christ it is so dirty here. Mud splatters halfway up the buildings, spit on the sidewalks; ugly faded colors, but too bright. . . .

Brian pushing me towards a Hook's drug store across a roar of heavy downtown traffic. We have the light. Maybe we don't.

"You want to make you a phone call," he reminds me. Brian holds the drug store's wide door open. A man is looking mean at him and Brian's looking back. I walk past them.

Too many people. Too much all over the place. All very loud and they smell wrong. Too many colors. Red. And the people are different colors, so many shades, not enough faces; features a blur and they keep changing shape, changing shade, changing costume. Moving quickly. Babble a buzzing roar. Droning machinery—blades on the ceiling churning round and round and going *hmmm*; refrigeration sounds, register sounds; *chink* and jingle—ding! Very bright colors, red to hurt my eyes. Aisles thick, close-containing; a room with orange, very bright, up from the tile floor halfway up the walls. The stench of broiling grease and sharp sausage; greasy popcorn, very sweet perfume. Hot sugar-sweets. Chocolate candy. Lime. Fire yellow. Pumpkin orange. Red. Stop.

"There is your phone," says Brian, speaking clearly.

A bright-sweet smell of soap in every color. Sweety-pink. . . .

He pulls my arm so I turn to face a phone about twenty feet away, on the wall underneath an exit sign.

"Now. You can't use it *now*," he says very clearly, holding me back. He pulls on my hand and we enter an aisle which almost touches me on both sides. "Now I want you to stay right here. I want you to—look here at me—I want you to stand right here in this aisle where I can see you. Now you hear? I'm going over this way to the drug counter and get my gin, and I don't want them thinking I'm buying it for no minor, you got that? Now you just stay in here where I can see you from that counter right there at the end of this aisle, right there in front of you. I won't be gone very long and there's somebody talking on that phone, so you stay right here and wait."

And I turn my face to the aisle, and there is soap. But I can't quite see it. I know however that even with all the pink and yellow creamy colors that if I just keep looking I'll eventually see some kind I recognize. Like square white Ivory soap for the shower. On the right hand edge of the several shelves are little heartshaped pieces. Blue and pink ones, yellow and chartreuse. To the left of them, brightsweetodored flowershapes; shapes like kids in violent, queasy colors. Shapes like bicycles and dogs and fireplugs. Like basketballs and squirrels and tennis shoes. There is a shape like Mrs. Pratt. There is a shape like Dr. Falgus. If you look into that little soft soap shape, you can see its little eyes, you can see its little chest go in and out. You can see that little white face like a dough-soft maggot, opening too-soft, wet white eyes to watch me telephone.

"Come on away from that stuff, 'fore they arrest you," says Brian.

And we wade down the aisle through the colors, through the noise. Do all these mouths make words like people do.

"Here's your phone," he says clearly, in my ear. I put out a hand and he sticks the receiver in it. "Where's your dime?"

I had one hidden on me when I left the ward.

"Where did you put your dime?" His voice is patient. His mouth is very wide and his lips are dry. A little chapped. Hard to understand.

His hand scoots around my coat pockets, feeling for a coin. It's in my skirt. This is the skirt with the pockets in it. I'm supposed to pay for the bus with script; even though I leave the ward I'm not supposed to handle any money. Heaven knows what I might do with it. "Okay. Do you have another pocket somewhere on you? Or down in your skirt, say? Maybe here in the other side of it . . . here. . . ." People passing by glance over at us. Ugly eyes.

Lifeoutside getting like this and it's only six months. Only a little while. And too many colors, too many choices. Noise not right. Different screams.

"You're going to call that friend of yours, what's-her-name. Tina." He's holding me up. "She's going to talk to you, I told her you was going to call her now. She's out. She's going to talk to you and tell you that everything is going to be okay and that I think we can get you out of here. You remember I told you that? You remember? Now, she's

180

going to tell you that everything's going to be okay, and she's wanting you to come back and you just work when you want to; maybe you'll get you some job. And she says she's going to East Chicago and you come with her—over a state line and you'll be fine, just fine. It's all over with. You never have to go back there again, and it's just going to be a little while longer, we'll get you out. Just a couple more privileges, a little more experience. You kind of need to get used to things again. You'll be fine. You go over the state line and won't nobody ever give a goddamn about you ever again. They got more runaways even than lunatics."

Hard to put the phone up to my ear. On the ward you do that and they really get you for it. Can't see a phone; never dial a number. Which is one of the reasons you can't ever handle any money. There are pay phones down in the hall outside the attendants' locker room. You might call somebody. A lawyer.

Brian dials.

After I finally remember the number.

T-a-a-a-ck! The hollow phone sounds.

I am waiting.

T-a-a-a-ck! That ending clink! so clipped, so clear.

Tina had only been able to get a couple of messages to me, through Brian. They took my mail from her and threw it out; they took what I wrote her and threw it back to me. Staring at the hearts and phone numbers scribbled on the wall behind the phone, trying to imagine what she looks like.

Is anybody there. Could she want me.

T-a-a-a-ck!

No one is answering.

"They nobody home?" Brian is nervous; we have to get the bus again. He has to take me. Supposedly I didn't get off the bus this time. "Hey is there nobody home?" he says. He thinks I'm spacing out on him. I am.

Click!

A someone on the other end is about to speak to me; words dry up. "What number did you dial?" an operator asks me. "What number were you trying to reach? Hello?"

"*Would* you say something!" Brian says impatiently. Across the room, in a checkout line, two deaf boys are signing with their mother.

I hang up the phone.

No one I wanted to speak to.

17

*S*IGNS AND *portents*. That's what my mom would say when two bad things would happen. She'd be waiting around and waiting around for fate to sort of drop the other shoe. And she'd start to wait at one bad thing, of course. There's always something gone wrong somewhere in your life, so it wasn't hard to start the count-down from two. And I know I had learned that way of thinking from her, to dread all the signs and portents of bad luck; and that's how I put that memory in my mind, that memory of the trip: bad luck, don't think about that. And I didn't. Try not to think about bad luck (even if it adds up to *signs* for you). I'd been having all good luck and if you just live by luck like me, having no other way to live, you shouldn't ever bitch if it goes sour on you. You're still lucky. What do you want? You're still riding the same horse, it's just the backside goes with it.

And that bus trip was definitely the backside of luck; when I let that memory enter my head, what came in with it was that pressure feeling. Which who needs? So I mostly forgot it. I mostly didn't have any intention of remembering it happening.

I told Anna about it:

—*I/go-to/B-U-S. How/sign/B-U-S?*

My fingerspelling was rotten, but she follows my stupid fingers. Immediately starts in answering my question: face goes *big, serious masculine-concentration*; spreads her arms, hands wide open, grabs a huge imaginary steering wheel; laboriously she turns it: *drive/great-big-thing*.

I look question marks:—*sign/B-U-S.*

She repeats the motions, twisting her mouth awry like *ooh, is this hard*; nods vigorously yes, that sign's *BUS*.

—*I/go-to/bus-that-way.*

Pointer finger circling at the ceiling: *where?*

—*Bus.*

Bus/you/go-to/where?

—*. . . There. . . .* (Away, far away. . . .)

You/go-out?

—Yes.

Go-away/disappear/here-not/disappear/free!?   You/free/ come-back/WHY?

—Never-mind.

WHY?

(Shrug shoulders.)

Crazy. You/crazy.

(Nod.)

CRAZY!

(Shrug; nod a little: so?)

BAH!

So who wants to talk about it anyway.

I avoided Brian. He kept wanting to make up all these plans. I didn't want to hear them. Wanted to think. A while. Or to not think, and that will take a while.

I was besides finding that I couldn't really remember the trip very well anyway, and he'd want to talk about it. It's *really okay*, he'd say; *it just takes you time, is all.* But I wouldn't quite remember. And anyway I was finding increasingly that I couldn't quite remember what had happened even five minutes ago, not that anything ever did that was worth remembering. Probably I didn't remember because none of any of the things that happened in a day's time were worth the brain cells. I was always doing the same things, never anything that was important. Which can be comforting.

Avoiding Brian.

At the dance: playing this game where you try to throw your saved-up pills into a pop-bottle from about ten feet away. (Well dangerous, yes; but interesting.) Burning my hands again.

At the Snack Bar: look over my soda pop; bat my eyes at Wykowski, across the room: *bat-bat-bat.* Anna is stunned. Diane Brown, stunned. Wykowski furious. I laugh. *Bat-bat-bat.*

I didn't want to think about anything. Mostly I played cards. I really got into that.

Anna give me this little piece of blue glass; she knows I'm feeling strange; she got it in this package from some son of hers. What does it look like. Dark, the color of depth or no light; shiny. It's a little glass dog, or deer; the lines are rounded and kind of vague. Its little eyes are only jagged pieces of glass that are glued or fused. I kind of like it. It exactly fits into my hand and picks up my heat and radiates my warmth at me. I like it. I carry it around in my hand because you know you can't leave anything on the ward. I carry it everywhere: in the bathroom I hold it in my mouth, it won't fit in my pocket. At dinner I put it between my chest and the plate. It looks at me. I put it on the head. And at the dance that night there's a new guy minding them on G; I don't know him; he offers me some money for a blow-job; what do you want. Like I have all these things that I can spend it on, but five dollars is five dollars. And I start to stall around for a time while I think about it and I look down and there's that dog in my hand. Or whatever it is. No place to put it; this is not the skirt with the pockets. And back on the ward, I take it out on the dog-cage porch and break it up in pieces and strew the little blue shards like bird seed out through the diamonds of the chicken wire screen.

Anna, please try to understand: don't wait for your children to starve—cut their throats.

She doesn't understand.

We played cards. Incessantly:

My. She certainly is good at cards. Both of you.

—(?)

Yes. Her, I mean. I mean she may be deaf; she's deaf, isn't she? She may be deaf but she certainly seems to understand cards.

—Yeah.

How does she do that?

—(?)

Remember all those cards like that. When she can't talk.

I mean I've taken notes for the doctor, and you really can't understand her. How can she think, I mean, about cards?

—I dunno.

Does she think?

—Who?

Her. Anna, I mean. Does she think when she can't talk? She can't write any too well either. Do you imagine she thinks?

—I dunno. Why'nt you ask her?

Well. . . . Anna? ANNA? Hi! ah. . . . Good cards! I mean you're awful good at cards! Oh, she doesn't understand me.

(I mouth with exaggeration):—SHE SAYS YOU ARE A REAL GOOD CARD PLAYER. (And at the same time I

186

flick my middle fingers off my thumbs—a quick movement, almost looks like a natural one):—*bah*!

Rolls her eyes.

We were actually running out of people to beat. When they had shoved our wards together for Easter, Anna and I beat two teams of attendants and one combination team of an attendant and a lady patient who got so upset she ran out of the room and flew back in with a pencil, and sat there punching out all the designs on the cards. That made me uneasy. Particularly because every now and again she'd stick the pencil upright in her fist, like a movie artist, measuring my face against it with her thumb. Maybe she was fixing to draw a picture, but something told me not with a look like *that*. After that I didn't really want to play against her.

Anna makes a goon-face; thumb on nose and fingers in a C-shape: *crazy bug!*

Yeah.

We had beaten our evening shift once back in February and they wouldn't play with us again. Which was all right.

I was really getting off on cards; for one thing, all you have to remember is the cards from this hand. That frees you of the other things that might otherwise be occurring to you. We started to methodically beat teams of attendants. It was something to do, something arresting. We beat the day shift on our ward repeatedly. In part it's because day shift changes constantly; you barely get to know them and vice versa, which is all right. The people on Days are by definition the last hired, low guys on the totem pole. Nobody wants to work days, there's lots of work to do—this is a pretty lively place, sometimes. The day shift kept changing, and then there were the day-weekenders, who were from absolutely anywhere and were anybody they could possibly locate. And each new batch of them just thought we were a couple of loons they could pulverize at cards. Hah.

187

Attendants *love* to smash patients at cards. At horseshoes. At basketball. At pool. At pin-the-tail-on-the-donkey. Never give a sucker an even break. If they were different kinds of people, why'd they work here?

And we sure did have some funny people working here, like Rec Therapy. The last day he worked, there was this party for him. He went around like a man who's been banged in the head with a beam, like one of the shock patients. I looked at him walking around like that and I said to him: *hey, don't let anybody in the bus station bump into you.* He gets this terrified look: *what?* he says. *You know, when you're standing and waiting in a line, or in the hallway, sometimes people come along who are, uh, real clumsy. They touch you and apologize? Well don't let them touch you, that's all.* He licks his lips: *queers, you mean?*

Some people seem to get off on being hopeless.

Just don't keep your wallet in your back pocket, I told him. *Leave it with your mother.*

I had got this wrist watch off him once, just to see if he'd notice. But he didn't, and nobody wanted to wear it, and I wanted to return it to him. I thought maybe I'd send it in care of the Army. I mean, they got nothing better to do there. It's not like we're still at war in Korea.

What weird people we got here. I could ignore them.

Falling into the cards, I could ignore them. I could be a million miles away, ticking off the cards I had seen, which I had not yet seen, almost like if I listened they would talk to me. One-eyed faces, with or without swords; dull red, shiny black. Secure and always the same in what they said to me, but I always see them fresh. A new interest each time. I could focus on them; it was sometimes hard to focus on everything else.

Anna and I were winning right and left, although we never took on any (well—one or two) male attendants; they won't play anything sissy-like—never euchre, never bridge—which is fine because it kept them the hell away from us, and especially Anna felt that way. They were too handy for her; she never learned to separate the ways that people will grab onto you, about men especially. Sometimes they'll grab you in a sex way, or to stimulate themselves, like old men do— the kind that need an erector set to get it up. Those guys grab you one way. But then there's the usual way an attendant grabs onto you, which is not usually sexual. It is much less personal. It's the way a medical doctor (not a shrink) or if you had a normal father, the way he grabbed you when you were little and he was pissed off. The *you-are-a-thing-in-my-way* grab; the one that says: *move-this-item*. That kind is not a sex-grab, that's *make way for me*.

But she wasn't realistic about that; she either didn't see or pretended not to see any difference. Just don't touch her. What my mother would have called *touchy, touchy*. Something she used to say to me; I guess I was like that when I was little, but I made myself get used to it. I saw that none of the outside of you has anything to say to the inside of you, anymore than the people around you, who only care about your outsides, could possibly say anything to your heart. I made myself not care about grabbing. It wasn't me being grabbed, it was the *thing-in-the-way*. What of it. Attendants were in charge of you. They moved you around like so many bags of bones. You can tell when that is *personal* (some of them, yes). But Anna would not try to tell. *Maladaptive*. But anyway.

We were taking on squads of them. And mainly, I decided, because cards were so absorbing. How could we have helped but play. Funny how I had never noticed how much I had such a passion for cards. I even played solitaire a good deal, like during those infrequent times when Dr. Kim commanded Anna come into his office. You could hear his initially calm voice getting louder and higher and less and less at all like English sounds, hear it clean through the tight-shut door. And that had used to bother me; I used to almost listen through the door—not for the words, for the event of that: as if I could go through that with her, somehow help her stand it (which is dumb, it only exhausts you). But now I could fall into the cards so easily, tune all that out. But then this particular time she comes flying out of his office shredding paper and strewing it all over the floor like confetti: she's upset; I come up to her, looking *WHAT?* with my face. Makes a sneer, a disgusted gesture; shoves me away from her. . . . Don't treat me like that.

So I walk on into the restroom; it has one wall lined with sinks, a mirror over the middle two; stalls on the other, the windows in the back wall flooding the room with white light from the white sky over the black roof outside. Wykowski at the mirror fooling with her makeup. Very curving lady; much white light. That uniform that feels so good to my fingers. Smooth and crackly, rather cool to touch.

Seeing me in the mirror. Looks at me peculiarly: "What's the matter with *you?*"

Nothing.

Sitting next to her on the couch, after lights out. Pratt is sorting clothing onto a tray cart in the hall; you can barely see Hart, in the nurses' station, talking on the phone. Almost midnight. Almost time for the night shift guys to come on. My knee against her hip. . . .

"Be careful—!"

"Everybody's busy. Who's going to see?"

"Just *stop.*"

I touch her shiny hair.

She jumps up.

*   *   *

And. I'm standing in the shower; she comes in. All this steam is going to wilt that uniform.

"Listen, I need to talk to you. What's got into you, anyway?" (*I'm crazy*). . . . "Latisha. Listen! The last thing—listen—" (*drops her voice*). "The last thing I need is you playing footsie with Hart around."

"What?" (*Turn up the shower.*)

"Be more careful. I'm up for a promotion—I can get out of this dump in another year if old Hardy doesn't queer it. You know the Nursing Super? The old cow . . . anything sets her off. I don't need Hart giving her any ideas—'Tisha, get your head out of that shower."

(*Turn up the shower.*)

"Will you stick your head up here! I said . . . I don't want anything to screw this up. If I get that position I can practically name my own hours and I guess you can see how that hits you. You can take a furlough . . .'Tisha? You can see what that means, can't you?"

She stands leaning against the side of the stone wall which backs this shower. Outside the curtain, arms folded neatly, starched white cap is sagging from the steam.

" 'Tish? I'm going to see to it you get job training. Finally. A reaction. Like that? Good. I thought you would. Then help me out. Hart hates my guts, and nothing would please her more than—"

"Miss Hart . . . Miss Hart was . . . telling that new one on days. Stillwell? About this girl. It was last summer. That you sure paid a lot of attention to—"

"*What* was she saying?"

Turn down the shower a little to hear. A little.

"Did that girl *kill herself* for you? You changed your schedule and just ignored her and she—"

"You can't make anybody kill herself—you choose to live or you choose to die; and if you mean Karen, she killed herself because she was crazy. It was her choice."

191

"She choose to be crazy?"

"That's *one* theory of insani—"

"She choose to have you—?"

"What does that mean?" (*Turn the shower back up.*)

". . . Karen was a sweet little thing but I . . . well, she was just a classic depressive. One of the kind that goes down and stays down and I, I frankly think she was mishandled. She should have had shock first thi—Now what's the matter?"

"That's what I like about you." (*Turn up the shower full force.*)

"What did you say?"

That pressure in my head again. Drown it. . . .

"I said, what did you say, Latisha? Honestly."

I lean out of the shower. Almost touch her.

"Just now. What did you say? Oh the hell with it. Look, I felt bad enough to go to the funeral. I'll bet Hart didn't say that. Look, I'm realistic. You and I are a lot alike—what did you say? Well say it louder. Life isn't exactly rosebuds, and if you can enjoy yourself, you should—Don't touch me, for God's sake, you're all wet!"

And I'm dripping on her skirt. Handprint; dripmarks. Makes her face all flushed, which is prettier.

"Hands off! What's the matter—"

Pretty when she's angry, fascinating. Steps away, shrugging me off, her sleeve all wet.

"Look, you're getting me wet—I've got to go downstairs for a review and look at me—I said *stop.*"

She steps back and I am after her, completely dripping wet. I wrap her crisp cool whiteness in my dripping wet warm arms. Pressure choking me, my face against her shoulder. And she breaks my grip. But I'm fixed on her. I grip her wrist and press my lips against it and she yanks back.

"Stop!" Nurse orders, but I grab her hand.

She shoves me and I grab again and kiss the backs of her fingers—she slaps me.

"Hit me again," I laugh.

She stares.

But I grab her hand and before I can touch, she's slapped me again. Almost a punch. Very angry.

"Wait," I say. Very politely, very quietly. I am standing dripping on the floor. "Don't," I say. I reach for her hand very carefully, the one that slapped me. I kiss that hand.

"My God," she says, forgetting about the water. "What in hell has come over you, anyway?"

I laugh. . . .

I took showers, I played cards; with these things I could be a million miles away and that was rather pleasant. I was finding increasingly that I couldn't quite remember what had happened fifteen minutes ago, although whatever that had been probably had not been important. I didn't do anything very important and didn't usually much want to try to, although there was one time when I happened to look into the Nurses' station and saw that little ukelele of Miss Hart's lying on top of her sweater up over the radiator. And I said, why didn't she play for us again. Well I'm feeling not too chipper right now, she said. Maybe I'll play something later. And then she said: I didn't know you liked none of that kind, I thought you just liked that rock and roll music. And I couldn't think of anything to say, so I didn't say anything.

And that night I was dragged off to one of those programs in the auditorium. One of those nights where they made everybody leave the ward (Mrs. Pratt wanted to watch a TV show) except the biggest pain in the ass to deal with: in this case, Weird Diane.

Actually, I really didn't like to sit in that auditorium anymore; I was afraid they'd let that goon get at me again, and

I was afraid of the way I might act this time. I honestly had no idea how I was going to act anymore. That trip had surprised me. And I go into that place and there he is, down in front, and I start shaking.

Miss Hart is in the back of the room, talking to another black attendant from B, a good ward. I go and stand by them.

"What's the matter," asks Hart. "Do you need something?"

"Not really. . . ."

"Well why'nt you go on, sit somewhere?"

I shrug.

She looks down front, sees the goon there. "Oh. It's that man, is it?"

"You go on," shoos B ward. "He can't hurt you with all us here watching him."

I stand, my arms crossed tightly.

"Go on. They upped his medication. He can't hurt you—get on out of here."

"I don't imagine you want to go anywhere near him, do you?" says Hart.

"Why he's got his attendants," says B. "Look, they're right close to him."

"Oh *those* fools," says Miss Hart. "Save the catskin after the dog done ate it. Miss Lambert, I'm going to have to ask you to excuse me. I'm going to take Latisha here back home. No, I know you can go yourself, Latisha, but Miz Pratt isn't about to let any one of you back in there and annoy her any. And *annoy* . . . she don't cut that screaming out, and I'm going to give her something to scream about. Weird Diane indeed."

We walk around the corner; I say: "Thank you."

"That's all right. You don't have to put up with rough treatment. I don't believe in that."

"I mean it."

194

"I can't stand to see a woman treated that way."

And we walk.

"I made an error about that man the last time, and I, *well.* . . ." That's as close to apology as I get around here. It's a lot for Hart to have to say. "Anyway," she adds. "I hate to see them young as you. . . ."

"How many kids you got, Miss Hart?"

"Ten . . . well, I got nine left. I got the one down at the college but all the rest at home, and that's a handful . . . but the one at the college, that's Wakefield—was named after his daddy, Wakefield Williams. Guess that leaves me nine."

We walk a while.

"He was the handsomest man. Met that man right out of the Navy, and if he wasn't the handsomest thing. I was fourteen. . . . Well, that man. Too bossy. Can't stand a man who has to tell me how to do everything. The housework. The silverware. . . . Wasn't a lazy bone in that thick skull of his, though. Well. That's just like his son at college, too. Junior does work, I'll say he does work. Says he's going to be a *law*-yer now, what he thinks he's going to do with *that*, I don't know."

She hold the keys up to the light from inside the ward D door. "But he studies, now. Every time I call him, he be studying. Now at the outset, he had to stick his nose in everything, but he's just fine now."

"You miss him."

"Well, he is the oldest. You always think first of that one. . . ." She stops. I think she regrets having said so much to me. "But they don't belong to me. It's like the Reverend says. God just lends the children to you, they belong to Jesus. . . . A lawyer. I guess he'll be good at that."

I laugh. "Won't that be convenient next divorce you get?"

"You get on," she says, swinging the wide door open. "I got to get back, now. Well. . . ."

"You think sometime you could show me some guitar chords?"

"Well . . ." she says, "I don't know. Maybe sometime. Maybe over this long weekend coming up, maybe I get a chance to show you. We'll see. . . ."

Yes Ma'am.

Or maybe not.

Bad luck over the long weekend, surprisingly bad. Starting with the card game with the evening shift. With Hart, actually.

We had already beaten our evening shift, way back in February, but this was already a rotten weekend. Something crazy in the air. People snapping constantly at each other.

Partly the reason we had not played them very often was that I was off ward so much. Another reason was Wykowski. When she'd come up to us, Anna wouldn't play. But she was off that night—a Thursday night, but nothing had been scheduled. Nothing to do with us. It was the beginning of the inexpressible boredom of a long weekend. And around the table we had Hart (snappish), Pratt (bitchy); I was spacing, but Anna was hot stuff—Minnesota Fats of Eastern Central with those cards. We played four sets of four hands each.

Anna took every trick in the first two hands—*hot stuff.* The third hand, I spill coffee all over the table. Hart says words appropriate to the occasion, jumps up to get a cloth and a new deck of cards. Comes back and says, "Now whose hand was that?"

And Mrs. Pratt says, "Just give it to her, there—she done won everything else."

She means Anna.

Starting at 7:30, we have won the sets by 10:00. But they don't want to quit. Wanting to get a decent second, anyway, they want to play again. With different partners. Nope.

They go out and consult; come back in, and they're looking clever.

The same then, but they'll want a four times four.

Fine with us. (Anna smiling. I draw four columns with
the word "hand" four times written under each heading—
headings One, Two, Three, Four.)

The first hand is equivocal, it could have gone either way;
but by the second hand it dawns on me we're losing. Something's wrong. They're awfully lucky. I play low to Anna. As
I always do.

Mrs. Pratt looks up hard at Miss Hart and says: "I don't
believe I want to see her take that. . . ."

"Well," says Hart, fiddling with her cards.

"His nibs," says Pratt; and to Anna, she says: "WELL I
NEVER SEEN ANYBODY PLAY CARDS AS GOOD AS
YOU DO, HONEY, AND I'M SO GLAD TO SEE YOU
OUT HERE PLAYING WITH EVERYBODY. YOU
SURE PLAY GOOD CARDS!"

And I think: what on earth is *that* all about?

"She's just not the dis-tractable type, are you honey?" says
Hart. "You just CONCENTRATE cause you DEAF."

Anna catches the word *deaf*: she nods at this.

Hart leans forward to Anna: "You are CLEVER, DO
YOU KNOW THAT? YOU ARE REAL CLEVER."

And I know she's seen Anna's cards. Not that I saw
her; just that I know.

"Well, you get the other?" says Miss Hart to her partner.
Who is smiling.

"Yes," says Pratt. Who smiles and takes that trick. She
places the trick face-down against the table, reaches over and
takes Anna's fingertips, squeezes them in her fingers. Shakes
them like a bottle of magnesia. "YES, YOU PLAY SO
GOOD," she says, squeezing Anna's fingers. "We're SO
GLAD TO SEE YOU OUT HERE A-SOCIALIZING
WITH EVERYBODY."

197

Anna smiling; quizzical. Eyebrow lifting briefly; smiles again.

Pratt turns her smile on Hart. "Well I can't follow," she says.

I deal to her and stare at Anna's face. "Trump!" I say, too quickly.

Anna smiles.

Miss Hart's pancake makeup breaks at the edges—showing her own skin's somewhat browner than her toner is.

"Seeing red?" inquires Mrs. Pratt. Anna sees this—she's looking questioning. Mrs. Pratt takes her arm and starts to pat it: "Well let's us play? NICE GAME!" she tells her.

"Yes and so clever I think," says Miss Hart. "Why don't you knot that tiger, Mrs. Pratt?"

Anna looks from one to the other, smiling vaguely.

Hart deals.

We take our cards and fan them out. Anna's eyes come up to mine and I risk it. I sign:—*liar*. I don't know how to make a sign like "cheat."

Mrs. Pratt leads. I play low to Anna.

Hart trumps very high, but Anna takes it with a jack.

Smiling with just her lips, Hart pats her arm. Then Anna deals.

"Looks like a sailor," offers Mrs. Pratt. Immediately I reach for a cigarette—right next to Anna, catching her eye:—*talk-talk*, I sign.

The light in her face goes out: she's irritated. What on earth is wrong with me? Signing like that? Signing out here?—*Two girl*, I sign, very quick and sloppy.—*Little boy*, I try, hoping this will make some sense. The signs are small and quick, very simple ones.

Anna has one eyebrow raised. Thinking. Looks at her fanned cards carefully, now at me. Touches her thumb to her forehead, then her chest; now signs *two father*, I get—hoping I play it right for her.

198

I play high, thinking that's what she wants. Except it isn't.

But then we've got it. *Red* touch your lips; *black* touch your head; *Dad, Mom, little-boy, lots-of-fingers*. We are winning. We haven't cheated before. It's kind of fun.

Anna takes a trick I've set up to her, playing a king as low.

"YOU DO PLAY SO WELL TOGETHER," says Miss Hart, smiling at Anna.

Anna saying: *boy-fancy-black*. I get: left bower.

Hart puts a card down.

I put a card down.

Pratt puts a card down.

Anna with a one-eyed jack, and takes it.

I reach across to take the trick and add it to our pile but Miss Hart stops me. Places her hand across my hand, across the trick we've won.

"Now what was that she told you?" asks Miss Hart.

"You have been setting there talking to each other," said Mrs. Pratt. "We know nobody's that good at cards, and we been watching you. I think Dr. Kim is going to be real interested in this."

"Yes," says Miss Hart.

"I think he's going to be real interested to know you been encouraging her at that. After you've been told and told about it."

"Yes indeed," says Miss Hart.

"I guess we can imagine how good you are at cards," says Mrs. Pratt.

"Oyes," says Miss Hart.

I hate them.

18

THAT WAS on a long weekend; it got longer. Counting from the bus trip, I was waiting for a third bad thing to happen. There was too much time on a long weekend to think about your problems; too much time to compare with all the *should-have-beens* and *-dones*, and that's depressing. Which who needs. I knew they'd written something up for Kim about Anna and me; knew that I might have really blown my chance to leave before I terminally *adjusted*.

And what if they got his attention. What if he was reading some worse article in some magazine? I tried to put it out of my mind. Bad luck enough, waiting for the third thing. There was always at least the hope he'd misunderstood them. Which maybe he did.

Saturday night. Trying to ignore Anna. It is evening. I am waiting for Wykowski. Thinking about the game I'll invent.

I pick up the cards on the card table closest to the television set; but there's Anna. Her back to Mrs. Pratt (in front of the screen).

Come play, she says to me. *Now you play now.* Touches my sleeve.

No (I remove her hands).

Wykowski is late.

Play? Bad? Wrong?

I turn away with the cards and deal myself a solitaire game. Kindly go away.

Anna takes up a different deck of cards and places a jack on my ten, eight on my seven.

I slam down my cards, scatter them over the table and floor. "HEY!" yells Pratt—I've interrupted *Jack Benny*—and there, for a change, in the nick of time. Wykowski comes in the ward door. Wykowski waves at Anna and myself—Anna whirls away from her.

"We'd better be going for that medical," she calls cheerily. Looks like Pepsodent nurse, all white: all she needs is a cape.

I shrug (relieved; it's getting tense around here).

Pratt: "Pick up them cards!"

I pick.

Anna snatches them: frustrated. Wykowski heads toward us. Anna grabs my wrist.

"Hey!" yells Pratt.

"It's alright," I yell, but Anna snatches me completely around and signs something. I bang my head with my fist: *STUPID! DUMMY!* Start to follow Wykowski but Anna grabs me again and I shrug her off and she slaps!—rings against my left cheek.

"HEY!" goes Pratt and Wykowski drops my hand, backs up. "It was an accident," I yell when I get my breath.

"What the devil is going ON around here?" shouts Hart from the hall.

"She just tried to grab my hand that's all—I'm fine!"—

and Wykowski drags me out, down the hall. The entire hall-way is utterly deserted. "Liar," she says as we turn a corner. "You're bruised—maybe next time she'll hand you your teeth."

I shrug.

"She's crazy. Every deaf and dumb we get in here is—"

"Drop it!"

"I beg your pardon?"

"Drop it! Just drop it! You don't know her! You don't know how—"

"She your lover? I hope the answer's no because she obviously has no discretion—"

"That's disgusting! Lay off her!"

"Who," she says coldly, "Do you think you're talking. . . ."

But I've dropped to the floor, I'm on my knees, my hands half-way up her white stockings. "Wait," she says, delightedly shocked. "Wait. . . ."

I know who I'm talking to.

Waiting for the third thing. There was always at least a hope that Dr. Kim had misunderstood about the game and Sign, which maybe he did; it turned out he had a whole lot more to think about by then.

Like about my Sunday night shower.

Early that evening I had been playing dominoes with Wy-kowski, fiddling a bit when nobody was looking, which can make sex much more interesting. But unfortunately, things were pretty interesting already. It was one of those nights when you know you're on the Funny Farm. One of the Di-anes bit somebody, and Wykowski had to treat the furious victim, who was punching everyone else. And Spacey Shirley was running around collecting all the trash baskets and ash-trays till they figured out what for, which was to shove all the garbage under the covers on her bed. Who knows what for? Only stop it.

Everybody jumpy. Wykowski having to actually earn her keep—and that never sets too well with her. Diane Brown had a bloody mouth (because she's never learned to keep it shut) and when she came out to get Wykowski to do something about this, she made the comment that Weird Diane had said something like, *Do you know? Do you KNOW what that woman SAID to me?* meaning Vivian-who-never-talks, and whatever it was she imagined Vivian said, she kept it to herself after the big buildup and just pasted Diane Brown in the mouth.

So I decided the hell with them all; I decided to take a shower.

It was certainly time for a retreat, and I was grateful for it if only for the quiet: you couldn't hear the Muzak. And I always liked the cleanness, the open stone echo. Spare is clean, to me, and healing. You can rest your mind in spaces that aren't filled up with junk.

The shower room was formerly a men's-style john, but they had taken out all the urinals and stalls and most of the fixtures, and what they had left was a big white porcelain bathtub up on a low platform made of gray stone like the floors, the kind of bath you use for quadriplegics. The white tub was nice against the gray walls, which were smooth and slick and cold. Almost icy, picking up a matte of steam with the shower on. Over the tub was a big window which opened our onto a flat roof still piled with unmelted snow; it was so cold, though late April, that year. And with the snow white and the roof black and the sky dark grey, pushing the glow of lights from our hospital back on us, it was very peaceful to look there—if you just looked out and not downward; and I liked that. I'd stand in the shower stall and look straight across at the white tub and the white snow and the gray night sky and think that was almost peaceful. You can be peaceful. If people let you be.

The sweet strong metal smells of the stone vault shower. Water-and-iron, water-and-copper; strong and sweet.

I would turn the water up full and let it flatten me; or turn it HOT and stand outside the curtain till the place filled up with warm steam halfway up my legs, and then turn on the cold and step into it. Let it knock me over; that's just fine. Not a thin trickle like in my parent's house. Clean and really firm with you.

And you pull that plastic curtain and you're completely alone; completely as you can be in here; alone inside your ears without that Muzak. And I was just standing enjoying this with my arms crossed so I could feel my ribs in back of me, when somebody came in. I hated that. I thought it was Wykowski. Leave me alone. I'm being peaceful.

I could tell that somebody had opened the door off the hall, because the curtain blew in, cold and sloppy against me; and I reached up and pulled it all the way across. I turned the shower head so the water was full and hard against my neck. I closed my eyes and let it drum, massaging me.

But the person who had entered yanked the curtain back. The cold rushed in and the steam blew up around her face, weird and hazy; it was Vivian. Like only once before, she seemed to be looking at my face and actually seeing me. Her eyes were almost focused. The curtain was halfway back, and her big frame completely occupied the opening. I had never before realized how big she was—maybe six-foot-three: farmer-lady with forearms like a man's. With the steam blown out of the shower stall, I was chilly.

She stuck her head in the stall with me. She was fully dressed. "CHRIST DIED TO SAVE THE SINNERS," she said suddenly.

Her eyes were fixed on a point above my shoulder. She

204

always stared, but this time what she was watching must have been worse. "That's good, Viv!" I said; and twitched the curtain back. It made a breeze, cold on my wet skin. And it came to me that I had never heard her say anything ever before. Nothing and Never.

She had not moved when I had pulled the curtain. It covered her face and body like a blanket. She stood outlined in the curtain, perfectly motionless, not even moving with breathing. Body-under-sheet, great farmwoman breasts of hers in the shower with me—pushing me back a little from the opening. From behind the curtain, staring me into the wall.

And she yanked the curtain.

Jerked back, the cloth snapped freezing and fat white rolls of steam boiled out around her, sucking away my heat. Not so wonderful. I carefully reached above her hand for the curtain and took a grip on it. I began to speak to Vivian very slowly. That seemed right.

"Cut it out . . . would you . . . Viv . . . ?" I said, and tried to pull the curtain to. "ALL SINNERS!" she said.

"That's nice," I said. "Let's talk about this later. Why don't we all just talk about this a little later, Vivian? Then I guess everybody will want to hear about it. Let's us talk about it later, Viv. Okay?"

Now I could see her body move beside the dripping curtain. Breathing like a person in a marathon, although I could not hear it. Not with the shower. Which seemed deafening. And the lighting seemed much brighter. She still had a fist full of curtain. And I watched.

When after a while she had still not said anything else, I reached out carefully and tugged on the curtain, like it had maybe only snagged on a thing, like a branch, and twitched it back again. It fell closed across her face and she let it stay there, sticking flat against her skull. I was freezing now. I couldn't quite get warm.

But she was really close to me and I backed away from her. The wall was slimy and rock-cold; the water had not warmed it up at all, and away from the center of the stall the flagstone floor was gummy, treacherously slimy, till up at the joint between the wall and floor there was a coating of thick goo. Hard to stand on. I redirected the water toward the wall to warm me up. I turned it hotter. But cold air was coming around the curtain, across my feet and crawling up my thighs.

The curtain—back.

"YOU'RE A SINNER," she said.

I could see her face through the water as I kept flat back against the wall. We stood that way. The curtain fell shut. The water splattered down, warm on my face and neck and chest; by the time it hit my stomach, it was cold. I started counting. I started counting by ones up to 500, and finally decided that she was just going to stay there, feet in the water, plastered with the curtain like that. It was too cold to stay like this. I stood in the center again and turned up the water—HOT.

But it was hard to get any sense of peace that way. And it was hard to get any kind of warmth.

She yanked the curtain.

"You want to get in here?" I asked her. "Look, if you want to get in here, just let me out, okay?"

It was easy, looking at her face like that, to imagine what she sees. Don't ever do that. She was directly in my way. I couldn't pass her without touching her.

"You want to let me through?" I said; and her face did not say anything. Staring at her devils, or whatever, on the wall behind my head. "Viv?" I said; I started edging past her. "Viv, you want to maybe let me through?" I was sliding my right leg around her, very carefully. And she grabbed. Very suddenly. My throat.

Ungodly strong, she was crushing my throat, and the heat

206

was suddenly in my head, my eyes thrusting. I had my fingers trying to pry into the grip, digging frantically into my own flesh, trying to get under that grip to break it. But I couldn't. It didn't come to me to try to break her fingers, all I wanted was to breathe again. Ears exploding; haloed lights; fighting hard, but my feet kept slipping on the slimy stone, couldn't get a purchase; blackening edges. She kept crushing and my eyes exploding outward but her face was like a statue. I kept slipping. I couldn't stop her.

The curtain blew in: someone had opened the hall door, someone shouting; much more shouting.

Light disappeared.

19

AFTER YOU have been throttled, your throat hurts. And your eyes hurt; they feel like they have been gouged-at. Your voice box hurts, you can hardly make a sound; it hurts to breathe. Your mouth is dry but liquids cannot help you. What you put down your throat comes right back out your nose. And the headache, the bruises and scratches, the torn-off finger-and-toenails keep you awake at night.

You don't feel very good. People tend to stare at you.

Wow, Wykowski says; *well what did you DO to her?*

You can't scream; your throat hurts. My face contorts but I can't say enough of my hate with it. I stop trying. *Nothing*, I whisper; *nothing*.

Dr. Kim, in rare form, had all these offenses fully digested by Monday afternoon. Everything clear. All these orders I was disobeying; all these wonderful privileges I was taking advantage of. After his leniency. After all his trouble. I didn't deserve them. Fooling him, making other patients sick.

There were in fact a lot of little resentful pissant charges, but the main two, those were the ones he was dangerous about. His special orders. Don't be queer, and don't use sign language.

I was using the manuals with that Anna.

—*What?*

I was the signing, the animal way and not the speech with words when all of the orders clearly; not at all what the directed had been.

—*Howzzat again?*

Agitation simply shot his English.

I had not been talking, as was his directed; I had been the violation of that rule. I had helped that violation. (We had cheated at cards, yes. We had been oppressing the attendants. Denying them a major compensation of such work.) I had helped the violation which was making the sick worse now in this woman, the lesser cooperative than when entering. I knew better than doing this; yes I did.

And I was using the sickways, the lesbianisms which I must have then lied about.

—*What?*

I have say that I have the boy interest, that the girl interest was just a child thing; I must have been lying!

—WHAT are you TALKING about?

That Vivian is the evidence! That girl is never to the violence without provoke, and now all over again many shock treatments, which are so my fault. And what have I got to say for these things!

—*Look, all I know about it is, she was strangling me! I was in the shower and she came in and started babbling about sinners and then she was strangling me! That's all there was to it!*

I must to have provoke her, that is finally.

*   *   *

That I had not was immaterial. At least it had not had anything to do with my relationship with Wykowski. Or even
Rec Therapy. Thank heavens. He could interpret my *advance*
to Vivian as a momentary thing, a piece of childishness
(whether or not it happened, it *might* have happened). I
should make more attempt to *socialize* with guys, spending
more time off my ward. At least, where the fault in all this
lay was clear. Anna couldn't talk, so she was stupid. She's
let off. And it couldn't be Vivian's fault (her strangling me):
everybody knew she was completely out of her mind. Didn't
know, after all, what she was doing. And nobody else had
been there, which leaves me, so I was strangling myself,
which you have to admit is really kinky stuff.

Well, nothing is fair. It wasn't fair my being in a body
other people wanted more than I did, either. But what can
you do about that but get out of it. And maybe you can go
live in heaven, but maybe you can't. Or maybe some people
are right and you're born right back into the place you ran
away from, which is hell for you. Nobody said that anything
was fair.

I could not have any dealings with Anna. Maybe they
would transfer me if they had an opening elsewhere in the
hospital. Maybe they would not. I had to prove I was not
corrupting Anna away from communicating with English. I
had to do this right; I do it right, I can keep my passes, keep
the still-theoretical Rehabilitation; I could keep my mind. I
do this wrong they take everything away, they keep me in a
sideroom, maybe shock my head off. Well we had a hospital
full of shock-zombies, and to hell with that. You can lock
me up, but I'll still be free in my head. Stay out of it.

It was hard on Anna.

When I see her come out the ward door, I turn and go
down the hall; when she comes into the washroom, I lock

the stall. They have told her something. God knows what it is.

A note floats over the top of the stall:
YOU ARE MAD ME WHY?

Writing had never really taken with Anna.

When she joins a group where I am, I either leave or look around at someone else. I keep away. But I leave a note on her pillow, which I cover with a blanket:
I AM NOT MAD. DR. KIM IS MAD.
HE WILL NOT LET ME TALK TO YOU.
I AM SORRY.

Her room is down and across the hall from mine. I wait for her to read the note. I watch for her to come, to catch her eye. But I don't see her. A while has passed and she doesn't come. I go do something else; I soon forget it.

Anyway, my memory wasn't all that good anymore.

She'd come out; I'd go in. I went outside in the yard a lot. We continued like that. I had the pink pass; I used it. I pretended to have an enormous interest in woodburning. And it was interesting making burn marks on my hands. There are stages you go through: pain, sweats; numbness . . . hyperpain. That was interesting. And I walked around in the yard a very great deal.

There was mud where the snow had melted, and drifts of dirty sooty piles of shoveled snow. I walked around without a coat a lot; first the cold shakes. Then the numbs, where your hands stop working. Then you get warm, so warm outside, but your bones are frozen and your hands and feet swell up. Then I'd go in the shower and stay in the heat, absorbing heat. They watched to make sure Anna didn't come in when I was in there. They were suspicious of what had really happened.

I look up over my plate—she's got my eye: *You-me friends?*

I look away. (Attendants watching.)

Every day I walked out on the grounds and all around them. I made paths of X's and O's in the snow or in the mud, whichever was out that day. Once I marked out FUCK EVERYBODY in the snow but stomped it out. I was going to be there a long long long long time, why make it worse. I look over toward the west wing and think I see Anna, out in the dog run, out in the cage. Maybe looking at me. I go in.

The new Recreation Therapy person is a woman, middle-aged. She catches me with the woodburning iron resting on my hands; I am clumsy, I tell her—very, very clumsy.

Wykowski dressing the burns; she's pissed at me and maybe thinks, she says, she'll tell my doctor. You just do that; I'll take up the New Jerusalem like you've never heard of. Get religion and babble out more jazz then they got in New Orleans—wait'll I confess. They'll sell tickets. Especially for Doctor; especially about you. *Our privileged relationship.* Call a priest; somebody baptize me.

Backs way off. Case closed.

I play solitaire. And because I was feeling so closed-in-on, claustrophobic, I had to carefully take that feeling apart. You can fight those walls away from yourself, with effort.

When you come into a small room and that oppresses you, this is because what you are noticing is the smallness of the room. Notice otherwise. Sit on a chair, sit in a corner, climb up onto a table; look around you. After a while, you'll find that the room gets bigger. The more you look, the more you'll find to see.

You see places into which you think you could fit yourself. Into the corner, maybe under that shelf. Turning sideways maybe, between two chairs. Where at first your eyes hang into the walls—something blocking you—where at first those stand in the way of the room, then you see the range. You see where you can go. Rest your eyes on the space between two chairs. The width of each leg takes up a certain area, but there is plenty left. Look at the space, at the number of blocks inside it. Look at the cracks that circumscribe each block. Look how deep; see how wide. What could fit there. Is there anything to that crack on the top of the middle block. Is there a little hairline fracture within it, moisture creeping in. Little bugs. A little fine hairline; several of them, featherlike. A pin could fit in there or several hairs. Several of yours; some of your eyelashes; some part of yourself. One of your fingernails. . . .

And so. You walk in and at first there isn't any surface for you, it's too crowded, and then you see all the surface; only surface; looking till that's all that you can see. So many places you can rest your eyes. But looking outside after that can upset you.

Playing solitaire. Red queen on black king. Black king on red ace. Red ace on black two and it goes around again. Round again.

In the Snack Bar, Brian sits across from me:

"I have got," he says, "hold of what's-her-name."

—?

"Tina," he says, "what's-her-name. O'Halloran. She says come on ahead, she's waiting. She's got her a brother living over on Prescott, you might say in the same line of work. She's told him about you, and that you're coming over to see him sometime real soon. Now you are, aren't you? 'Course you are. Your throat still hurt?"

—(Croak).

"I had somebody do that for me once, ruined one of my vocal chords. Now I'll never get into any opera. Now you go see this brother of hers, his name is Leo. Don't you have a brother named Leo? That's what I told her. She said you never said anything about your family. Well this brother will give you a hop up there and you and her's going to—guess what? San Francisco!"

—?

213

I try real hard to remember what she looks like.

"She'll take you just as soon as you adjust. I said you maybe need a little rest period. Then you both just go live happily ever after. . . ."

. . . San Francisco. Northern California. A place as weird as Mars and twice as far. Holly trees. An ocean somewhere near it. There's a bridge and it doesn't snow, and there are street cars like you see on ads for noodles. Asian people. Lots of queers. I don't believe there is a California. Nobody from around here ever does.

"Look, you don't think about that part. Not till you get out of here. You just think about getting out. Okay? You just think about that part."

But I didn't think about that part. I played solitaire.

I had met Tina in a bus depot, when I was very hungry. She told me I looked like a hungry baby bird, that she would feed me. She was twenty. That seemed really very old. I looked at her and knew that she was something like myself, and I had longed for that. Really longed for that.

There had been a time when I thought I loved her. In the beginning, she was good to me. And then one day I came in off the street—I'd been trying to get a waitress job, but all the guy really wanted was to screw—and she said that I just had to start bringing in money. I said I was trying. And she said well I put out, what's with you—is your ass golden? And then she hit me. I'm pretty much used to that, but she hurt my feelings. I had thought there was something special about when she made love with me.

Incorrigible just means you make them pay.

There was another freaky April snowstorm the Thursday after that weekend, and I went out in the dog run to watch it. Very heavy, very wet; gray-white skyline. Not exactly very

214

cold. It was like the sweet warm casual snows you get in mid-December. Big white flakes, snagging fast on the diamond cage wires, making a pattern that filtered sunlight blue.

The kids in the yard.

I was waiting to get cold. I thought maybe I would get really cold and then go in and take a shower; I was looking down into the yard when somebody grabbed me from behind, and it was Anna. She yanked me around so I had to face her. She was cold-faced; really, almost ugly.

Wrong! she signed; she meant WHAT IS WRONG?

—*Can't . . . can't/talk*—

You-me/friend—she said; and something else. Something fast.

I didn't get it—and she looked ugly, furious with me.

—*Friend*, I repeated, idiotlike.

Want? Her eyebrows high—*Want? What!*

—*Can't/can't.* I stammered with my fingers. Never good at signs like this, I never had been worse.—*Doctor/tell/not*— Couldn't sign this fast enough.

—*Wait*—I said, and I mouthed this; but suddenly she seized both sides of my collar, jerking me toward her, slamming my mouth into her teeth in a kiss. I shoved back away from her. *WANT?* she said; *WANT?*

And I couldn't remember anything at all but I shook my head, shook it so hard my brains almost came out, but she slammed me with her teeth again, terribly in that kiss before I could shove her. I can't remember shoving anybody—I don't remember shoving anyone but her away—and then Hart grabbed me. Where she had come from I don't know, I will never know. I just went with her; she didn't have to twist my arm, though she did; she kicked the door back and forced me through it, and she turned and yelled something back to Anna.

"You!" she said to me. "You're ugly!" To Pratt, still in

215

the office, she shouted: "I want you to get that doctor on the phone and get him up here! He's in Admitting. You!" she said to me. "You just wait!"

She shoved me up to the green wall to the left of the nurses' station. Anna had followed along behind the both of us; I just stood there, back against the wall and Hart right next to me, poised to grab me if I made a move, but I felt nothing; I was not moving; absolutely nothing. In the station Pratt was dialing the phone, framed in the halfwindow, the phone in front of her, and next to the phone a big pot of colorless flowers.

Hart said to me again: "You are really ugly!"

Anna came up to her and Hart yelled into her face. "Go away!" she said. "I'm not thinking much of you, either!"

Anna tried to say something.

"Go away!" said Hart.

Anna's creaky sound that never came out right.

"Go away!" said Hart. "You just get out of here! Look what you've done!" she said to me. "Now you've gone and got her all upset!"

But Anna was trying to sign to me; I really did not know what she was saying. In spite of all that practicing, I wasn't very good; didn't know even half as much as anyone thought I did, including Anna. She signed some more. I didn't get it; shook my head:—*don't understand.*

"Stop that right now!" Hart shouted in her face.

Hart tuned her back on Anna; she was meaning to speak to me.

Anna was standing like a dancer—hands on hips—still athletic-looking after all those months, a little heavier; Hart said: "Well I—" And suddenly the nurses' flowerpot was in the air, a blue arc shattering on the deskedge; Anna grabbing shards in both hands and leaping, graceful, at Hart's throat; bright blood spurting all over the green wall, over the floor, over me; scarlet and crimson; everything red.

Red.

The only time you die like that immediately is on television. Time enough to watch the dreams go out; that face; the sounds. All her kids. My eyesight seemed to go out. Completely blind. Only red. A memory of red.

They dragged Anna out of there.

I never saw her again.

20

ASLEEP, TRYING *to think. Sometimes you will find that this is safest. Retracing a day exactly like any other. Retracing a day watching Anna drinking coffee. Because it helps. Because I like her. Something has happened; I can't remember. Something is wrong. A stick figure Hart is waving from down by the door to the hall. So far away. What is this that's happened. Please don't tell me.*

I wake up.

I was sometimes able to sleep in the next few days, and that was a great relief. However, that was not usually the case. A peculiar thing had happened to my consciousness. Usually your thinking is in two pieces, sometimes more. The outer shell is telling you what's happening. The inner shell is finding words to fit to this and making up predictions, pulling in your history. The top of the inner core will tell you stories. It's a monologue you have for yourself and it talks to you night and day. I did not have this anymore.

I did not know what was happening around me. If it had not been for the inner core I could not have moved around

218

the ward at all. When I saw that murder the outer shell stopped. The top of the inner shell stopped babbling. It was very quiet in me, which is unusual. Only the inner core continued functioning. It was doing double duty. It tried to monitor attendants' looks; it tried to keep aware of patients' faces, maybe one might hurt me, after all, if I didn't watch them. But it was dim in that core; it looked out at them across a great distance. Trying to read the faces as if across the street and through a window. Trying to figure out what time it was, what day it was, what I had to do in order to function. When mealtimes were; when bedtime. It was dim in there; it was as if all that was left was a little candle back behind a barred gate. All my light.

I took all those medications I had not been taking, that first night. I mean the ones prescribed. They gave them out; I swallowed them. It was then possible to sleep a little. I did not even mind that feeling of dragging around lead weights.

In any case there was hardly any around to drag. There was no way to understand what to do; there was no routine now. All my routines had centered somehow around Anna. My afternoon routines depended on Hart. You do not know how much you need routine until it shatters in your face.

Look up and think you see Anna—turning the bend in the hall; shutting the door to the john; clear across the auditorium. Blind again.

There was a blindness striking me when I saw Hart's face; within a few moments I could not see at all. That blindness persisted almost absolutely; and when they gave me those pills and I took them all, that knocked me stupid. I was not used to the dosage; I slept a little bit. Woke up again about 3:00 in the morning—cold awake in a sweat, had it really happened. It couldn't have happened. No one I love could do that. The morning would come and I'd go to Dr. Kim. I would ask permission to try to get her to talk. Anna, I mean. She was isolated, that was what was wrong. I was encouraging her to keep her isolation. That was what was wrong—maybe she'd work for me. Try for me. We'd make do. Everything be better. It had to be. That couldn't have happened.

I padded out to the nurses' station and there were the night attendants, laughing and talking. One of the three was white, so he made sexy talk at me. But I had no words. The others would have talked like this but they were black and the white one would have told on them and somebody might have got them; so the one of these said: *Guess you had some real excitement up here.* It had happened just to the left of where they were sitting. And suddenly I see it again and run into the shower room, up to the tub, my hands in my mouth but I can't scream, my throat too bruised, won't work. And when I open my eyes, that's when I realize.

The shower's a gray room: gray floor, white tub, white cracks in the masonry; over the tub through the window the sky very dark gray. But I look down at my shoes and they are gray as if by magic. They'd been brown. And my light blue nightgown is light gray. Everything's gray. Not one color left. Someone's taken it. By some witchmagic wand everything is gray all over the ward. Even the green walls.

I took the medicine the second night, too.

It was no longer possible to swallow. This was a curious thing, there was no longer any decision about it: I couldn't eat. This was a physical problem. What I put in my mouth hit a block of cement in my throat. Nothing went down there, even my own saliva. Most of the time I was spitting into a Kleenex . . . my ears rang, my head had a viselike bar crushing over my ears. My hands shook; my eyes seemed too far from the floor. I thought I was falling; don't look down. I was almost torturously thirsty, but I could not swallow anything. I'd go into the john, hold water in my mouth and spit it out. If I tried to swallow liquid, it came out my nostrils.

I kept seeing Anna everywhere. Hart. Both of them.

220

I was mostly sleepless but I lay down a lot; I was freezing cold. It had somehow turned May and now all the heat was off, though the weather was cold. Ordinarily staff will not let you get into bed during the day hours. That's a regressive sign; that's not done. Get up. You can lie on your bed but you cannot get under the covers and get warm. Except I did this. The staff around us was preoccupied. And newly frightened, they checked out rooms in pairs, which is inefficient. So they left me alone a lot. I could try to get warm, but I could not sleep.

I preferred to stay under the covers (though eventually they did make rounds and they will pull you out of there) because when I took a shower to warm up, two things went wrong. First I couldn't warm up, even though I actually burned myself with that water, which was amazingly painful. In that inner place inside there was a heat-sink, that candle packed in ice. All the heat went in and through that into nothing and I stayed freezing. Cold in the marrow.

The other thing was I kept hearing people come into the room. Hearing people talking. As soon as I turned that water on I heard Hart's voice. And what I thought was Anna's. I heard Anna's walk—quick like clockwork. Tak-tak-tak— stop that.

In the back of my head I was aware that I was being carefully watched by the staff. Don't act funny. Who knew what they might do about that. But there were meetings on meetings now for staff; even Wykowski constantly in meetings which was all right, who wants to talk. Endless meetings. Sometimes police, asking them these questions. This was keeping the staff away while I was trying to paralyze my memory. Don't think about it.

Every black attendant looked like Hart. Even the white ones. Even, out of the corner of your eye, the men.

All those kids.

Going stone blind.

Even the fifth night I took the medicine but woke up in the night anyway. The candle burns too steadily for sleeping.

Lie in the dark. Listen to your heart. Listen to your breathing. The inrushing air makes a bigness then a smallness in your chest; not enough air for you.

You feel the air rush in and you know there's less and less each time. Not enough air for you; can't take in enough. Slowly asphyxiating: count the breaths; will that they get bigger.

Stop that.

That morning, it was Monday. I had not slept much the night before and passed the morning smoking cigarettes, which didn't help my headache.

At noon I went to the lunchroom with everyone else. I could not eat, of course, and I passed off a good deal of the meal onto the plates of the morons sitting around me, but then there were the attendants who were supposed to watch us, neither of them from my ward—they came over and moved me to another table, close to them. They told me to eat. They were watching: eat. I opened a milk carton and tried to pour it down, but it did not go down; I almost strangled. They said drink it; I said I hated milk; I said I wasn't hungry. It came to me that those were the first words I had spoken in five days. That thought stunned me. They went on yammering. I picked a fight with one of them; they started taking notes. Lots of notes on me. One of them reached across and pinched up a small fold of the skin over my wrist; the skin stayed pouched. I pretended this had hurt me. I pretended they were abusing me and that I would go back to my ward. One tried to stop me. I waved my pass and I went back to my ward.

Walking, I was full of strange sensations. I knew that I was about to do something permanent, something irreversible. There were singing sounds in my head, almost a chorus. I felt as if I wasn't breathing in enough.

222

On the ward, an attendant on the telephone. She looked at me and promptly dropped her voice. The cafeteria. They had called. The other one was looking at me and scribbling down some notes. Time for Doctor.

Come here, said the scribbler. I never had known our day shifts very well, including these. *Come here, let me see your arm*. I did and she pinched my wrist like the other one had. I told her I was going to sign out of the ward and walk around for a while. The attendants looked at each other; one said *Okay, but only for a little while....* And when I came out with my coat, she took it away. I could not have my coat. When I get cold, I come in. Okay.

I walk downstairs. I walk back upstairs. I can't stop walking. Upstairs I pass the little hall which leads to the attendants' locker room. I turn and walk down it.

In the women's, on a wooden chair close to the door, was a white intern's coat. I put this on. I walked back down the stairs and out into the yard and it was snowing. Clear in May. Big white flakes of it. I was freezing. For an hour or so I walk around in a circle. A week before, Diane Brown and her lawyer had got her out of there. Two days after that, all hell broke loose. Too much to think about; I didn't think, I only walked around. In the pockets of the coat were various items: a comb, a prescription pad, a pen—two dimes. Good.

I hid the coat in a garbage can and went back into the building. I took a stroll through every open room. Occupational Therapy, Recreational Therapy, the auditorium, the snack bar in the gym. In the back of my head I was waiting to hear my name called over the PA system. At the corner of my eye I kept thinking I saw Miss Hart, to take me back. She didn't come.

In the snack bar I met Brian. I was still pacing.

He just looked at me and said—*You leaving?* I didn't answer. He said: *You really got that leaving look. You shouldn't leave without planning. Why don't you wait?* I looked down and, amazed, saw that I was shaking hands with him. *Goodbye,* he said. *They always bring you back. That'll be in contempt of court. You know what they'll do to you after they get you back. Why don't you wait? It'll be so much harder to get you out of here when you don't have those passes and things. And you won't get any more passes, honey.* I nodded that I knew. *Well, you go on if you got to. I'll probably see you tonight. If they'll let me visit you.*

I turned and left him.

It was by then three-thirty—rush hour out on busy 54th street. Out past the guardhouses you could see a smoky crush of bumper-to-bumper traffic.

I fetched the white coat back out of the garbage can, and as I was about to walk down the steps, out of the door behind me came a big laughing and talking clump of young medical students and nurses, heading for a white van out past the guardhouses. That was the van that goes to the downtown Medical Center for the evening clinics; I fell in behind them. Luck and luck. They sauntered along and me behind them, my hands in my pockets not thinking anything at all, don't think; and we got to the van and I kept on walking. Straight into the street of bumper-to-bumper gray smoggy traffic all the way to Chicago, picking my way across.

Attendants won't chase you on foot unless they're angry; that's no fun: no flashing lights, no siren. And nobody could have driven across that traffic.

I looked down and watched my feet walk out of there.

Luck and luck. I stuck my thumb out three streets away and the second driver going by stopped. This was a big dirty dump-truck that I had to jump up and climb into, and the driver had the radio half pulled out of the dashboard playing Ernie Ford's *Sixteen Tons.* He was a little runt. And he pulled way out into traffic without even asking me where I was going, and that told me.

And he drives like a maniac for about a mile and a half,

and suddenly turns down a side street into a housing project and up into the middle of an enormous churned-up mud lot covered with piles of lumber and scrap, and he stops the truck.

He takes out a pocket fish knife and opens it out in his fingers, very efficient, and lays it open on the dashboard under the window. There is snow piling up outside on the windshield wipers. And it's May. He tells me I'm going to blow him and automatically I hear my voice come on. I hear my still bruised voice saying:—"Hey now lover, you don't need a *knife.* . . ." But then before he has finished unzipping himself, before he has completely disentangled himself from that steering wheel in his way; I don't understand—this comes so suddenly—one second I am seeing his little pig eyes and the blue pulse pumping above his collar, very blue; one second I am seeing his throat and the next I have that knife and it is stuck in him. Through his trousers, the inner thigh, and just below the balls. We look at this, his mouth is hanging open. Like a marvelous miracle. How easily.

In his eyes there is a look of blank surprise. The blank of his eyes enframed with great sad eyebrows. Like heart-broken.

It comes to me suddenly that he must not be very much hurt. I should have hurt him; and I grab out the knife, throw open the door and jump, landing running.

I was fastwalking and sometimes running across that great lot with stars firing in my head. Stars ablaze; my mind ablaze; in my head there was a 21-gun salute to me. Stars and rockets, sprays and bursts of bright-colored roostertail 4th of July explosions, my head pounding. Explosions in my head, lightning fireworks, striding like King Kong. And then that wore off and I was freezing.

21

AND ACROSS that muddy field it was terribly cold, completely exposed to the wind which flayed vivid my sweating skin. The mud sucked at me, and across the field I was looking down into ruts and wide and small footprints of dogs and big men, in the deep part of them standing water with a white reflection of the bright sky. I was aware of the whiteness of my coat and the sky and the water down below me in the ruts of heavy black mud, and this was blinding. And I reached the edge of the lot, at a big dirty pile of black and brown mud and rocks with a faint film of snow, and turned around to look back at the truck, which had not moved. I couldn't see anyone in it. Looking down I saw the long fish knife, red stickiness two-thirds up the blade, on my fingers, I thought: *blood!* like a punch. I thought how he wanted to cut me and I had not killed him and I hated myself: I wanted to stab myself. I looked back and the dump truck had not moved. And all the juice drained out.

I walked miles.

All the juice and the stars in my head just seeped away

and left my body hollow, dizzy—sick and not just cold. I began to feel like I would fall at any moment; I had walked miles and without food for so long. A little milk. I began feeling like falling, and up ahead of me was some kind of an eating place in a shopping mall, which smelled like melted hot bread and hot meat grease and hot real sweet stuff and coffee, especially coffee and hot meat grease. And I walked into its glassed-in entry and there was bright light, a double reflection off the inside windows from the white sky outside; and I walked on into the restaurant itself, all dark wine-red with a red tile floor, and in front of me a thick pane of brighter glass over a counter; behind it there were people cooking. Men. There was a big white block of light from the windows and the sky behind me across the glass. A sky in the counter window, and I stand staring through its white blur at the french fries, at these cheeseburgers in front of the cooks wearing red aprons. As I stood looking, I could see an image of myself, a reflection. I could see that white coat on the white sky patch and the way my hair was cut exactly like a patient's. A long time looking.

And my hands sagging in the pockets, half my collar up and half down; and over my reflected shoulder two faces. Two people were behind me, looking at themselves and me in the counter glass.

They are old. A gray old man; a short and gray old lady, standing in the window behind my shoulder. What do they want.

"Pardon me," says the man.

I don't.

He is old and too-well dressed for an afternoon at a place like this. His hat in his fingers. The woman has a little hat with a little veil and she twists her little gloves round and round. They look to each other. Back to me. What attracts them. I cuddle the long-bladed knife in my pocket. My friend.

227

"Hem," he ahems.

The red cooks look through the glass at me, at each other. All that food. Grease and sweet; the sweet smell twists in my belly.

"Hem," says the man.

"Par-don us . . ." says the lady.

I stare at them in the glass. So gray.

"I, we, we notice you for a little while now. We hate to interrupt you—" They talk like Chicago Jews. "We are wondering if perhaps you—might like to, to join . . ."

"Are you hungry, dear?" says the lady.

"Could we get you a little something to eat," he says. "Just a little something. If that would be all right with you."

I turn.

"Would you like a little something?"

They are as frail as two old pieces of paper. He keeps his wallet in his inner left breast pocket. She has little jewels in her ears to match her necklace. Which is crystal. Or—? You could tear the old birds with your hands. *"Sure,"* I say.

I eat a meat-thing, covered with orange cheese. I eat a red sweet dough thing that is like plastic stuffed with sugar. What does it matter. I drink an orange shake and a cup of coffee and they watch me eat this stuff. And more coffee. Do I want more. I drink coffee. I am seated across the booth from them and watch them. When my fingers are greasy I dip them in the coffee and wipe them on my coat. I'm supposed to feel something.

Could they offer me a ride? North they're going. Yes, I say.

I give them a north address and we go to the car. I stop, keep away from them. Stand.

The old man holds a back door for me and backs very gently away: "There you are," he says. "You can have the back seat. You have quite a lot of room . . . see? There are

228

two doors and you can open both locks. See? You can lock them, too."

I climb in.

The lady leans in as he holds the door, and he gets in the driver's side. The upholstery has no color. Nor the car. Nor the couple.

They sit in the big front seat, and the cars go by them past the windshield. The snow is turning fast to rain and sleet; a little mist, a little fog. It is a new car that could run everything off the road but he drives old, carefully; his ears stick out beneath his hat over the throbbing thin skin of the throat; her head makes tiny nods. I know this part of town. I know this place.

"Just let us know where you want to go, if there is any oth-er place, too," says the lady. "We had a granddaughter, she ran away. We, we sometimes think maybe she might be tired, she might be hungry somewhere. We hope that maybe some kind stranger—"

"Stop the car!" I yell.

He begins to stop but I yell, "Right here, pull over!"

"It's alright," he says. "We're stopping, we're coming right here to a stop; it's—" his foot on the brake, he's gripping the wheel tightly and adds: "but are you su-ure that you want us to—"

"Here's fine!" I clutch my knife and we're safe at the curb and I'm halfway out the door on the lady's side, my foot on the curb.

"Wait," manages the lady, "maybe you could use a lit-tle something?"

And I jump back from the car. I grip the door and throw it slam into the frame. Sick in my stomach. And she's rolling down her window. The old man leans across his wife to her window and extends his hand through it. "Take this," he says. "Please."

After an instant, he lets it fall.

I am walking backwards.

"God bless you," she says; and the window goes up and the car is in motion and it's raining now, the snow has turned to rain. I pick up the bill and cram it down my blouse. It's a five.

I turn around and begin to walk away.

I was out. I was alive; I had succeeded. I would put those people out of my head with all the inconvenient things. Tina had a brother on the northside somewhere near. I could make him take me in; I could be useful. I knew I could do what I needed to do; that it would work. I had proved that I had no problem with anything I might need to help myself. I was nothing like the boring people and nothing like the stubborn ones. . . .

The stubborn ones. . . .

I've got the slick knife out and open and slashing across my palm. . . . Again. I have to stop. Because it *hurts*. . . .

Anna; because of Anna.

One of the best things you can have is a bad memory. But if you've been in a place like that, if you've seen these things, you can't always keep that forgotten. It will come sometimes. I don't mean at times you expect, like when somebody's telling Little Moron jokes or when some lunatic shoots himself a president; but sometime when you're in a crowd and suddenly everyone around you pulls back and there you are, very sudden, in the middle of a stand of strangers with an old bag lady jabbering about her devils or what not; and in the strangers' eyes you see the *Insanity That Doesn't Happen to Us;* the *Way No Real Person (ME) Could Become.* That those people have a superior ability to misidentify what really happens; that maybe it never could happen to them, but it happened to people you knew; it happened to you. Or almost did—it was only a matter of time. It may still happen.

You put that out of your mind; you keep away from people who grab at your coat on the street but wherever you find yourself you know that if anybody ever knew what was in back of you they would stare at you that same way. And be angry with you—maybe because you've fooled them. They thought you were real but here you were only fooling them. They hate to be fooled except sometimes. Some ways. Or is that it?

Pretend that they love you.